Danger Lighthouse

Laura File's husband is killed suddenly and she finds herself alienated from her law student son, Gary. She tries to put her life back together in Granton Wisconsin with her closest companion being a big black dog named King. After facing death in an armed bank robbery Laura no longer wants to put off her dream to buy a Scottish Lighthouse. She purchases Gealach Head Lighthouse on a remote island in the Western Isles, which is a part of the Scottish Hebrides. On the airplane trip to her new Scottish home she meets Jim Green who helps her through the trauma of putting King in the UK mandatory six-month rabies quarantine. Jim volunteers to lend a hand setting up the lighthouse. Frightened and alone Laura accepts his offer.

Arriving in Scotland they hear rumors of danger at the lighthouse. Reassured by Ian Webster, the island's police constable, they move into the lighthouse. Laura and Jim begin seeing lights on the beach at night near Gealach Head. The police constable finally admits he wasn't totally honest about the situation. He is worried about the night activity around the lighthouse. The danger escalates with the killing of a Custom and Excise officer and the ransacking of Laura's living quarters at the lighthouse. Danger is everywhere and Laura does not know whom to trust or what to do.

Sharma Krauskopf a world-renowned author who lives in a remote lighthouse in Scotland brings the excitement of lighthouse living to each page. Millions have read and treasured her other books such as Scotland A Complete Guide, Scottish Lighthouses, Irish Lighthouses, The Last Lighthouse, A Year at the Lighthouse, Moonbeam Cow, and Northern Lights. Her first novel Danger Lighthouse is another of her great books.

Danger Lighthouse

Also by Sharma Krauskopf

Non-fiction
Scotland A Complete Guide
The Last Lighthouse
Scottish Lighthouses
Irish Lighthouse
A Year at the Lighthouse
Scotland's Northern Lights – Lighthouses of Orkney and
Shetland

Children
The Moonbeam Cow

Danger Lighthouse

By
Sharma Krauskopf

Published by Scottish Radiance Publications
USA
1832 Litle Road
Parma, MI 49269

ISBN: 09543367-1-2

First Printing January 2003
Second Printing October 2003
Printed in the USA

Publisher's Note
This is a work of fiction. Names, characters, places and incidents either are the products of the author's imagination or are used fictitiously, and any resemblance to actual persons, living or dead, business establishments, events, or locales is entirely coincidental.

This book is dedicated to my beautiful dog, Kiri and Grand dog, Maxx, who died recently.

CHAPTER ONE

Torrents of rain persisted as the minister finished the graveside blessing. Laura File held tightly to her umbrella. She continued to look in the distance searching for an answer. What would she do next? Could she recover from the tragedy of her husband Peter's death? Never one to accept defeat or to give into life's setbacks but Peter being gone seemed unbearable. If her friends and neighbors could have seen the trials she would experience in the next year the pity they felt for her would have been replaced by terror. Laura turned slowly toward her son, Gary. With the determination of a lifetime, she placed her arm around Gary's shoulder and led the grown man up the hill as if he were a small child. It was difficult to tell whether the two mourners were crying or was it rain blowing under the umbrella that made their faces shine with glassy wetness. Their steps were determined but slow. As they slipped into the car neither looked back toward the tent and the flower draped coffin.

Rushing from the protective canopy to their cars their friends and family would follow Laura and Gary back to the house for a lavish meal, prepared by the neighbors. Granton, Wisconsin was a small Midwestern town of about six thousand people. Its economy was based on the surrounding farms. The Files had moved to Granton from Chicago to get away from the hustle of the city after Laura's Mother died. Peter was an orphan and Laura an only child so they had no family except Gary. Vacationing near Granton one summer they decided it was perfect place for them.

In small Midwestern towns it was tradition to gather at the grieving family's home for food and to offer support. Laura and Peter had lived in Granton for six years so they had many friends. Peter had taught history at a consolidated high school ten miles from their house. The area was too rural for each town to have a secondary school so Peter's served seven small communities. Laura was a graphic designer who did free lance work for local businesses. Recently she had begun to specialize in the design of computer graphics. Both Files had been very active in civic affairs and Peter's job brought him in contact with many people. Gary had been away at law school since they had moved to Granton so he was a stranger to the town folks. Four days ago Peter was driving to work when a car going to fast down the middle of a dirt road had forced him into the sand on the road's verge. Not being able to regain control of the car he had collided with a oak tree. The coroner said he was killed instantly.

The File's large old house was bustling with activity when Laura and Gary entered the front door. The house echoed with the sounds of clanging dishes and many voices. When it became known that Laura and Gary were home a silence settled over the house. Larry Madison, the File's next-door neighbor, and one of Laura's clients rushed forward to take their coats and offer them a cup of coffee. Laura smiled and thanked Larry but Gary went up stairs. Laura wondered how she could convince Gary to give these generous people a chance. He had told Laura in the car on the way to the house.

"Mom, I just do not feel like Granton is home. It makes me nervous to have strangers doing so much for us. When I got in the car to drive here from the University I pretended it was just another holiday. I am visiting just like all of the other times. But when I walked in the door Dad was gone. The house was full of strangers. I still cannot accept Dad will never be here to greet me. The strange people remind me he is dead. I do not want to be reminded."

"Gary, I can understand how difficult it is to understand all this. I still can't acknowledge your father is gone. In time we will come to accept it. Maybe it is not so important to accept it today. As each day passes without him we will come to realize he is gone. The people of Granton have lost him too. Their loss is not as great as ours but just as real. We should let them do what they feel is right. Even if it means nothing to you please don't tell them how you feel.

Gary's quick exit upstairs demonstrated how uncomfortable he was. Laura was thankful at least he hadn't verbally offended any of the neighbors. Heading for the kitchen Laura sought the one piece of reality she desperately needed at this moment. "King, where are you?" She shouted. King, the big black Labrador retriever that had been a part of the family for ten years, came bounding through the kitchen door. When they had first gotten him from the dog pound he had been beaten and starved. The Files had nursed him back to health and in doing so King had become an important member of the family.

"Oh, King," she sobbed. "What are we going to do? It just you and me now." King seemed to understand what Laura was saying. He rubbed against her legs and put his giant paw in her lap. Larry Madison with a cup of coffee in one hand leaned over to stroke King's head. He gently raised Laura and handed her the coffee like it would make everything better. Accepting the coffee Laura smiled through her tears and thanked Larry for his kindness. Sitting down at the table she slowly drank her coffee continuing to stroke King's big black ears. The far off look exhibited at the cemetery returned to her face. Sitting at the chair in the kitchen her thoughts wandered. Larry Madison afraid she would become more upset chatted at her about the terrible weather and how King was refusing to go out. Laura slowly returned to the present with the sound of his voice. Hearing his comments about King she led the dog to the door and pushed him out into the back yard with a word of reassurance.

"Go quickly and when you get back you can have a dog biscuit."

King jumped into the rain and found the nearest corner to do his business. As soon as he finished he ran straight for the door and Laura. Letting him in she dried his muddy feet as he crunched on his dog biscuit. Somehow the familiar activity of tending to King and watching him eat his treat made her realize somehow she would find a way to make things bearable without Peter. Buy how? What would she do? These were the terrifying thoughts she had been fighting all day. Thoughts that held no answer only more questions. She had depended completely on Peter. They were only ten years away from retirement. They had so many plans including purchasing a lighthouse and moving to Scotland where she would continue to do graphic designs via the Internet and he would study the history the area. Now that would never be. She and King were alone. Gary was going to finish law school and join a law firm to get some experience before sitting up his own practice. He certainly wouldn't want to become involved in his mother's life. She was not even sure she wanted him involved in her life. She wasn't sure what she wanted.

The always-present Larry Madison brought her back to the kitchen by introducing a family whose children had been in Peter's classes. It made Laura proud they had cared enough to come to the house and tell her how much Peter had done for them. The thought of what Peter had accomplished with his students and that he would never do again brought anguish so Laura excused her self from the family and went up stairs to find Gary.

She knocked on his door but there was no answer so she gently said, "Gary, are you in there? Its Mom."

"Go away, Mom. I just want to be alone," he answered.

"Gary, I need to talk to you. I know how hard this is for you. Open the door, please."

She heard footsteps and at last the door opened. Gary stood at the door with a strange look in his eyes. Laura could smell a sweet odor in the room. "Come on in, Mom," he said with a doorman like bow.

"Gary, do I smell marijuana in this room? How dare you use drugs in this house when you know how much your father was against it? He has only been gone a few days and you are tramping on his memory by doing something he fought against all of his life."

"Oh, come off it Mom. It is just a little something to help me get through this celebration you and the neighbors are having down stairs."

"Gary, in away it is a celebration. They are here to honor your father as well as help us get through a hard time. They are good people and are only trying to lend a hand. We need to talk about what we are going to do in the future."

Turning his back to her he pointed toward a half-packed suitcase on the bed. "I am leaving in a few minutes to go back to law school. That is what I am doing in the future."

"Why so soon?" Laura cried. "I need you here to help deal with your father's clothes and legal matters including his will. I cannot go through this alone. You know all about legal documents and what we should do next."

"Sorry Mom but I just can't handle all the sadness and strange people. I need to get back to school where I can surround myself with my friends and keep busy with things I understand. Did Dad have a lawyer and a will?"

"When we sold our first Granton house without a realtor we used attorney Alan Fitch but he only handles real estate. I don't think your Father ever wrote a will. If he did, he didn't tell me. It was just not something we thought about being so young. How do I find out?"

Gary replied as he returned to his packing, "Call Mr. Fitch and begin there."

"Gary, please don't leave now. I need your support. In a few days everyone will forget the new widow. Then I truly will be alone. I had been married to your father for over 27 years. I can't even remember what it is like to be on my own."

"Sorry, Mom you will just have to cope because in a few minutes I am out of here. You had better get back to your guests. They have gone to all this effort to be with you."

Laura realized her only son had dismissed her. Feeling dizzy like she was going to faint she reluctantly turned toward the door. "You will say good-by before you go?" She begged.

"Oh, come on, Mom. Of course I will. I am not the type that would sneak out without letting you know." He replied.

Laura automatically turned toward the door but inside she was panicked and wanted to rush somewhere. The problem was where to run and knowing when she got there she would still be alone.

As she started slowly down the stairs Laura straightened her shoulders. When she reached her guests she wanted to be more in control. Bewildered she had no idea what she was going to do in the future. Actually, she didn't know what she was going to do in the next few days. The most frightening point was she didn't know what she was going to do in the next few minutes with Gary leaving.

At the bottom of the stairs King was waiting. She was wrong when she told Gary she had no family left. The black lab wagged his tail and jumped with excitement when he saw her. Laura moved quickly to the one member of the family who would stand beside her.

Laura helped Susan Madison wash the dishes after everyone had gone. They discussed the various people who had been so nice to come to the house. It had been an interesting group and it helped Laura keep her mind occupied. Suddenly she realized she had not seen Gary. Could he have left without letting her know? He had promised he wouldn't. With panic she ran to the window to see if his car was still there. The car was in the driveway. He hadn't come down while all the visitors were still at the house. Laura excused herself and ran back upstairs to check Gary's room. Opening Gary's door the odor of marijuana was strong and the room was dark with the curtains shut so no light would enter. After a couple of seconds Laura's eyes adjusted to the dim and she saw Gary sprawled beside his suitcase on the bed. His shoulder length brown hair was lying in a fan around his pale face. His tan skin seemed to have faded like someone had scrubbed him with bleach.

"Gary, are you alright?" She shouted as she rushed to the bed. Watching for any sign of life she saw he was breathing normally. Her fear was quickly replaced with rage. She shook him hard and kept yelling his name. It was all she could do to keep from slapping him.

"What?" Gary mumbled as he slowly opened his dark hazelnut eyes.

"How could you?" Laura yelled. "What if someone had come into this room by mistake and found you like this? I don't know what you have been doing in college. It is evident you have learned some bad things you didn't learn from your parents."

"Vicki, is that you?" Gary mumbled.

"Who is Vicki?" Laura asked.

Finally coming out of his drugged sleep Gary

realized where he was and his mother was standing over him.

"Mom, I am sorry," he stuttered. "I don't know what came over me. I guess I missed Dad more than I thought. Please forgive me."

"There are a lot better ways to express your grief than drugs." Laura yelled. "I do not understand you at all. I am so embarrassed. How could you do this?"

Gary realized his Mother was not going to understand. In her current state he was just making it worse, so he got up and closed the suitcase. He gazed around the room to make sure he had not left anything. As his eyes quickly inspected every corner of the darkened room he realized it felt like a hotel room not "his" room in "his" home. This thought made him sad and he felt tears beginning to gather in his eyes. He did not want his Mom to see him cry again so he quickly picked up his suitcase and started toward the door.

Realizing she had been overly harsh with him Laura grabbed his shoulder in an attempt to stop him. Gary side stepped his Mother's grasp and continued toward the door.

"Gary, please, won't you even give me a hug?" Laura pleaded.

Knowing if he touched his mom he would completely loose it, Gary ignored his Mom's request. He rushed out the door shutting it with a loud bang. As he ran down the stairs he saw King sitting at the bottom.

"King, I love you." He cried as he stooped to hug the dog. Gary knew he was saying to the dog what he should have said to his Mother. For just a moment he considered going back up stairs to tell her. It was just too hard to be around his Mother, experiencing her grief and confusion when he had so much of his own. He was afraid to let go of King because it felt like it would be letting go of his Dad and his home. If he didn't move fast his Mother would come down the stairs. He would have to deal with her anger and emotion all over again. Reluctantly he gave King a final big kiss between his big black ears and picked up the suitcase. As he opened the door to the porch he looked once more at the dog. The tears he has been trying to stop spilled down his face like someone had opened a dam's floodgates.

Upstairs Gary's hurried exit was the last in a series of things that Laura found unreal. She fell onto the bed and curled up in a ball. Hugging her knees close to her chest she felt like a new baby born in a foreign and harsh environment. Gary was a stranger. She no longer had a husband. Oh, my God, she thought I have to take care of myself because there is no one left. Laura felt like shedding more tears but no more seemed to come. Lying with the smell of Gary still very close she did not want to move. Her mind traveled back over the years when Gary was living at home. They had been a happy family and done lots of things together. Peter, King and Gary were inseparable on weekends doing "guy things." She smiled as she thought of those family times. Peter's death had ended that. The last few days resembled a horror video that she wanted to turn off but couldn't. "Laura," she heard in the distance. Her neighbor was calling from downstairs. She knew she didn't want Susan to come into this room that smelled of pot. She hesitantly got up and dragged herself to the mirror to see if she could do anything about repairing her appearance. Looking in the mirror she saw a plain 47-year-old lady with short curly reddish blonde hair that had not begun to show any sign of gray. The face starring back at her was drawn and there were dark circles under her bright jade green eyes. Her face was puffy and her mascara had run down her checks.

"Oh, Laura you look like an old Hag." she whispered and rushed to the bathroom where she washed her face and combed her hair with a brush that Gary had forgotten. Looking in the mirror she thought, "I will deal with this somehow."

"I can handle this," she said out loud as she straightened her shoulders and turned to face the future without Gary or Peter.

CHAPTER TWO

As Laura descended the stairs, her next-door neighbors were waiting at the bottom with their raincoats draped over their arms. The sun had come out and was low in the horizon. Laura had not even realized it had stopped raining.

"Everything is all cleaned up and we put the extra food in the refrigerator." Susan explained. "If you need anything give us a call. I know the next few days will be difficult. We will touch base with you every day to see if there is anything you need. I once heard on the radio, it is a good idea to plan your activities a day at a time to help get through the first few days after a loss like yours. So, what are you going to do tomorrow?"

"I don't know. I suppose I should start to pack Peter's things. I don't feel like I can live with all so many reminders surrounding me." Laura responded.

"Would you like help doing that?"

"No, it is a personal thing. I must take it at my own pace but thanks anyway. I will keep in touch and please don't worry about me. I will get through all of this. I still have a life to live." Laura stuttered as if she knew those were the right words even if she didn't believe them.

"Okay, we'll talk to you tomorrow." Larry said as they stepped out the door.

The slamming of the door sounded like an exploding cannon to Laura. This was the beginning of her life alone. Panicking she decided she must get busy doing something. What would keep her mind occupied and was not too much of a reminder of the things she had to do in the next few days? Looking out the window she noticed the roses had many tattered blooms from the day's hard rain.

"There is still enough light to take off those sad looking flowers and pull a few weeds," she told King. "Come on boy, let's do it." Grabbing her scissors, she went into the back yard. Cutting off the dead blooms she put them in a plastic garbage bag, the ones which were still beautiful went in a jar of water she has brought along. Every time she saw a weed that was invading the flowerbed she pulled it with a vengeance. King lay beside her and supervised. Before Laura realized, it was too dark to see the weeds or to tell which blooms were worth keeping. Picking up her jar full of fragrant blossoms she called King and they returned to the house. As she placed the flowers on the kitchen table, she noticed she had not changed her clothes. Her best shoes were covered with mud and her suit was snagged in many places from rose thorns.

"Oh, dear. I am going to have to do better than this." She groaned. "I must start thinking things through."

Completely used up, she turned off the lights and headed upstairs to bed. Ever since Peter was killed, she had been sleeping on the pull out couch in the third bedroom that served, as her workplace. Again not being able to face the bed she had shared with her husband she headed for the office. Too exhausted to even hang up her ruined clothes, she threw them on the chair and slipped into her nightshirt.

"King, come." She called as she lay down on the couch. King jumped up, gave her a big lap with his tongue, and settled down at the end of the make shift bed.

Laura was afraid sleep would be difficult and wondered if she should take the sleeping pills the doctor had given her the night Peter was killed. As she thought about whether to get up and take them she drifted into a sleep brought on by complete exhaustion.

The next morning Laura woke to bright sunshine. As she opened her eyes, she saw the sun shown on her picture of Scotland's Neist Point lighthouse that hung over her desk. It had been placed above her desk as a daily reminder of Peter and her goal to retire to Scotland. For a few minutes Laura remembered the happy visit to Neist Point. They had a lovely time walking back that evening with the light rotating into the dark hills they were climbing. Peter had held her hand and they talked about how the sheep's eyes resembled shiny pieces of coal in the light's rays.

Shaking her head she said to herself. "Stop it, Laura! Peter is dead. Those plans are gone. You are alone and must find a new way to live. King, come its time to go out."

The dog was not anxious to get up but dutifully followed his mistress down the stairs. After putting King in the back yard, Laura fixed some coffee and toast. Sitting at the table beside the fragrant roses she picked last night Laura decided to make a list of the things she had to do. The first item was to find whether Peter had a will, which meant calling the lawyer. She'd also go through Peter's clothes. She would donate them to local charities, which might be able to use them. It was important to get them out of the house so she could truly face Peter was gone. After the clothes were sorted she would sketch how to redecorate the bedroom. It was important to her to remove any reference to her old life. Every time she thought about Peter it hurt so much she wanted to cry. After she got the house in shape she would have to decide how she would support herself and the house without Peter's income. Would she even be able to keep up the house payments? Fright gripped Laura as she thought about supporting herself. At least Gary was on a scholarship and self-sufficient in law school. Shaking her head Laura decided that was enough list making and thinking of the future. It was time to begin doing. Seeing the first item on the list was to call the lawyer, she looked at the clock and was shocked to see it was only 6:00 am.

"Its too early to call the lawyer. I will get cleaned up and begin going through Peter's things. Maybe if I am lucky I will even find a copy of a will and won't have to call the lawyer." She declared as she poured some more coffee and let King in from the back yard. "King, you must help me get through the next few hours. I am petrified of taking Peter's things from this house but I just can't go on with them here." The dog seemed to understand. He stood at attention and looked like he was ready to attack anything.

After Laura showered and changed into blue jeans and a sweatshirt she stood at the master bedroom door afraid to enter. Tossing her red gold hair she whispered to herself, "It takes only one step after another to advance. It takes only one step after another..." she repeated as she slowly opened Peter's side of the closet to begin the task of sorting his things. The sight of his neatly organized clothes brought back memories of the times Peter urged her to be more methodical about her clothes. She wouldn't have any trouble finding anything the way he had his closet organized. Reaching out to touch his favorite sweater they had bought at a woolen mill in Edinburgh, memories seemed to run her down with the force of a locomotive barreling down a track.

"No!" she proclaimed. "I will not get bogged down in self pity. I have a job to do and I must get on with it."

She took every thing off the hangers and folded them neatly in three different piles. One for the charity, one for Gary and one with things she wanted to keep. As the piles grew she noticed only one item in her pile. The sweater from Edinburgh seemed to be the only thing she wanted.

After an hour the bed had no more space to pile things. She would have to go downstairs and get a box or a plastic garbage bag to put the charity things into. Eighty percent of the material piled on the bed was going to them. Reluctantly she went to the garage to get some of the boxes that were always stacked in the back. She hated the empty garage. Her car was parked out front and Peter's was gone forever. For the first time since she had gotten up sorrow overwhelmed her as she left the empty garage with three big boxes. Passing through the kitchen from the garage all she think of were reasons why she should be doing something else besides sorting the clothes. She could have a cup of coffee; clean up the plate and knife she left from breakfast, or wash the suit she probably ruined last night. As she struggled up the stairs with the boxes she realized she must complete sorting now or it would never get done.

"This is the hardest step the next one will be easier. I seem to be talking to myself a lot. Is that sign of shock or am I losing my mind?" Laura said to no one in particular. "Maybe I need to see that counselor Larry Madison said specialized in death and dying. I will add making an appointment with him to my things to do this morning. Yes, I will see that counselor." The idea of talking with the counselor gave Laura a little peace and she swiftly went upstairs and began to pack the clothes into the boxes.

"The one thing left to go through is Peter's desk. After I have a cup of coffee I will attack the desk." She muttered to herself as she carried the first of the heavy boxes down the stairs. Putting coffee on to brew she went upstairs and retrieved the other two boxes. Looking at the empty closet, she felt a mixture of pride for getting the job done along with sadness at how bare the closet looked. Wanting to shut away the sight, she slammed the closet door, picked up the boxes, and moved quickly down stairs.

With her freshly brewed mug of coffee she sat at Peter's desk. The first thing she noticed was a picture taken three years ago on a family vacation in Scotland. It was the last trip Gary would make with them before his studies kept him at school full time. Laura pondered what had happened to cause Gary to act the way he did last night. They were always so close.

Beginning with the desk's bottom drawer, she found most of them full of school information and newsletters from the various organizations Peter belonged to. She put the school stuff in a brown paper grocery bag and dumped out the rest. The narrow middle drawer she left until last because it probably contained only odds and ends. She always threw things in her middle drawer when she didn't know where else to put it. Opening the drawer she was amazed how organized it is. Everything was arranged in a logical order. She smiled because it was so like Peter. On the right hand side were some papers. One was an insurance policy, another a retirement policy from the school district, and the final one looked like a will.

"Just like Peter to have the important papers where he knew I would easily find them," she said. Even after he was gone Peter seemed to be taking care of her just like he did all their years of their marriage.

The insurance policy paid off the mortgage on the house upon the death of either her or Peter. She laid it aside and looked at the retirement policy. After weeding through the details of the retirement legalize, she came to the part, which said. "Benefits Upon Death of Employee." Laura was shocked. Right there in black and white it said she was to inherit $150,000 in case of accidental death. "Well, money is not going to be a problem for a while with the house paid off and $150,000 in addition." she said with a sigh of relief.

She put the will off to last. A will was so personal. Laura did not want to read Peter's words in her now empty world. It was important she knew what it contained so she slowly opened the document and began to read. It was a standard format leaving everything to her and in case of a joint death to Gary. She skipped through it until she came to the last item. Peter had bought some stocks in a local utility company without telling her. The sole purpose of the investment was to buy a lighthouse when they retired.

"I wonder what they are worth?" Laura contemplated.

Knowing a good way to find out she called her neighbor, Larry Madison, who was a stockbroker.

"Larry, its Laura. I was wondering if you could tell me what 200 shares of Greenly Utilities are worth on today's market. It seems Peter bought the stock as an investment to help pay for the lighthouse in Scotland."

"I'll look it up and get back to you as soon as I have an answer. How are you today?" He asked.

"I am making it," she answered since she really didn't know how she was supposed to be.

"Good. I'll call you back when I know the exact the worth of the stock. Wait, I have a better idea. Would you like to come over for lunch and I can give you the answer then?"

"Yikes it is twelve-thirty. It is almost lunchtime and I haven't even cleaned up the breakfast dishes. Yes, I would love to come over for lunch. It would get me out of the house for a while and King would love to romp with Maxx. I haven't even taken time to walk him this morning. See you in a few minutes."

"King, where are you?" Laura called when she realized she has not seen the dog since she came down stairs. Searching downstairs she did not find him so she went upstairs. Looking in the master bedroom she saw the gigantic dog curled up as tightly as he could on the sweater from Edinburgh. "King, get off that sweater. You know you are not allowed to lie on people's clothes. I know you miss Peter but that sweater is important to me. Anyway we are going next door for lunch and Maxx will be waiting."

Hearing the name of his favorite playmate, King jumped quickly off the sweater and ran down the stairs. As soon as he reached the bottom he impatiently looked up at Laura like he had been waiting for hours.

Laura took a few minutes to clean up and change into some better clothes. Her reflection in the mirror seemed healthier and more positive. She thought about what she had been doing all morning. The best therapy was to keep busy and not to think about the past or problems in the future. Some how she would get through the next few weeks just like she was able to sort Peter's clothes this morning. No matter how difficult the situation she would make it. Realizing this encouraged Laura. It would be interesting to see how much the stock that Peter had bought for the lighthouse was worth.

Susan Madison answered the door and handed Laura a cup of wonderful smelling coffee. "I just brewed this. It is a new blend and quite strong but I felt you might like it," she said as she offered the coffee to Laura.

"Thanks, it smells fantastic. You know how much I like different types of coffee." Laura replied all the time wondering if the Madisons had gone out and gotten the coffee just to make her feel better. Since Susan didn't mention it she felt she would just accept the gift, no matter what the reason. Sometimes, you just had to let people do things for you because it made them feel better.

"Where's Larry?" Laura asked.

"He's at the computer working on the value of that stock you found. Why don't you join him in the office while I put the finishing touches on lunch? Will pasta salad be okay?

"Great," Laura answered. "I am hungry for the first time in days." Laura realized what she told Susan was true. She was hungry. "I'll go find Larry. Give us a call when you are ready or need any help."

Laura tentatively knocked on Larry's door fearing he might be involved with client on the telephone.

"Come in, rich person." Larry answered.

"Rich person?" Laura questioned. "The stock must have been worth something."

"Yes, it has increased in value a lot since Peter originally purchase it. Would you believe if you sold it today you would get somewhere around $150,000 for it. Peter certainly knew what he was doing when he chose this particular stock. I never knew he was into investing. When did he start doing it? Is there more stock?"

"I don't think there is any more. He bought this according to his will to be used to purchase a lighthouse when we retired to Scotland. I suppose he felt there would be no other way we could get the lighthouse. And it looks like his idea worked because the stock value is more than enough for a lighthouse."

"What are you going to do with this stock, Laura?" Larry asked.

"I have no idea. What do you suggest? Will it increase in value or should I sell now?"

"I feel the stock may go down in the next few years as Greenly has been having some financial troubles. They lost a suit to an environmental group on their nuclear reactor plant. If you need the money right now it would be a good time to sell. You could also gamble and leave it until you need it." Larry answered.

Laura is overwhelmed, "Larry, with this stock and Peter's retirement through the school I have over $300,000. I don't even know what I am going to do tomorrow. How am I supposed to know what to do with $300,000? Peter thought ahead. All of sudden I have a lot of money. My life is in chaos and all I want is for it to return to normal. Now I am rich and things are not the same. In some ways the money makes it worse?" The thought of Peter's wisdom and how well he had taken care of her brought a terrible pain inside Laura. She doubled over and dropped into the chair beside Larry's desk.

"Laura, are you alright?" Larry asked. "I know it is a shock but you don't have to decide now. The stock can just sit until you make a decision."

"Larry, I am completely surrounded with Peter's love. I wish he were here to thank him for doing so much to make my life easier. But, the problem is in some ways it just makes it harder. I don't have to worry about paying the bills but I still have to worry about how I am going to live without him. I can't even imagine the next few years."

"Lunch." Susan called from the kitchen. Larry was thankful his wife had come to his rescue since he had no idea how to answer Laura.

"Lets, go eat. No decisions are necessary now and we can discuss all of this later when a little time has helped to heal some of the hurt."

Laura straightened up, smiled through the fog of her tears, and realized Larry was right. She didn't have to make a decision right now and she found she still was hungry. She grabbed the hand Larry offered to pull her from the chair and followed him into the kitchen.

CHAPTER THREE

The last few days had been busy as Laura began her life alone. After giving Peter's clothes to Goodwill Laura started redecorating the master bedroom. She had given all the curtains and matching bed linens to Goodwill along with the clothes. All of the furniture she had repainted a basic white. A new set of matching bed linens and curtains had been purchased. Looking in from the door at the redecorated room Laura concluded she once more could sleep in this like new room. She felt a little unfaithful to Peter's memory but she knew this was the only way she would heal. Some people need to hold tightly to all the things that remind them of what they have lost. Laura was only interested in moving on with her life. The memories tormented her. She needed a new beginning.

The check from the retirement policy had come. Without knowing which direction she wanted to go, she had put it in a regular savings account so the money would be easily accessible. Laura had spent many sleepless nights thinking about the stock wondering whether she should sell. Desperate for guidance she had called Gary to ask his opinion. All she reached was his answering machine. Feeling separated from her son she had left many messages for him to call her. He still had not called. Not hearing from him was beginning to worry her. She called twice today and there still was no human answer.

"Where could he be? Laura asked King as if the dog had an answer.

"We will call again tonight. Would you like to go for a ride in the car big guy? I need to go to the bank and deposit a check. Maybe if you are good, we will go by the drive-in and get an ice cream cone for both of us."

Laura had noticed her eating was out of control since Peter died. She had always worn a perfect size 10 but most of her clothes were a little tight these days. She was confident it was her reaction to the stress of the situation and would go away in time. Tomorrow she would start exercising more. Exercise would relieve the stress and reduce her appetite.

Driving to the bank she began thinking about the stock again. "Peter wanted that money to go for a lighthouse. For five years we had been planning our retirement around buying a lighthouse in Scotland. It still was a perfect dream. I would be happy in a historic old building at the edge of the sea with no one for company but the wind, waves and the birds. Some people need to be around people all the time. I am happy alone or with just few people around me. All I need to keep me content is my computer. The Internet gives me contact with the whole world and yet I am still in isolation." Laura thought.

"Stop it. It was a dream that died with Peter. If only he were here now that the money for the lighthouse is available," Laura whispered to herself. Suddenly Laura realized the stock money had been there before Peter died. He had been so busy he hadn't even taken time to check.

"I guess that is what happens to all of us," she told King. "We get preoccupied with day to day things like running to the bank. We forget to reexamine the things we say are important in our lives. I'm promising you since there is no one else to say this to. We are not going to neglect the important things in the future. We will focus on what is important without getting distracted. Peter got in the car to drive to practice. A few minutes later his life was over. The same thing could happen to us. Something could happen today and we would not return from the bank."

Seeing the drive-in window was occupied Laura parked the car and gathered up her deposit to take inside.

"Stay put King. I will be right back." She said as she shut the car door.

Seeing a friend across the street coming her way Laura waited to have a little chat before she shoved the bank door open.

"Get down on the floor."

Laura looked up to see a shot gun pointed at her by a man dressed in bid overalls, an artificial red bird mask and sun glasses. It took Laura a couple of seconds until she comprehended she has walked into a bank robbery.

"I said get down on the floor. And I do not want to tell you again." The stranger shouted.

Laura began to shake all over and her legs went weak. She sank to the floor more out of desperation to stop the shaking than because the man with the gun had told her to do it.

As she laid face down on the floor, she heard the man ordering the tellers to put the cash quickly in the bag. Laura didn't even attempt to look up. The words she had spoken to King in the car about not returning from the bank echoed in her mind. If this man shoots me, King will be left without anyone. Realizing she was jumping to conclusions she laid as still as possible. Remembering a TV documentary about hostage taking that said you should try not to draw attention to yourself she laid perfectly still. She listened to the sound of footsteps advancing toward her.

"Oh, my God, he is coming towards me." she thought.

The footsteps paused right beside her. Laura knew the man was going to shoot her. All she thought about was poor King alone in the car and Gary who she had not been able to reach. Gary was going to lose his Mother and Dad all in the same month. What would he do?

Laura perceived the man bending down towards her. Saying the Lord's Prayer repeatedly in her mind, she hoped it would help her accept what ever was going to happen. When you are about to die it seemed the best thing to do. She waited for the sound of the gun, which would end her life.

The man seemed to be picking up something beside her. Laura heard no shots or felt any pain. A click resembling a lock springing shut was all she heard over the thudding of her heart. The footsteps started again but this time away from her. The man now behind her said. "Don't move or contact anyone for five minutes. My partner outside will shoot you if he sees any of you make a wrong move." The footsteps faded. Laura heard a door open and shut.

Frozen like a block of ice by her fear, Laura waited for something to happen. Finally she heard a teller pick up the telephone and call the police. Some one was coming toward her. Laura wanted to cry out but could not move. A lock clicked. Hands reached down and touched her. Laura screamed.

"He's gone. Mrs. File please get up. You are safe now," the head teller mumbled. Laura felt herself being lifted from the place of cold terror to a standing position "Are you alright?"

"Yes, I think so. I thought he was going to shoot me when he stopped beside me."

"No, he had left his gun case near where you were lying. He stopped to put the gun in the case. I suppose so when he was outside no one would notice."

As Laura got to her feet she felt like life was starting over. "Thank God, you are alive." She whispered to the teller. "I tried to stay as quiet as possible so he wouldn't shoot any of you. I was terrified for the three of you. I didn't want him to shoot you because I did any thing out of line."

"Mrs. File, we appreciate your concern but we were in no danger. The glass in front of us is bullet proof. If he had pulled the trigger he would not have been able to injury us. Now, you were a different story. My heart just about stopped when I saw you walk in the door. There was nothing to protect you. Thank God you did exactly what he told you so he didn't get upset and shoot."

Laura felt her knees give way, as she comprehended how near she had come to death. The teller anticipating Laura's reaction led her gently to a chair on the far side of the room. Laura fell into the chair and was extremely cold again. She commenced to shiver although the room was actually hot. The icy fear had returned.

"Don't worry Mrs. File," the teller told her. "It is all over. It is normal for you to experience shock after what you have been through. I will get you a glass of water. You just set there and rest. The police will be here soon and then you can go home."

Laura dropped into the chair and drank her water. The tellers begin going through what looked like a written procedure. They were extremely busy. Laura yearned for something to do except sit and wait for the police. Time was frozen in her icy fear. Laura was sure it had been at least a thirty minutes since they called the police.

"What is taking the police so long?" Laura asked.

"It has only been five minutes. Time seems slow after such a huge shock. I hear the sirens. It soon will be over Mrs. File." One of the tellers answered.

The teller was right. A police car came screeching to a halt in front of the bank. Two uniformed officers jumped out. One of the tellers ran to the door to let one of the them into the bank. The other policeman placed a yellow tape around the sidewalk in front of the bank. The policeman who came inside immediately began to question the tellers and record their answers in a little notebook. The second officer stayed outside by the door so no one could enter. Neither of them paid any attention to Laura who was hunched over in her chair watching. Another car arrived and a tall handsome gentleman in a suit entered. He asked a few questions of the two officers and then he noticed the despondent Laura.

"I am Sergeant Grant of the Sheriff's department, Mrs. File. Are you all right? Would you like us to call someone for you? I have just a few questions and then you will be allowed to go." Laura thought for a second. She really didn't want to drive home but whom would she call. With Peter gone and Gary unavailable she was totally alone. "No, officer, my dog is waiting in the car. I will drive myself home as soon as you have completed your questions."

The Sergeant asked her to describe the man and a few other details about what she had seen. Laura was positive he sensed how desperately she wanted to flee the bank. When he was finished Laura got up to escape to her car. As she stood she realized she still held her deposit in her hand.

"Officer, can I make my deposit?"

"No, the bank is officially closed but a teller can give you a night deposit slip. You put it in the drop box and they will process it first thing tomorrow."

Laura placed the deposit in the drop box and dashed to her car. Poor King had been shut up in the car for such a long time. Looking at her watch she was bewildered. It had only been 45 minutes since she went into the bank. She felt like it had been hours.

"Oh, King, I thought I would never see you again."

Laura muttered as she put her arms around the dog and buried her face in his sleek fur. Inside the bank Laura had shed no tears. The minute she was in the car she began to cry. Laura had lied to the police when she told them she was not badly frightened. Hysteria was a breath away. She started the car and automatically went through the steps necessary to get King home.

When she arrived home she called Susan Madison to see if she would come over and keep her company. Susan wasn't home. Desperate to talk to someone she dialed Gary's number again hoping that just by chance he would be there. The answering machine clicked in on the fourth ring.

"Gary, it is Mom. I need you. This afternoon I was involved in an armed bank robbery. I am so scared. Please call me as soon as you can." Laura pleaded.

Laura having failed to reach anyone sat in the living room and stared at the wall. Since Peter's death she has known she was alone but not until this moment did she comprehend just how alone. A few minutes ago she had almost been killed. She had no one to even talk with. She wasn't paranoid enough to believe no one cared. There just wasn't anyone, whose life was closely linked with hers any more. When Peter had been killed she had become like a baseball free agent - not attached to anyone. She was totally on her own. People cared but no one was available when she desperately needed support.

Laura felt abandoned but strangely it did not bring more panic. It was the way things were. As she thought about it Laura began to feel a new type of freedom. She could do anything she wanted because no one cared. Except for King no one was dependent on her. If she had been shot this afternoon all her opportunities would have been over. There would have been no decisions to make or scary future. She would not have to decide what to do with the stock or figure out how to deal with Gary. Suddenly Laura knew there was something she yearned to do. For years it had been her wish to go to Scotland and live in a lighthouse. When she and Peter had decided to retire in Scotland it hadn't been Peter's idea but hers. Peter had caught the dream from her. He was gone. Laura still had the dream. No one would be affected by what she did except King and he would go with her. Peter's wise investments had given her the money and opportunity to make the dream come true. All she had to do was do it. Laura had heard life-threatening events helped people become more conscious of what really matters. Laura knew what she wanted. She was going to buy a lighthouse and move to Scotland before something happened to take the opportunity away from her.

CHAPTER FOUR

Around 9:30 the evening the day after the bank robbery Laura was putting on her nightgown when the telephone rang. Exhausted from answering everyone's questions about the robbery, she was reluctant to answer. All the calls had been from "friends," some of which had not even contacted her when Peter died. They all asked how she was but it was obvious the callers were more curious about details of the robbery than her welfare. "Maybe I am being unfair," Laura thought as she answered the telephone.

"Mom, its Gary. I called as soon as I got your message. Are you okay? Were you hurt?"

"Gary, I am shook up but I not physically hurt. I have been worried about you. I have left at least ten messages without a reply. A more appropriate question is how are you and where have you been?"

"Mom, there is something I been wanting to tell you. I should have told you when I was in Granton for Dad's funeral but I didn't want to upset you any more than you already were. I have met this girl. Her name is Vicki Wells. She is a law student too. We have been ... spending a lot of time together."

"That is good news but it still does not explain why you didn't return my calls"

"Yes, it does. I am not just spending time with her. I am living with her. I have been for the last three months."

"Why didn't you tell me? Is it serious relationship? Are you planning on marrying her? Why didn't you bring her to your Father's funeral?"

"I didn't tell you because I was afraid you would jump to the wrong conclusion. I am not in love with her and have no plans to marry her. To be perfectly honest she is just a lot of fun to be around, quite good in bed, and it is cheaper to live together." Laura could not believe what she was hearing.

"Gary, I hope you know what you are doing. You can't be involved with someone over long period of time without severe emotional consequences. You are an adult so I won't try to lecture - just be careful."

"Don't worry, Mom. I know what I am doing."

"When do I get to meet her?"

"That is not such a good idea right now. Maybe by the end of the school term we can get together. Now, back to the bank robbery, did they catch the gunman? It was a man wasn't it?"

"No, they haven't caught the person. I honestly don't know whether it was a man or a woman. It really doesn't matter. I am just thankful it is over. Gary, I have a few things I need to tell you related to your father's estate." Laura casually explains about the $150,000 retirement benefit and the Greenly stock.

"What are you going to do with all that money?" Gary asked quietly.

"First, I want to know if you will be needing help with school or living expenses before I decide anything."

"I have a full scholarship. Now that I am living with Vicki I have hardly any living expenses. I might need cash when I get out of law school to help set up my own practice. I haven't decided whether I want to go into private practice. Everyone says it is better to work for a big firm first. I will do that if I get the right offer which means I might not have any use for the money for a long time. What do you want to do with it?"

Laura thought carefully before she answered. She wanted to spell out her plan precisely so Gary wouldn't think she was foolish. "I am going to sell the stock and do what your Dad intended and buy a lighthouse in Scotland. King and I will move over there. I plan to talk to a real estate agent in Granton tomorrow about putting this house on the market. Today I searched the Internet for lighthouse property. I may have found some strong leads. I hope to hear something tomorrow from one of the Scottish estate agents."

"Mom, you're being irrational. You don't just pick up, sell your house, and move to a lighthouse in Scotland. What about supporting yourself and being close to me? What about King?"

"I can support myself over there just like I do here. I will design computer graphics and keep in touch with clients by Internet. You are involved with your new girl friend and finishing law school. There is plenty of money if we want to see each other. We can just jump on a plane. King is going with me. Gary, I am so thrilled about all of this. It is exactly what I want. Please support me while I try to make all of this happen. Your father's death along with the bank robbery where I had a shot gun aimed at my head helped me see I am no longer want to put my hopes and dreams off."

"To be perfectly honest, Mom, I think you should see a counselor before you do anything. Dad's death and now this bank robbery, I believe has been too much stress for you. What you are considering is insane. Have you told anyone else?"

"Not yet." Laura answered. "I wanted you to tell you first. No matter what anyone says, including you I am going to buy a lighthouse. I need your support. The only close family I have is you and King."

"I will help you as much as I can if you stay in the US but not if you leave for Scotland. It sounds like there is nothing I can say to stop you. Let me know when you are ready to leave the country and I'll send you a post card." Gary said as he promptly hung up.

Laura stood for a long time with the telephone in her hand before she put it back on the wall. She needed Gary's support and the opportunity to share her new adventure with him. If her own son thought she was crazy she wondered if anyone would understand and support her going to Scotland? Peter would understand if he were here. Not wanting to become overwhelmed with apprehension she sat down at the computer and began to list what she needed to do to make this all happen in her new planning software.

As her plan developed it was obvious many things had to be done before she would get very far. Finding a lighthouse was number one. Hopefully, she would hear from one of the estate agents tomorrow. When she found the right lighthouse, she would sell the Granton house. If she couldn't sell the house maybe, she could rent it. Money was not a big issue thanks to Peter. Selling the Greenly stock and putting the money in the bank should be done right away. After the house was sold or rented then she must decide what to take to Scotland with her. King was going for sure. The most difficult part of the plan was King would have to go into quarantine. The United Kingdom had stiff laws against rabies. They required all animals that entered the country be held in confinement for six months. King not being with her would be one of the hardest parts of this process.

The different electrical current in Scotland meant she would have to buy all new electrical appliances including a new computer. A while back someone had offered to buy her computer so she could begin there. A well-designed page on the Internet would help find new clients for her graphic design business. Why had she not thought about that before now? It didn't matter where she lived as long as people can reach her via the World Wide Web. All she needed was an Internet Service Provider (ISP) to provide space for her web pages and to allow her to receive E-mail. A search on the Internet for an ISP located in Scotland was added to her things to do. She wasn't sure she could select a server until she knew where she would be living but she would check. The planning software wasn't like talking it out with someone but it would be a big help getting her to Scotland. She would make this come to pass she decided as she saved her additions.

Laura was so excited she started the development of her home page even thought it is already going on midnight. She hardly even noticed the time as she drafted the design. She already had a company logo so she did not need to develop a new one. Did she need to establish a corporation in Scotland or can she keep her business incorporated in the US? Suddenly she knew she didn't want to keep her business in the US. She wanted a total break. Laura brought up the planning software and added incorporation in Scotland to the list. The distraction from the development of the home page made her to look at her watch. It was 3:00 a. m. Suddenly Laura felt very tired. She was so excited she was not sure she could sleep.

"I must get some sleep so I can take care of all these important things tomorrow. I know what will help me sleep. Peter's supply of Scottish single malt whisky, which she had not given away, would put her to sleep in no time. One 'wee dram' of malt and I will sleep like a baby." She said to herself. "I must stop talking to myself and King all the time. Gary thinks I am crazy. He is wrong but I must be careful to act like a normal person. People may question my sanity. I must be careful to make sure everything I do is well thought out and logical. I will drink my scotch and when I get up tomorrow, oops, today, I will begin working on my list."

Laura put King out for his nightly trip when the telephone rang. Laura looked at her watch. It was 3:30 a.m. It could be the estate agent in Scotland. There was a 6-hour time difference between Granton and Scotland so she hurried to answer the telephone.

"Mrs. File," someone with a deep Scotch voiced asked.

"Yes, this is Laura File."

"My name is Tom Morrison. I work for Morrison & McNeill Estate Agents in Edinburgh. Your E-mail to the Northern Lighthouse Board inquiring if they had any lighthouse accommodations currently on the market was referred to me. We handle all their property. There is a lighthouse currently on the market on the Island of Gealach in the Outer Hebrides. Robert Stevenson built it in 1814. The keeper's accommodations are small with only one house with two bedrooms. A private five-car ferry runs twice a day from the Isle of Lewis to the island. Ferry service operates from Ullapool to the Isle of Lewis two times daily from the mainland so Gealach is quite accessible for such a small island. The Island of Gealach consists of 7,400 acres and a population of 150 crofters and fishermen. There is a post office in the local shop, which is also a petrol station. Most of the main shopping must be done in Stornoway on the Isle of Lewis. Have you been to Stornoway?

"Yes, I've been there three times in the last two years."

"It would be your primary spot for shopping and services. It has a good hospital and there is helicopter ambulance service from Stornoway to Gealach so the lighthouse is not far from anything you would need."

"What price is the Northern Lighthouse Board

asking for the property?"

"They are looking for offers more than £75,000."

"Has a bid closing date been set?"

"That is why I am calling as the bid closing is in two weeks. It may be too short of notice for you to respond but we wanted you to know about this property. It seemed to meet the description contained in your E-mail."

"How fast can you get me the brochure on the property? What surveyor would you suggest I use to have the property inspected?" An excited Laura responded.

"I sent the brochure this morning air post. Do you have a fax? I can fax you a copy of the brochure as well."

"Please do so immediately." Laura answered giving him the fax number and trying not to let her excitement show. "Is there someone on the island who I could contact to take some pictures for me? Is there anyone who would scan them and put them on the Internet?"

"Larry Macdonald is the attendant to the lighthouse and quite a good photographer. I will call him and have him take the pictures today."

"Fine. Have him do it and look for someone who will put them on the Internet? Naturally I will pay for that service. You did not answer me about the surveyor. Can you recommend a surveyor?"

"I will have to get back to you on that. I imagine there are come good ones in Stornoway but I am not familiar with any personally." Mr. Morrison replied.

"Look forward to hearing from you soon." Laura replied. "Please fax the brochure immediately so I can evaluate whether I want to continue looking at this property."

"My secretary is preparing the fax as we speak, Mrs. File and we look forward to hearing from you."

As Laura hung up she could not contain her excitement. A lighthouse was available immediately. She hurriedly looked for her map of Scotland. Finding the map, she searched for the Island of Gealach. She found a small dot on the map marked Gealach. It was a little south and east of Lewis in the Minch. Lewis sheltered the island from the Atlantic's fury.

"Woof, woof."

"Oh, King, I forgot all about you." Laura said as she let the distressed dog back into the house. She locked the door and hurried off to the new bed in the master bedroom. As excited as she was, she fell to sleep immediately.

The ringing of the telephone woke Laura. She looked at the clock. It was only 6:15 in the morning. She had slept less than three hours. She decided to let the machine answer and then she remembered Mr. Morrison's promise to fax the information on the lighthouse.

"The brochure." Laura shouted as she ran to the fax and watched as a picture of a typical Scottish lighthouse appeared on the emerging paper. Laura hoped this was going to be the perfect place for her and King. She waited impatiently as the brochure continued to snake out of the machine. Peering over the machine she saw more pictures but she was afraid to tear the paper off, as she would smear part of the income message. After what seemed like hours the machine beeped to indicate the entire message has been received. She carefully tore the paper and hurried to her desk for scissors to cut the long roll of paper into pages. If she wasn't so tight she would have a plain paper fax and it wouldn't be necessary to cut the pages she thought impatiently. Cutting each page, she piled them face down so they would be in order when she went to read them. Her eagerness was so intense she wanted to read each page as she cut it instead of waiting until all were in order. Knowing she should take notes and list questions she forced herself to go to the kitchen and make a cup of tea. After the tea was all made, she placed the fax, still face down, her teapot and a plate of scones onto a tray to take out to the rose garden. It was one of those unusual warm sunny days which sometimes appear in the late fall. Realizing she was forgetting a dog biscuit for King she placed one on the tray and headed for the rose garden.

The early morning sun touched the rose blossoms, which had survived the first frost. The garden was sparkling with reds, yellows, pinks and white. Dew was still on the hearty petals so they look fresh and crisp. After wiping moisture off the wrought iron table Laura sat down. It was pleasant to be surrounded by the wonderful sweet floral fragrance. The beauty of the spot helped Laura relax as she seeped her tea. Picking up the fax she read. "Gealach Head Keeper's Accommodations." A small flat roofed cottage with a large white tower to the right stared out from the fax. The tower looked about three times as high as the cottage. A stonewall surrounded the cottage and the tower. Laura could tell the buildings were trimmed in black and a lighter color not possible to distinguish in a black and white fax. Knowing the Northern Lighthouse Board, the color was probably yellow as most of their properties were trimmed in that color. The general description of the area was exactly what Mr. Morrison had told her on the telephone. The 7,400-acre Isle of Gealach lay off the southeast tip of the Isle of Lewis. The keepers' accommodations included twelve acres of ground. Laura skipped quickly over the ferry information since Mr. Morrison had been so specific about the accessibility. The next section describing the keeper's house was what she really wanted to see. The cottage had an entryway with a small sitting room with a solid fuel Rayburn, which provided heat and hot water on the left. A small eating area was a part of the sitting room, which had a window looking out on the water. Behind the tiny room was a kitchen with stove, a refrigerator, built in cupboards and a sink with double windows looking out toward the sea. The bathroom was behind the kitchen. The hall turned right to form an "L" shape. On the right of the long hall was a formal living room with fireplace. At the end of the hall was the entry to the master bedroom, which though small had a large window, looking out across the sea toward the islands of Skye and North and South Uist. Perfect thought Laura, she could stand and do dishes while watching the whales swim by the lighthouse. Reading on she found included in the sale were a garage, a Land Rover, a walled garden and a glass house to raise vegetables. Laura was amazed. She would need to have a survey done and see the pictures but it sounded just like what she and Peter had dreamed of. The price was only £75,000 and with current exchange rate she would have more than enough money when she sold the stock to buy the house and the furniture necessary to live.

"Oh, King, we have found our new home." She said as she looked at the picture again with tears of joy streaming down her face.

CHAPTER FIVE

Laura sat for a long time staring at the picture of the small lighthouse. Often people dream about something knowing it will never come true. In many ways that was how Laura had felt about buying a lighthouse. It was something, which might happen in the future and was fun to talk about. On her lap was a picture of the real thing. It could be hers. Laura felt sad realizing Peter would never see it or be with her at the lighthouse. The big dog at her feet recognized something was wrong. He nuzzled Laura's hand with his head. The warm touch of King's head brought Laura back to the present. Looking at the dog, Laura tried to think about the future not the past.

"Thanks, King." She said. "It's just you and me. I must remember that. I do wish Gary would take more interest in what I am trying to do. His new girl friend seems more important than we are. Hopefully some day he will recognize his mistake. Where did I file that list I made of things to do? We will get things started by tackling some of the tasks on that list."

Laura searched for a few minutes until she found the list on the computer. Contacting the real estate agent about selling the house was first. Finding the number in the telephone book, Laura called Lucy Mann, the agent who had sold them this house. Lucy was not there. Her secretary said she would contact Lucy on her cellular telephone and get her to call Laura right back. Not being able to contact the real estate agent was disappointing, so Laura continued with the list. The next item was selling the Greenly stock. This was a difficult because it meant Laura would have to tell the Madisons she was moving.

Reluctantly she dialed Larry's number hoping he would not be there so she could leave a message on his voice mail and not have to explain.

"This is Larry Madison. May I help you?" A cheerful voice answered.

"Larry it is Laura. I have decided to sell the Greenly stock as quickly as possible."

"Let me see what the value is right now." Larry

replied as he typed. "It is higher than it was when we looked the other day. Are you sure you want to sell? You could wait a few months to see if it gets any better?"

"Since it is strong just go ahead and sell." Laura responded.

"Will do it right away. But what's the rush? You must have made up your mind what you are going to do with the money." Larry quarried.

"Yes, I have. I hope you and Susan being my best friends and neighbors will support my decision. My son isn't."

"Of course we will. What are you going to do?"

"Larry, I am going to use the funds to buy a lighthouse in Scotland. It is why Peter invested the money. I've always really wanted to own a lighthouse."

"I can't see why Gary was so upset. We have discussed this many times and a self catering lighthouse is a good investment." Larry happily replied.

"The lighthouse will not be self catering. King and I are going to live there. Larry, I am moving to Scotland." Laura enthusiastically explained.

The telephone was silent for a few seconds. Finally Larry answered quietly. "Laura, Susan and I will miss you. I know how much you have always wanted to live in Scotland. I will not be selfish by trying to talk you out of it. We will help you in any way we can. Have you found a lighthouse to buy?"

"Yes or at least one that looks promising. It is on a small island called Gealach in the Outer Hebrides. Just a small house but it would fine for the dog and I." Laura happily replied.

"Why don't you come over for supper and bring all the information so Susan and I can share your excitement."

"King and I would love to come. By then, I may have more information. You will never know how much this means to me. Gary just hung up when I told him."

"Why do you think Gary is so upset about it?" Larry asked.

"I hoped it was because he would miss us. More and more I believe he is concerned about what people will think. His mother selling everything and moving off to Scotland a short time after her husband's death. You know what Larry, I just don't care what other people think." Laura was surprised how angry she sounded.

"It is your life and I agree with you, Laura. We can talk more about it tonight. I will get busy and sell the stock. Tonight I may even have a check for you. See you then." Larry answered as he hung up.

Laura was grateful for Larry's support. It gave her new enthusiasm to work on the design of her home page. She would have liked to go on the Internet to see if she could find any more information on the Isle of Gealach. Being online would tie up the telephone line so the real estate agent would not be able to reach her. Laura created a new layout for her home page design with a picture of a Gealach Head lighthouse. A link to information about the location of the lighthouse was added to the information about her. "It is important to not get too involved with any particular lighthouse and location until things were more definite." Laura thought and removed the link. As she began to save her design the telephone rang.

"Mrs. File? This is Lucy Mann. First, I want to express my condolences upon the death of your husband. He was a nice man and we will all miss him. My secretary said you called and are interested in selling your house."

Although Laura felt Lucy was being a little too congenial she replied with enthusiasm. "Thank you for the kind words, Lucy. I need to sell my house as quickly as possible. I have identified a piece of property outside the country and want to be in a position to place an offer on it immediately. How long do you think it will take to sell this house?"

"Houses on an average take 90 days to sell in today's market. There is no way of knowing for sure. If you want to do it quickly we should get started. When can I come over and go through the comparable properties to set the price so we can get it on the market?"

"How about later this afternoon?" Laura answered.

"You are in a hurry. I believe I can work up a price by then. How about 4:00?"

"Fine, see you then." Laura replied as you put the telephone down. The more she thought about it the more sure she was that she didn't like that women. The good part was she wouldn't have to deal with her after the sale. She would be in Scotland. Now that the important calls were completed she could get on the Internet to find out more about the Gealach Island and maybe the lighthouse. Her Internet search revealed Gealach was one of the smaller inhabited islands in the Hebrides. The population has been slowly declining as the younger residents were leaving the island and the number of older people who had stayed was declining as death took them one by one. The island's one claim to fame was the mysterious disappearance of a lighthouse keeper's wife. The local rumor said she was a silkie. A "silkie" was a seal that at certain times can come back as a woman. The only documented fact was the lighthouse keeper's wife had disappeared. Some believe the lighthouse is revisited by the "silkie" on a periodic basis. Laura was thrilled by the thought of a haunted lighthouse. She didn't believe in witches, ghosts, or silkies so the legend excited her more than frightened her. It would be exciting to investigate to see if she could find the true story.

The other important piece of information she found was the Western Isles Regional Council had obtained a grant to help the islanders learn computer skills, to establish a cottage industry based on retyping information for publishers, and using the Internet as a communication tool for the isolated islands.

"Every one involved will need web pages. Once they start making a living with their computers on the World Wide Web they will need my services." Laura chuckled. "There I go again talking to myself. I am really going to have to learn to keep my thoughts to myself." Laura grumbled.

Just as she finished rebuking herself the doorbell rang. Laura looked at her watch. It wasn't time for the real estate agent. Who could it be? She ran to the door and there stood her neighbor. Larry had completed the sale of the stock. He was so excited he could not wait until tonight to give Laura the check.

"I have something for you Laura." Larry said with a gleam in his eye.

"Come in." She answered.

"Haven't got time but here is a present for you."

Larry pulled from behind his back a miniature lighthouse with an envelope attached to it. Laura couldn't believe her eyes. It was so unlike Larry to do something like this. She took the wee lighthouse and looked at it.

"For heaven's sake Laura open the envelope. The lighthouse is not the important part of this." Larry hollered.

Not entirely agreeing with Larry but not wanting to frustrate him after all his trouble she opened the envelope and draw out a cashiers check for $163,412. "Larry, you got a lot more than the $150,000 we originally talked about. How did you do it?"

Beaming Larry responded, "I watched the stock closely all day. Around noon it started to take a swing upward. I see these trends all the time. When I thought it was about time for it to start coming down, I sold. And it worked. A few minutes after I sold your stock it did drop back almost to where it started this morning. So, you have almost $15,000 more to buy furniture."

Laura threw her arms around her neighbor and hugged him; "You are truly the best friend a person could have. Thank you."

As Larry left Laura stared at the little lighthouse. Before she left Granton, she had to do something special for the Madisons. She put the check in her lock box and sat down at her computer to continue her exploration of the Internet. Her thoughts kept returning to her son. What was she going to do about Gary? Would she see him before she left for Scotland? Would he ever come to Scotland? All bothersome unanswered questions that only time would resolve. Laura knew if she kept thinking about Gary, she would never get anything finished. Trying hard to get back into the mood for working on the computer she found she couldn't. A cup of tea out in the rose garden would help clear her mind. She started there this morning. She might as well finish her day there.

Just as the teakettle whistled there was another

knock on the door. Knowing it was almost time for Lucy Mann, the real estate agent she put another cup on the tray and went to answer the door. Lucy was dressed for success in a severe dark blue business suit. Her blue jeans and T-shirt embarrassed Laura.

"I worked up figures on you house. I think you will be pleasantly surprised." Lucy offered.

"I was just going to have a cup of tea in the rose garden why don't you join me. We can go over your figures out there." Laura offered. Lucy nodded her head and followed Laura outside.

"What a beautiful garden you have. This will help sell the house. I evaluated the prices of houses similar to yours sold in Granton last year. After looking through all of them I came up with a selling price of $175,000. It may be a little bit high but I like to start high. You can always lower the price but it is impossible to raise the price." Laura heard greed in Lucy's voice.

Laura looked over the figures that Lucy had prepared and could find no fault with the pricing. She kept trying to grasp what it was about Lucy she disliked so much. Lucy reminded her of the typical insurance salesperson although Laura knew there was no such thing as a typical insurance salesperson. Lucy seemed only interested in money and could care less about Laura. It took only a few minutes to sign the papers and Lucy was off to place the "For Sale" sign in front of the house. After Lucy was gone Laura noticed Lucy had never even touched her tea. Laura chuckled to herself and wondered what it was like to be so driven by success. Reflecting back over the day she examined the contrast between the real estate agent and her stockbroker. People sure do business differently. She felt Larry Madison's manner made it a lot easier to continue doing business with him. This was something she would try to remember when she was working with her own clients.

She realized as she sipped her tea every thought today was focusing on what life would be like after her move to Scotland. The placing of the house on the market did not seem to bother Laura at all. Everything was falling into place. She had found a possible lighthouse home, the stock had sold well and the house was on the market. Everything except her relationship with her son was going in the right direction. She yearned to tell Gary all her exciting news. Dialing his number she hoped he was there. Gary voice answered but it was recorded not live. "He should have given me Vicki Wells telephone number then I could call him there." Laura thought. Her biggest fear was Gary would not change his mind about her plans before it was time to leave the country.

CHAPTER SIX

The last four weeks had raced by for Laura. All the details of purchasing the lighthouse including getting the survey done, selecting a solicitor, and securing the backing of a Scottish bank were complete. She was only hours away from the bid being presented to the lighthouse board. After much discussion with the surveyor she decided to offer £78,000 for the property. The estate agents were saying they had many potential bidders. But estate agents always said that. Laura's attitude about estate agents was they were worse than real estate agents in the USA. Maybe they were a necessary evil but she would be glad when she was done with them. Ever since she put the house on the market in Granton she had to nudge Lucy Mann to get her to follow through. After Lucy got the listing, she seemed too busy with other properties to pay much attention to the File house. In desperation Laura had been going to Lucy's office every other day to check what had been done since the last visit. Lucy had said yesterday that she felt they would receive an offer today. If an offer was received on the Granton house and the bid was submitted on the lighthouse, this would be a real important day indeed. With luck she would complete her home page also. Laura had found a good Internet service provider in Scotland that served the island with a national number. During her search for an ISP, she had a lucky break. She had stumbled on Mark FitzSimmon's email address. Mark headed the District Council's grant to develop computer technology in the Western Isles. He was interested in her buying the lighthouse and thought he might have a job for her. Everything was falling perfectly into place. If she got the lighthouse and the house had a buyer she could begin the final stages of her plan that included selling her household items and booking the plane tickets to Scotland. The six-month separation from King still haunted her. The only other alternative was to leave him here. Her dog was an important part of her life. Laura could handle six months without him if the alternative was not having King at all. Her greatest worry was her son. Gary was still not returning any of her calls. He sent a Mother's Day card so she knew he was alive. He had written no message on the card just signed it. Laura wrote every week telling him what she was doing. One letter included a passbook for the account she had established for him. She had put $25,000 in a joint savings account just in case he needed it and could not reach her. She checked periodically to see if he had accessed the funds. So far he was ignoring their existence. Gary's telephone had been disconnected a week after he told her about Vicki Wells. She looked up Vicki Wells in the telephone book but there was no listing and no new listing for Gary File. Gary had disappeared. Laura even considered hiring a private detective to find him. If she did not hear from him before she left the country she would hire someone to find him. Laura knew he was upset with her but surely he would want to talk to her before she left for Scotland. The ringing of the telephone interrupted her thoughts about Gary. She ran to answer it.

"Mrs. File?" A pleasant Scotch voice asked.

"Yes, this is Laura File. Is that you Mr. Morrison? Did we get the lighthouse?" Laura anxiously inquired.

"My name is Gregory MacDuff. I am an associate of Mr. Morrison. He is on the telephone with the lighthouse board's solicitors. They are negotiating your offer. It looks like they are going to accept it if you are willing to pay half of the maintenance for the mile long road leading to the lighthouse. Mr. Morrison wants to know if you will agree to that small change. If so the board will accept the offer as amended."

"Yes. Yes." Laura answered as her racing heart felt like it might explode.

"Mr. Morrison will call you as soon as he has all the details worked out." Mr. MacDuff answered.

Laura ran to her desk. She searched for the pictures sent by the lighthouse's attendant. In just a few minutes wonderful Gealach Head would be hers. She knew every picture by heart but she still took the time to go through each one: The beautiful walled garden where she was going to plant the cuttings from Peter's roses she had been growing on the window sill; the quaint kitchen she was going to paint first thing when she arrived: the glass house where she would grow flowers and tomatoes; and the small front bedroom she would turn into an office with her desk facing a window looking out on the mountains of Harris.

Ring. Laura hand shook as she answered the telephone. "Mrs. File Mr. Morrison, here. We were one of four bids. There was one higher but for some reason the Board turned it down. I believe it was a local bid from someone on the island. We will never know for sure since they are not required to tell us. Congratulations the lighthouse will soon be yours. Do you have any questions? If not I will be in touch as we begin to process the papers"

"No." An overwhelmed Laura answered.

"Okay. Cheers for now." Mr. Morrison said as he hung up.

Laura sat staring into space with the pictures of the lighthouse in her hand. Sitting without moving for several minutes, Laura began to laugh. She was to become the owner of a lighthouse in Scotland. Suddenly Laura stopped laughing. She thought of Peter and how he would not be with her. It made her sad.

"Peter, you should be here. Our lighthouse, we finally have our lighthouse. It is no longer a dream." Laura whispered. She missed him so much. He was responsible for this. The stock and the retirement policy were making it all possible. Knowing Peter, he would be proud of what she had done and approve. So she began to hum "Flower of Scotland." For five minutes Laura looked at the lighthouse pictures and hummed. The telephone rang again.

This time it was Lucy Mann asking for an appointment with Laura to bring over an offer on the house. Lucy explained some of the details of the offer on the telephone and Laura realized it is a full price offer with no contingencies. She had bought a lighthouse and was well on her way to selling the house in Granton all in one day. Everything was falling into place. Laura was excited but anxious and fearful at the same time. Was she doing the right thing? Would she be able to live in a foreign country by herself? Gary, what was she going to do about Gary? All of a sudden doubts overwhelmed her. Laura could feel the misgivings taking over. If Laura did not stop thinking like this, the fear would become totally debilitating.

"This won't do." Laura said to King. "Lets go into the rose garden and share that split of champagne I got for the minute we knew the lighthouse was ours. This is a wonderful moment. I refuse to sit here and let my doubts keep us from enjoying it." Retrieving the champagne from the refrigerator, she got a crystal goblet from the cabinet and one of her best china bowls for King, which she carried to the rose garden. The minute the bright sun hit her face Laura knew it was a day for celebration. The garden was polka dotted with bright cheerful colors of the last roses of the summer. The place was brimming with warm soft peace. As she sat her tray on the table she picked one of the brightest and reddest roses to fasten in her bright golden hair. Pouring champagne for King in the china bowl she filled her crystal goblet and raised it in a toast. "To our new home." Laura proclaimed. Once she had drank the champagne she began to make mental notes about what she should do next. She would need to decide what she wanted to sell and what she would ship to Scotland. This was not going to be so hard as she actually wanted to keep very few things. The most important were her memories and they would go with her. She had already started the incorporation of her business in Scotland. The papers would be processed next week so she could start working as soon as she arrived. Before she went to the island, she would shop for a few things in Stornoway. The rest she would purchase after she had seen the property. Suddenly she realized she was moving too fast. Coming back to what had happened today, she got a calendar to estimate the date she could take possession of the lighthouse and when she would be able to vacate this house. Looking at the calendar she realized she could arrive in Scotland the end of November or the first of Dec. Should she wait and have Christmas with Gary or have Christmas in Scotland? Fearing if she stayed here, Gary would not come home for Christmas she decided to invite him for Thanksgiving and she would tentatively leave for Scotland on Dec. 10th, which would give her time to get partially settled before Christmas. If she could maintain this schedule King would come out of quarantine in early May and be at the lighthouse for the summer. It seemed like a good plan so she penciled all of the dates on her calendar. Thinking of King's quarantine she looked at the big dog and realized he hadn't touched the champagne. King must not be fond of champagne. The next time she had a celebration she would get milk for the dog. He loved milk. It was a shame to waste good champagne Laura thought as she threw King's portion on some of the roses.

While the house sale was being processed, Laura spent most of her time going through and marking what she would sell at a garage sale, what would go to auction and what she would keep. She would sell all the small things at her garage sale and the big items by auction. All she wanted were books, old pictures, clothes and her rose cuttings from Peter's garden. Susan Madison was willing to help with the garage sale and came over every day to help mark the merchandise.

Immediately after she accepted the offer on the house, Laura had written Gary inviting him for Thanksgiving. She still had not heard from him. Being busy with the garage sale she hadn't had time to worry about it. Gary would come. Laura just knew he would come see her.

The day of the garage sale turned out to be windy and raining making it truly a garage sale. Even with the bad weather a lot of people came and to Laura's delight she sold almost every thing. The few things left she could give to the Salvation Army or Goodwill. After she and Susan counted the money, Laura decided to take a break and check the mail. As she opened the mailbox, the first correspondence she saw was a letter from Gary. Not being able to wait she ripped open the letter and read.

"Dear Mom,

Thank you very much for the money you placed in savings for me. I do not need it right now but I will keep it in reserve.

I appreciate the offer to come home for Thanksgiving but I am spending the day with Vicki's family. I know you are busy getting ready to leave for Scotland so this will be easier for you. As I told you before Granton is not home to me so I have no desire to be there for

Thanksgiving.

Since you are continuing forward with leaving our country, I wish you well although I still think you are making a big mistake.

Gary"

"Granton being home is not the issue. What about coming to see your Mother before she leaves the country?" Laura shouted. Laura did not want to believe Gary was not going to see her before she left for the UK. She desperately wanted to see her son. Suddenly Laura was cold and she could not stop shaking. It was obvious Gary would not come to Granton. If she tried to go to him it would just make things worse. Laura was frightened once she was in Scotland her son would break all contact with her. Not wanting this to happen she began immediately to reply to Gary's note. Knowing her son it would be better if she did not accuse him or even nag him about seeing her before she left. Instead she would take a positive approach telling him how exciting everything was and it is too bad he was not a part of it. She copied all the information on HER lighthouse and included it with the letter hoping it would help him understand. Taking out an unused calendar she marked in ink all the important dates including Dec. 10th, the day she would leave the country and put it in the envelope with her letter. As she sealed the envelope, she realized how excited she was.

After putting the letter in the mailbox for pickup she dialed British Airlines. "I need a one way ticket to Glasgow Scotland and to reserve a space for a large dog carrier for Dec. 10th. Do you have space and what it the cost?"

CHAPTER SEVEN

Laura looked at the possessions spread across the floor of the room, which used to be her office. There were so few things; from her old life she wanted to take to her new one. In one corner were a tiny stack of clothes, a small box containing computer floppy disks and King's favorite toys and his leash. Her gaze lingered on King's toys. Depression seized Laura as she thought about King going into quarantine for six months. He would not be there when she saw Gealach Head for the first time. During the winter she would be alone at the lighthouse while the dog was secluded at the kennel. It seemed so unfair. Dwelling on the upcoming separation made her feel worse so she was off to scrub the kitchen floor. In a short time the house was be turned over to the new owners. She wanted it to be in perfect condition. "Why did people always clean up the house to make it look better for others?" She pondered as she walked to the kitchen. Laura glanced around the empty house. Surprisingly she knew she would not miss it. Peter and Laura had wonderful times in this house. The memories will always be hers. Nothing could take them away. The house was just a house.

As she scrubbed the kitchen floor, she looked out the window at the rose garden now covered in a soft fleecy blanket of snow. One of her better ideas had been to start the rose cuttings. They were well established in their pots. She had a permit to take them into the United Kingdom. She would have missed Peter's roses if she had not been able to take them to the UK. When King joined her in May they would plant the roses. Until then she would keep them in the glass house at her new home. Peter had been so proud of his roses. As she looked at the roses that were now white mounds in the bright sunshine, she suddenly thought about her son. Would she see him before she left for Scotland? Unless a miracle occurred it was unlikely. She would probably not even talk to him. As she continued to scrub the floor the telephone interrupted.

Picking up a the receiver she hears a Scottish accent on the other end say "Mrs. File?"

"Yes, Mr. Morrison what can I do for you?"

"I just wanted to let you know Larry Macdonald has the keys. When you reach the island go to the local store and he should be waiting for you. Something has happened I believe you should be aware of before you arrive. The last few nights there have been reports of strange lights near the lighthouse. Larry and the local police constable, Ian Mitchell, are look into it. They think some youngsters found the place deserted and are hanging out there. You should ask Larry about it when you get to Gealach. It would be a good idea to check with Ian Mitchell immediately after arriving since you will be a single woman alone in a remote area."

Laura felt anger erupting but she kept herself controlled. Mr. Morrison was only one among many who felt a woman should not be living alone at a secluded lighthouse. Controlling her anger she thanked Mr. Morrison for all he had done and promised when she came to Stornoway to shop she would drop in to say hello. The idea of the strange lights near her new home was disturbing. Probably just kids having fun but she would check with the police as soon as she arrived.

Her cleaning of the kitchen interrupted by the telephone call she decided to have a cup of tea. Sitting on the box spring mattress she was using as both chair and bed until she left on Thursday she found the spot already taken by a big black dog. Gently pushing King over she sat beside him. King moved his head under Laura's hand so she had no option but to pet him. It was difficult for Laura to even look at King. In a few days she would be turning him over to complete strangers for six months. Their only separations before this were short term. The thought of the dog being alone with strangers was upsetting. She had many times contemplated not taking King with her and leaving him with the Madisons. They had offered to keep him with Maxx. Selfishly Laura wanted King with her. Some how they would handle the separation. Drinking her tea, she noticed it had started to snow. The huge wet flakes were beginning to cover the red velvet bows the Madisons had tied around the bottom of the wreaths on their windows. Christmas. Laura was doing every thing she could to avoid the upcoming holiday. All of her friends said she should wait until after the Christmas to move to Scotland. What they did not understand was going to Scotland meant no memories. She could celebrate Christmas or not and that was the way she wanted it. This was her first Christmas without Peter. Laura didn't want a family Christmas. With no contact from Gary she felt she had no family except King. Definitely she would not celebrate Christmas this year. As she finished her tea the doorbell rings. Reluctantly Laura got up to answer.

When she opened the door, she found a United Parcel Service man with a package. She signed his sheet trying to figure out who could be sending her something so near her move. The label on the box was a mail order company. She went back to join King on the bed. Opening the box she found a big black British style umbrella. Hunting around for a card she found it buried in the bottom of the box. Opening it, she read.

"Merry Christmas and Bon Voyage.

Gary"

Laura stared at the card. Was this going to be her only communication from her son - no telephone calls, surprise visits or anything? Just a card typed by someone else and sent by some mail order company. Both anger and sadness overwhelmed Laura as she looked at the black umbrella. She started to cry, shook her head and stopped. Realizing there was nothing she would do to change Gary she was not going to waste any more tears or energy on him. If he wanted it this way and so be it. A slight smile actually began to cross her face as she looked at the "bumbershoot." It is just like Gary to make a final snide comment about the weather in Scotland. "This will be very useful at a lighthouse where the winds blows all the time." She sniggered to herself. "I will put it with my carry on items." The umbrella was carefully laid beside her camera and the things, which she would carry on the airplane with her. Looking at her watch she realized the day was half gone and she still had not finished scrubbing the floor. Laura was scheduled to sign all the papers for this house at 1:00 p.m. after which she must arrange for an electronic transfer of the money to Scotland.

Late in the afternoon Laura arrived home to find a

note stuck in the door. "Please join us for dinner. Signed Susan and Larry." Laura was touched by the continuing support of her neighbors. Not once through the entire process had they tried to convince her to stay or make her feel guilty for leaving them. She picked up the telephone and called Susan to ask what time she was planning dinner. Realizing the telephone was to be disconnected tomorrow, she called both the electric and gas company to double check the utilities would be shut off on the day after she left. That task completed she began a sincere letter of thanks to Gary for the umbrella and once again give him all the contact numbers. Not wanting to change out of her dress she laid on the bed beside King for a few minutes before she went next door for dinner. Drifting off to sleep, Laura saw in her mind a small white lighthouse.

When Laura arrived at the Madison's, the house was ablaze with Christmas lights and Christmas Carols could be heard inside. In many ways she wished the Madison weren't so much into Christmas. What she needed was a quiet dinner without all the reminders of Christmas past. Knowing the Madisons were only trying to be helpful Laura would pretend to enjoy their Christmas. As Susan opened the door she handed Laura a glass of sparkling wine and said, "Bon Voyage Laura."

"Thank you." Laura answered deeply touched. "It is impossible for me to express how much you and Larry's support has meant to me since Peter's death. I am going to miss you desperately. You plan to visit Scotland next summer for a long stay and I will hold onto that thought."

"We will be there. We have already started our lighthouse travel fund to make sure. Now, come in and have some snacks in front of the fire before we sit down to dinner."

When they entered the living room Laura found many of her neighbors and business clients gathered under a computer sign saying "Farewell to our favorite lighthouse keeper." Laura was dumbfounded. All her friends from Granton were here. Larry and Susan had gone to a lot of trouble to arrange a farewell party for her. To keep from crying she gave Susan a bear hug before she began greeting all of her friends. After talking to everyone in the room Laura returned to Susan for another glass of wine. Susan took this as a sign it was time for Laura to open her presents. She handed Laura a stack of ten envelopes. Each envelope contains a note from a friend with a description of an item already sent to Scotland. It was helpful to have the gifts sent to her new home instead of making it necessary for her to carry them. Each gift was well thought out and would serve a useful purpose in her remote location. They contained such things as pots and pans, a weather station to monitor the conditions, and from Larry and Susan was a telescope to look at the stars along with the passing ships and whales. Only true friends would have remembered one of her goals was to study the stars in the huge expanse of sky above the lighthouse. She would find a special spot away from the light where she would watch the stars with her friend's gift.

"Thank you everyone." a dumfounded Laura replied. "I will never forget you. You all know you are welcome to visit me in Scotland any time. It would be a cheap vacation. All you have to do is get yourself there since room and board would be on me. The airfares are often cheaper to Glasgow than to the West Coast of this country."

As they sat down to dinner Laura wondered how many of her friends would be brave enough to come see her. Looking around the room she knew none of them had been outside the country. She really hoped they would take her up on her invitation. In some ways the evening seemed to go forever. Saying good-by was difficult. Laura was relieved when people started to leave. After everyone left Susan and Larry asked Laura to sit by the fire and have a cup of hot chocolate while they finalize the arrangements for tomorrow. The Madisons were taking her to the airport to catch her British Airways flight to London. The conversation was a matter of fact arrangements of details. Again, Laura understood how understanding the Madison's were being. No last minute emotional scene just simple plans for the future were discussed. Sure they had the details straight Laura got up to leave. For the first time Susan showed how tough loosing Laura was for her. She threw her arms around

Laura and held tight. Laura knew Susan was softly crying because her shoulder was wet. Next Larry took his turn at hugging his long time friend. And that was it. The two friends with their arms around Laura's shoulder led her to the hall and helped her with her coat.

"That is our good-by for now." Larry added. "Tomorrow when we take you to the airport we will handle the situation like you are going on a short trip. We know how excited you are and how much you are dreading leaving King in quarantine. There will be no more emotional stuff at the airport. We will pick you up at 1:00 p.m. which should get us to the airport in plenty of time."

"Sounds good to me." Laura replied softly.

As Laura let herself into her Granton house for the last time she felt no regret about leaving the house but she would miss her friends. Letting King outside she sat down on the bed to think. It was too late for regrets but actually she had none. In 36 hours she would be on the Isle of Gealach taking possession of her new home. She would be unpacking her things and deciding what new furniture needed to be purchased to make her house into a home. It was very difficult to visualize what the house was going to look like on the inside since the photographs the attendant sent had not shown the small rooms very well. King was barking at the door so she went to let in him in. The worst part of the whole business was King having to be in quarantine. "It is only for six months," Laura thought. I will be so busy getting the lighthouse all set the time would fly." Although she believed what she was telling herself she put her arms around the big animal and nuzzled up in his fur. King seemed to know something exciting was going to happen as he waged his tail and curled up next to Laura.

CHAPTER EIGHT

Last night sleep had been a stranger to Laura. It had to be all of the excitement of leaving for Scotland. She made herself a cup of instant coffee and began to organize the packing of her luggage in her mind. Her plan was to take only one large bag and a box. Since she would be alone she felt she would not be able to handle more. When she arrived in Glasgow she had to transfer onto a bus that would take her on the four-hour trip to the ferry. King would be with her until Glasgow. He would be put in his cage at the airport and kept in a heated luggage compartment. Yesterday she purchased some new toys she knew he would really like to keep him entertained during the long flight. The airlines did not want him to have food because he might get sick. The cage had a water dish so he would get plenty to drink. Laura wanted to run from the terrible feelings she had inside when she thought about what was ahead for King. Was she being self-centered? Would King be better off left in the United States? She stared at the dog lying on the bed. His trusting eyes reflected deep affection for her. She knew he would never understand if she went off and left him behind. The kennel where he would be quarantined was one of the best. King liked being around the other dogs. "King we will have such a good time in Scotland. You can roam the beach every day if you like," Laura said as she began packing. She knew dwelling on the situation about the dog and her fears was not wise. All the decisions were made. She would carry them out. This was not time to doubt.

Laura found she was able to get everything she planned to take into the suitcase and a small box. As she closed the suitcase the click echoed in the empty house. Somewhere she read when you decide to make a major change in your life you hear the door of your old life close with a gigantic bang. The shutting of the suitcase represented the closing of her old life and the beginning of a new one. She moved all of her luggage to the front door and sat it beside the big cage that would be King's home during the trip. Suddenly she wondered if she had all of King's papers with her travel documents in her purse. Panic seized her when she couldn't find the vaccination papers. She looked all through her purse and they were just not there. She shook the contents of her purse onto the floor but no vaccination papers. Where could she have put them? She opened her suitcase again and looked in the envelope that contained all of the settlement papers on the lighthouse. Each page was documentation of her new life. She was now the owner of Gealach Head lighthouse keeper's accommodations on the Isle of Gealach in Scotland. She saw her name but it didn't feel like it was truly she. The very last paper she came to was King's vaccination record. "Oh, thank goodness. I could not leave here without King and he can not enter the United Kingdom without his vaccinations I would just have to postpone the trip if I did not have these." Thinking about King she decided to take him for a long walk around Granton. He would be restricted to his cage for almost ten hours so the exercise would do him good. It would be a great way for both of them to say good-by to the town.

For the first time today Laura looked outside and saw it was snowing softly. "Perfect. She told King. "In Scotland we will not have much snow especially on the island. We will take this opportunity to enjoy it because it could be the last snow we see for awhile." When King saw Laura put on her coat and boots he jumped off the bed and stood by the door. He was ready for a walk in the snow.

Outside Laura and King found although it was snowing it was not very cold. In fact, the snow was melting on the sidewalks and streets. The big snowflakes lingered when they landed on the area that was already covered with a hard layer of packed snow. The sidewalks were snow-free as Laura and King walked along at a good clip. King as usual kept his nose to the ground but Laura looked at every house and tree. She wanted to take a mental picture so she could remember Granton. She and Peter had chosen the town when he accepted the job at the high school. It was a wise choice. Laura had always liked the feeling of community and the friendliness of the people. Only three bad things had happened in Granton. The worst being she lost Peter in the car accident. Thoughts of Peter still caused her pain. She had been so involved with her move to Scotland she thought of Peter's less and less every day. The second negative was Gary's refusal to accept the town and to be a part of their life here. One of Laura's biggest fears was Gary would refuse to accept Scotland in the same way. He certainly was giving every indication he intended to do just that. The bank robbery was the third thing but maybe it was more of a plus than a minus since it forced her to do what she really wanted.

Almost everyone Laura and King met stopped to talk and to wish them well. The people of this small town had supported Laura in her decision to move. Without their support she might not even have considered going since Gary was so against it. Her neighbors expressed no disapproval or rejections of her decision. Most of them were excited as Laura. She was not sure she would have been able to carry out the details necessary to sell the house and buy the lighthouse without their support.

After about an hour and half Laura realized King was starting to limp. He had a tendency to get ice in between his toes when he had been a long time in the snow. "King, let's stop at the cafe and have lunch. That should get us back to the house in plenty of time to wait for Susan and Larry to pick us up. Laura was aware she didn't call the house "home" but just the house. It was no longer home. Home was across the Atlantic and she was ready to get there.

When she arrived back at the house the telephone was ringing but by the time she reached it who ever was on the other end had gone. Maybe it was Larry or Susan with a change of plans for today. After taking off her wet clothes she called Susan. Susan indicated Larry had left to get gas in the car. They should be over in a few minutes. Who could have been on the telephone? Could it have possibly been Gary? Laura could not bear the thought she may have missed her son's telephone call. She sat on the floor by the telephone praying if it were Gary, he would call again. The next noise she heard was the doorbell. If her son was trying to reach her it was not going to happen as she opened the door to Larry Madison.

The trip to Chicago O'Hare airport took approximately 2 hours. Laura and King sat in the back seat as close together as they could get. Laura talked constantly to King. Susan and Larry had tried at the beginning of the trip to talk to Laura but she was in a world that included only the dog. The Madisons knew how hard it was for Laura to put King into quarantine. They talked quietly to each other and allowed Laura and King their time. When Larry pulled up to the curb and motioned for the skycap Laura began to cry.

"Larry, I don't think I can put King in that cage and check him in. I feel almost as bad as I did when Peter was killed. Maybe even a little bit worse since this is my choice where Peter's death was not."

"I have an idea. Why don't you go check in? After you get your boarding pass Susan will take you for a cup of coffee. King and I will go to the baggage area and get him all settled. How does that sound?

"Am I being a coward to not want to go with him? I feel like I am just disposing of him earlier."

"Laura, you are not deserting him. Think. Even if he could go with you to the lighthouse right away he would have to ride across the ocean in his comfortable cage. It is not abandonment it is just the first leg of the trip to the lighthouse. Aren't you the one who kept saying you and King are traveling to your new home guided by Gealach Head lighthouse's beacon? This is the first segment. That is all. King must become an UK dog; you must claim the property and make it a home for King to come to when he is ready. So you go get checked in. Susan will go with you. King and I will wait here. When you come back King and I will go find the baggage area."

Larry's words made so much sense Laura stopped crying and grabbed Susan's hand as they joined the international check in line. The processing took only a few minutes because they were early. The slowest procedure was having King's papers checked. As soon as Susan and Laura were back Larry took the papers from Laura. With King on his leash in one hand and the big cage in his other Larry started walking toward the elevator. Laura wanted to stop him so she could say "Good-by" to the big dog but she knew she would just get upset again. She stood and watched until the elevator doors closed.

Susan pushed Laura toward the coffee shop and said; "You will see him in Glasgow before you catch your bus so lets have no more tears. King is going on his first airplane ride and he will love it. What if there is a beautiful female in the next cage? King will spend the entire time trying to make friends. You know he has always been such a flirt."

Laura could not keep from laughing because it was true. King was a big flirt. When ever they went for walks and he saw a female dog he become very difficult to handle. "Susan, you are right. King will be sure to find something to pass the time in his cage. He has all of those new toys and I hid a dog biscuit under his water dish that he will sniff out right away. I am going to stop acting like something has died. Nothing has died. A great adventure is about to begin."

Sitting over a cup of a coffee the two old friends talked about Laura's plans when she reached Scotland. Laura promised to send them an email as soon as her new computer was at the lighthouse. She had signed on to "American On Line" which was available in Scotland. She could call the Madisons if she wanted to since the phone was already installed. Larry joined them and reported King was happy in his cage because one of the new toys Laura made a strange squeak. It was a good the dog was not going to be in the main cabin. The noise was obnoxious. "Leave it to King to find something to do the second he arrives a new place. Oh, thank you, Larry I was being so silly. I would have been sure to upset the dog if I had taken him down there." King's owner admitted.

"No problem. I see by the monitors it is time to head for your plane. Do you have your passport, all the closing papers on the lighthouse and the passbook for your bank accounts in Stornoway? You know how conservative those Scottish bankers can be?"

"Larry, I have everything. I checked three times before I left the house. This is not my first trip to Scotland and not my first trip alone. Twice I flew over before Peter and met him there. I am experienced at all of this. Why don't you and Susan take off now? I do not need anyone to put me on the plane. It is so boring sitting in airports."

"No way are you going to take away our chance to watch all those people getting on that big plane to Glasgow. It is one of the best places in the world to people watch. Besides if we watch you we will know what to do when it comes our turn next summer to go to Scotland."   He laughingly answered.

Knowing she could not talk them out of going with her, Laura agreed. Besides it would be nice for Laura to have someone to talk to until they called the plane. Peter never left until after she was on the plane and she believed he probably waited until the plane took off before he would leave the boarding area. When they reach the boarding area Larry suggested they have a Bon Voyage glass of wine together. Sitting at the bar sipping her wine Laura felt very much at ease. It might be the wine. Maybe it was final acceptance she was doing exactly what she wanted.

"British Airways Flight 38 Non Stop for Glasgow is now ready for boarding. Please have your tickets and passports out for the attendant."

Laura got up and looked at her two friends. "I have said thank you so many times I must sound like I do not know any other words but thank you. It will be so much fun when you come to visit next year. We will use the telescope you gave me to watch the stars while we listen to the ocean. Until then remember dear friends I love you."   With that Laura turned her back on her two friends and joined the long line at the gate.

Susan and Larry stood holding hands until Laura disappeared. Then they reluctantly turned their backs and started down the escalator. Susan had tears in her eyes and Larry seemed worried.

"Susan, I have not said this before but do you think it is safe for a single woman to live at a remote light house all by herself. For the first six months, she won't even have King."

"I have been worrying about that myself."   Susan answered.

CHAPTER NINE

As Laura settled into the seat that would be her home for the next seven hours she wondered how King was getting along in the baggage section for dogs. Would she hear him if he barked? Feeling foolish Laura laughed at her strange thoughts. Once everyone was seated they started the usual routine of the stewardess welcoming everyone on board and giving a brief rundown of the flight time to London. Laura found she was not listening. She had heard it so many times she knew it by heart. In the seat next to her was a young man with long blonde hair and freckles. In many ways he reminded her of Gary. The coloring wasn't the same but he was about the same build as her son but younger. He said "Hello" when Laura sat down but had not attempted to start a conversation. He was having trouble understanding all of the buttons on the arm of his seat. Laura carefully explained how they worked. He thanked her but did not volunteer any information about himself. "Oh, well, it will be a quiet trip and I can get some sleep," Laura, thought.

The giant jet crawled to the entrance of the runway. The captain announced they were ready for take off and all the cabin crew should be seated. The gigantic metallic bird took off with ease. The four hundred and seventy four passengers were on their way to London. Laura began to read the book she brought with her when the intercom interrupted.

"This is the captain again and we have a light indicating a small fuel leak in one of the engines. I am sending the first officer back to visually inspect it. It could be just a faulty light. As soon as we know something more I will let you know."

Laura heard the captain's words but had no reaction. On a couple of her other flights the planes had had mechanical problems. They were usually fixed right away so Laura was not concerned. Remembering King she hoped it would not affect him. All the passengers watched as the copilot appeared and pointed a flashlight out the window two rows behind Laura. The passengers sitting near Laura showed signs of fright with the inspection going on so close to where they were seated.

"This is the captain again. It seems we do have a small fuel leak in one engine. We will need to return to Chicago O'Hare. We cannot land there until we have discharged the huge amount of fuel we have on board for the transatlantic crossing. This means we will have to fly around in circles gradually dumping the fuel. Once we reach the correct weight we will be allowed to land. I am estimating it will take approximately 20 to 30 minutes to eject the necessary fuel. Do not be concerned if you do not hear from the me for a while. We will be extremely busy making the necessary corrections for a safe landing. The cabin crew will answer any questions you have. Meanwhile just sit back and relax."

"Relax." Laura thought. "How can anyone relax when thousands of gallons of jet fuel was being poured from their plane into the night sky. What about King? Was he near the fuel leak?" Laura pushed the cabin crew call button. No one came so she pushed it again. Looking around she realized the cabin crew were busy trying to calm many disturbed passengers. Laura wasn't worried for herself. She was concerned about her dog. He was alone and would not understand what was happening. Finally, one of the cabin crew turned off her call light and asked, "May I help you."

"My dog is in a cage in the baggage area. Is he safe from the leaking fuel? Can I reach him and sit with him so he won't be frightened?" She appealed.

"Your dog is on the other side of the plane from the problem. We cannot allow anyone to go into the baggage area. We are all too busy right now to check on a dog. I promise when it slows down I will check." The kind man replied.

"Thank you."

"You're welcome. Since you are so calm you could help us by talking to the passengers around you, it may help them."

For the first time since the captain's announcement she noticed the man beside her. His hands were gripping the armrests so hard his knuckles were white. His breathing was rapid. It was obvious he was petrified. Laura turned towards him and said, "My name is Laura Fine and I am moving to Scotland."

At first he did not reply but then as if he was coming out of some kind of trance he said. "Moving to Scotland must be terribly exciting. I have never been outside the United States. In fact, I have never been out of the Midwest. My parents gave me this trip as a graduation present. I am on my way to London then Paris and finally Rome. My name is Jim Greene."

"That is a lot of excitement for someone who just graduated from high school."

"I graduated from Northwestern. Do I look so immature you think I just got out of high school?"

Realizing what a terrible mistake she had made, Laura assured the young man he clearly looked like a college man. Inside she thought how as she got older college graduates looked younger and younger. Gary who was already in law school looked more like a teenager than a twenty five year old. If only he was still in high school, Gary would be on this trip to Scotland. The thought of Gary depressed Laura so she turned her attention to the man sitting beside her. "What did you study in college and what are you going to do after your trip?

"I studied pre-law and I am going to law school at Northwestern when I get back."

"My son is in his last year of law school at Northwestern. He should be ready to take the bar in another six months. I am so proud of him. He had to work hard to get where he is. We helped him some financially but most of it he did himself. His name is Gary File. If you ever meet him tell him you sat beside me on the trip to Scotland." Laura yearned for Gary to be beside her instead of this nice young man. And yet Gary's stubbornness made her angry.

"Attention, ladies and gentlemen, this is your captain again. We still have more fuel to unload. It is taking a lot longer than I thought to empty this bird. It looks like it could take another hour"

The young man next to Laura was getting more disturbed. To take his mind off of the situation she questioned him about his career goals and what he expected to see in Europe. He was ecstatic about studying law. His eyes sparkled bright with determination and pleasure rang in his voice when he described what kind of lawyer he wanted to become. He didn't sound confident when he talked about the trip to Europe. He made it sound more like punishment instead of a gift. Laura felt sorry him. He was an adult and didn't have to take this trip. He could have said no. Driven by the thought if Gary had been in the same situation she would have wanted someone to help him, Laura invited Jim Greene to visit her at Gealach Head if he had time during his trip. The young man seemed enthused by the offer and said he might on his way home.

"Ladies and Gentleman this is your first officer. We have begun our descent into O'Hare field. I want to warn you that fire trucks and ambulances will be meeting the plane. Do not be alarmed. This is standard operating procedure in situations like this. It is only a precaution. Technicians will check the plane. If we meet prescribed standards we will be allowed to proceed to the terminal. We should be safely down and at the gate in approximately twenty minutes."

Jim appeared to be the color of his last name. Laura did not know what to say to him since she was also terrified. Fire trucks and rescue squads meant there was danger or they wouldn't be there. To keep her mind off of what was going on around them she quickly ask Jim, "Would you like to see pictures of my lighthouse?"

"Yes, I would like that very much."

While the rest of the passengers did what they could to get through the next few tense moments, Jim and Laura looked at Larry Macdonald's pictures. Laura explained every detail of each photo. Jim seemed genuinely interested asking lots of questions. Laura's pride in her little home helped her forget what was going on around her. The next thing she noticed was applause. They had landed and the passengers were applauding the pilot for the safe landing. Putting the pictures down, Laura and Jim looked out the window. Red and yellow lights were dancing on the wet pavement. Small figures in shiny yellow covers were walking around the plane. In the distance they could see the terminal. Many planes sat silently at jet ways and nothing was moving. The only activity was their arrival in the middle of the concrete isolation of the big runway.

"It looks so spooky no one is moving around the terminal. Do you suppose they evacuated it because of fear we might explode?" Jim said.

"No, look at your watch. It is 1:30 in the morning. They haven't evacuated the terminal. Everyone has gone home. It is the middle of the night." Laura explained.

"I must have really enjoyed your company because I haven't looked at my watch once." Jim replied. "What do you suppose will happen once we get to the terminal? Will we get on another flight tonight or will we have to wait until tomorrow? I really don't want to spend the night at O'Hare and go through all the hassle to get another plane."

Suddenly Laura remembered King. "Oh, I can't wait until tomorrow. My poor dog would be shut up in a small cage all that time. It would cruel for him to spend so much time in that cage. It was bad enough that he has to spend eight hours to get to Glasgow. I hope they load us on another plane and send us on our way. Just so it isn't this plane."

"I wouldn't go any where on this plane if they paid me big bucks to do it." Jim admitted.

They watched the red and yellow strobe light display outside the window until suddenly they went out. Darkness claimed the isolated jetliner sitting on the runway in the deserted airport. The trucks and men in their yellow slickers began to leave.

"Ladies and Gentlemen we have been cleared to proceed to the terminal. I have been advised they are getting another airplane ready. As soon as they have transferred the bags, we will be on our way to Glasgow. They estimate we should depart in approximately two hours."

"Two hours," a frustrated passenger screamed.

Laura was worried about King who would have to spend another two hours in his cage. Once they were in the terminal she would demand to see her dog. There should be no reason she couldn't since they will have to unload him before they can place him on the next plane.

As soon as Laura arrived in the main terminal she went to the desk and asked the reservation agent to see her dog. The agent was busy answering other passengers' questions but she told Laura she would check. A few minutes later Laura again approached the agent to ask if she could see King. The agent looked at her like she had no idea what Laura was talking about. Laura calmly explained again. The agent replied she would check. Inside Laura something snapped and she started screaming and pounding her fist on the desk. "I want to see my dog. I do not want you to say you'll check. I want you to check." Finally the agent paid attention to the hysterical woman in front of her. Picking up the telephone she called a supervisor to check if Laura could see King. When she got off the telephone she announced King had already been reloaded on the new plane.

"Why didn't you check the first time I asked? I might have been able to see my dog and take him for a short walk." Laura screamed. Two strong hands on her shoulder turned Laura away from the agent. Jim Greene gently pleaded. "Laura, why don't you come and have a cup of coffee with me. There is nothing you can do now but wait until we land in Scotland to see your dog."

Laura allowed Jim to lead her to the coffee machine since everything else in the airport was closed. She sat with a cup of disgusting instant coffee in her hand and stared at the floor. She had been wrong to take King and leave Granton. Laura was frightened and the only person she had to rely on was a young stranger who only a few moments ago was scared to death.

CHAPTER TEN

"Laura, anyone who had a member of their family in the baggage compartment of this airplane would be upset. Actually, anyone who is on this plane has a right to be upset. Don't be too hard on yourself and don't get discouraged. It is just one of those things that happens. I am sure King is fine. In a few minutes you will be on our way to Scotland, your island and your new home again."

Laura thought it remarkable. A complete stranger who only a few minutes ago she was counseling was consoling her. Jim Greene was being sympathetic considering they had just met. He reminded her so much of her son or at least how she wanted Gary to be. She was not sure at this point whether Jim was right. Some of upset passengers were canceling their trip. That was not an option for Laura. There was no place to go back to so she could only go forward. Scotland was going to be home. She had committed all of her emotional and financial resources to that end.

"Ladies and Gentlemen we are now ready to board. The plane is a DC 10 identical to the first one except there is no fuel leak. You should take the same seat you were assigned before."

Jim chuckled, "I hope it is a lot better than the one we got of. If not I think I will stay right here in the good US of A."

"Come on Jim lets get this trip over. I have a lighthouse waiting for me," a fully recovered Laura said as she grabbed his arm and towed him with her onto the plane.

Once they were settled the cabin crew brought soft drinks. Jim looked at Laura and winked. "This is not a good sign. We are going to be delayed some more because we can not have soft drinks in our hands during take off." It turned out Jim was right. They sat in their seats for another hour. The captain announced they were loading luggage and as soon as it was completed they could take off. Laura felt her anger returning remembering how the agent told her King was already on the plane. She wondered if that was true or a convenient excuse to get rid of a distressed passenger. "What if they forget to load King? What if he becomes lost baggage?" Laura shouted at Jim. She punched the call button. The lead steward answered. With a voice quaking with fear she asked him, "My dog is in a cage in the baggage compartment. Is their any way you can find out if he is okay and if he has been loaded?"

Sensing her fright the steward smiled and said, "I will check immediately. I have a dog. If she were in the same situation I would want to know for sure she had been loaded. I will be right back." Tears begin to trickle down Laura's face. The kindness of this man after everyone else had been so rude was welcome. She knew he would return as soon as he could locate King. In less than five minutes the steward was back.

"Your dog is fine. One of the baggage handlers took him for a walk while we were one the ground. He hasn't been barking and they changed the papers in the cage and his water. They said he seemed content and to enjoy watching everything that was going on around him. He was loaded on a few minutes ago with the last of the luggage."

"That's King - always curious. He must think this is a rather strange show." Laura answered but she made a mental note to write a letter to the airline complaining about the gate agent who was so rude and complementing them on the lead flight attendant.

Laura's muscles began to unknot and relax with the news of King's safety. All of a sudden she was exhausted. It wasn't surprising when she looked at her watch and saw it was 3:30 in the morning. The captain announced they were finally ready to close the doors. With that announcement Laura started to doze off when screaming woke her. A passenger was banging on the closed door. "Let me out," she yelled. The nice attendant who had gotten the information on King tried to convince the lady to stay on the plane. She would have no part of it. After a few minutes the door opened and the passenger got off. The door shut immediately. Laura fell asleep and she did not hear the captain announce there would be another delay while they retrieved the luggage of the passenger who left.

"Would you like some dinner?" interrupted Laura's

dream about her new home. Opening her eyes she saw the kind steward standing beside her with the dinner cart. Rubbing her eyes Laura realized she was hungry and eagerly accepted the tray he handed to her. Airplane food was not always the best but Laura was so hungry it tasted good to her. She turned to ask Jim Greene how he liked it to find him softly snoring. Laura thought he must really be tired. At the airport he said he would eat anything he was so hungry.

After finishing her meal Laura fell back to sleep and did not wake until the same steward asked her if she wanted breakfast. Laura knew the routine so touch down in Glasgow was only an hour away. She would soon be in Scotland her new home. Excitement took over as Laura realized her dream of a lifetime was about to happen. She turned to Jim Greene who having missed supper had already finished his breakfast. Laura offered him some of hers and with appreciation he accepted.

Laura had been thinking of asking Jim to help her with King at the airport. She dreaded leaving King so much she felt someone to talk to might make it easier. Deep inside she knew she was attached to Jim because he reminded her of Gary. Gary was not there and Jim was. It was as simple as that so she asked. "Jim, I have a favor to ask of you. Do you need to get on your way immediately upon landing?"

"No, I was going to ask someone how to get a bus into downtown Glasgow."

"I can explain all of that but can I ask a favor?"

"What do you need?"

"I have to turn King over to the manager of the kennel who will be taking care of him while he is quarantined. I dread it. It would be so helpful if I were not alone when I do it. It will only take a few minutes."

"No problem, I would like to meet this dog you are so fond of. I wanted to ask you if you would like company on your trip to Gealach but felt you might be afraid to have a stranger accompany you. I don't have any special time schedule and you have talked so much about your lighthouse I am dying to see it. I could be a big help getting furniture moved. You know the kind of stuff that needs big muscles."

He said as he showed her his strong-arm muscles. Laura wondered if was wise to travel with someone she had just met. Jim had been kind and helpful. He would be an asset in helping her move the furniture and fixing the place up. Most of all he reminded her so much of her son she hated to part from him.

"I don't want to impose but if you would like to come along I could use the help. I have no idea what kind of accommodations we will find on the island until we get the house set up. They could be rustic."

"I can handle that. So is it a deal?"

Shaking her head yes, Laura felt a big black cloud of confusion has been removed from the horizon. The help of this young stranger would make it easier to say good-by to King and to settle into the lighthouse. She decided she would pay Jim when they were done. She looked out the window and she could see nothing but clouds below. Never had she landed at Glasgow airport that it wasn't either raining or foggy. It was even more of a sure thing in December. Noticing Jim had his nose squashed against the window she explained all the clouds probably meant either rain or fog on the ground. Jim laughed and continued to stare out the window as the cabin crew collected their headsets.

The pilot announced they would be landing in approximately 30 minutes. Laura was correct about the weather. The pilot said there was mist and fog on the ground and a temperature of 55 degrees. Laura became ecstatic. She had actually done it. She was on her way to her lighthouse. It was difficult to believe dreams do come true but right now her biggest dream was coming true. She knew it would not be easy but she was making it happen. As far as the difficulties she would just take them one at a time until all settled into place. The first extremely difficult step was turning King over to the kennel for his visit. A visit sounded better than quarantine. Besides she would not be able to watch over King while she was getting the lighthouse ready and he might come to harm in the new environment.

"Laura, look the ground!" Jim squealed. "It is so green. It can't be December."

Looking out the window Laura saw the familiar grayish green fields of Scotland. The fog subdued all the colors and gave them a tranquil and restful appearance. She loved the quiet of the color and realized she was felt like she was coming home. Jim being so excited was an added joy for Laura. She tried to point out some points of interest. Glasgow's airport was 12 miles out of town so mostly the scenery was farms and fields.

"Excuse me Madam you need to fill out a landing card." The steward said as he handed her a card.

"Thank you for being so helpful the entire trip" she told the steward as she took a card for herself and Jim.

Laura helped Jim fill out his card and then filled out hers. Always before she had been a tourist this time she would be a resident. She had an immigration permit to show passport control. She explained to Jim what would happen once they were on the ground. He should stay close to her. She would lead him through all of the steps. The big jumbo jet touched down and everyone applauded. Laura had never been sure whether they were applauding a safe trip or that the trip is finally over but it was a custom she had come to like and joined in.

After gathering up her stuff including the box with the cuttings from Peter's roses she and Jim waited in line to get off the plane. She kept up a constant chatter about what they would see on the trip to Gealach. The excited Jim asked question after question making the wait seem shorter. As they began the long walk to passport control he continued to fire questions. As they got near the passport station she felt Jim getting fidgety.

"Don't worry about this part. They are just going to ask a few questions. You will be through in a couple of minutes. You may have to wait on me since I have to show them more documents like my papers on King, and my immigration papers since I am going to be staying."

As Laura had predicted Jim went right through. It took her over five minutes to process all of her papers and to explain to the official what her future plans were. The passport agent was nice and even supportive when she told him where she was going to live. It seemed he had relatives on Lewis so he knew her island. Finally, he stamped her passport. Jim and Laura were on their way to baggage claim. Laura ran down the hall. She was so anxious to see King and make sure he was all right. As she entered the baggage claim hall she saw King sitting in his cage on a large cart in one corner. The minute he saw her he started to bark and wag his tail. Running to him Laura stroked his ears and talked to him before she gave him a dog biscuit she had in her purse. She knew she could not take him out of the cage. Giving him as much affection as possible, she rubbed him all over. She introduced Jim. King accepted him gracefully with a big lap of his tongue. After they collected their bags Jim put the bags all on one cart, which he pushed. Laura pushed the cart with King's cage. Waiting at the door was a woman with a sign saying "King File." Laura headed that way. Seeing the dog, the woman waved.

"Welcome to Scotland. I am Margaret Johnson of the Lochside Kennels. I hope your trip was uneventful and you are excited about your move to Scotland." She said as she slipped King another dog cookie.

"The trip was more than exciting." Laura responded as she gave the Margaret a short explanation of their delay as well as the required paper work for King

"I have brought pictures of the kennel since you have never seen it. Here is my card so you can call and check on King. We will take special care of him and you should feel free to call whenever you want. A portable phone even makes it possible for you to talk to him and maybe he will bark. I know how hard it is for you to leave him so I suggest you give him a big hug and be on your way. It does not help to prolong this." Laura felt she should ask Ms. Johnson more questions. She had given Margaret Johnson the details of what King ate and his habits on the telephone at least three times. To do it again would only be a stall to avoid the moment when she must turn her back and walk away from King.

Knowing Margaret was right Laura looked at King and felt the tears welling up in her eyes. She was all of sudden doubting whether she had made the right decision. Was she being selfish? Would King miss her so much he would get sick? "Laura lets go. I am dying to see Scotland and to be on our way." Jim said to interrupt her thoughts. For just a second Laura was angry with Jim. Then she realized it was exactly what she had asked Jim to do. Giving King one bigger rub between his ears she turned and walked out the door behind Jim.

"Oh beautiful Scotland here I come." she said as squared her shoulders and dried her tears.

CHAPTER ELEVEN

The main section of the Glasgow terminal was crowded. Laura and Jim's first priority was to get British currency so they went directly to an ATM machine. Jim was amazed how easy it was to get money from his bank account back home. No different than when he used an ATM near the university. Knowing they would be riding a bus for another six hours Laura suggested they go to the "Granary" café and get sandwiches to take on the bus with them. Jim asked Laura to pick a chicken something for him while he called home to tell his parents his change of plans.

"There is a telephone right outside the buffet. You can pick out your sandwich. I will have a cup of tea while you make your call." Laura suggested.

Jim appeared very uncomfortable with Laura's suggestion. He explained he would like a more secluded place than near a restaurant. He wanted to be able to hear his parents over the noise of the crowd. His answer was not out of line but his manner bothered Laura. Jim was acting guilty about something. Laura decided not to make an issue of it and agreed to meet him at the Granary. A little time alone with a cup of tea would help her recover from leaving King. On her way to the Granary she got a paper to check the weather for the next few days. Before she drank another cup of tea she would need to find a toilet. As she headed for the bathroom she saw Jim in the corner on the telephone. Walking by she overheard him say, "It is all worked out without any problem."

"What has all worked out without a problem? It certainly was not the flight?" Laura speculated. "Had she make a mistake agreeing to travel with a perfect stranger? Up until now she had found Jim to be a big help and not the least bit suspicious. Besides she just over heard part of the conversation and it probably had nothing to do with her or the trip."

Just as Laura sat down with her tea Jim joined her. They discussed the food Laura had bought. Laura could not detect any uneasiness in Jim. He raved about how good Laura's crisps were so he went off to get some more. Laura decided she wouldn't pressure Jim for more information about the telephone call besides it was none of her business. When Jim returned Laura laid out the plans for the rest of the day. As soon as they finished their tea they would take the airport bus to Buchanan Bus Station. The Skyeways bus to the Isle of Skye left from Buchanan. The bus linked with the Caledonia MacBrayne ferry at Uig on Skye. From there they would ride the ferry to Tarbet on the Isle of Harris. They would have to stay over night at Tarbet, as there was no public transportation to Stornoway after their ferry's arrival. The next morning they would go to Stornoway where the Gealach Ferry departed about noon. Larry Macdonald would be waiting on the dock in Gealach to meet them with the keys to the house. As Laura explained it to Jim it still seemed like she was a character in a novel and this could not really be happening.

"Let's get to it." Jim declared. "I came all this way to see Scotland not to sit in an airport drinking a cup of tea."

Laura laughed as they headed into the heavy mist to catch the bus. The mist was more like a fine rain. It covered all the cars and buildings with a shiny finish. Laura always found the misty calming. She laughed inside at the alarm caused by over hearing Jim's telephone call. Jim was not a sinister character but only a kid who was on his first trip to Scotland. Luck was with them as they found a bus to downtown Glasgow immediately. Jim was fascinated by the driver being on the other side of the car from home. More and more Laura felt she had made the right decision to have Jim accompany her. It was fun to see her beloved Scotland through the eyes of someone who had never been here. It was therapeutic to be a tour guide. It kept her from worrying about King and the unknown of the island. Jim almost broke his neck struggling to see all the buildings in downtown Glasgow. Reaching the bus station they found the Skye bus left in approximately twenty minutes. Laura went into a newsstand and bought a map of Scotland. It would be helpful in pointing things out to Jim on the bus trip. As they spread it out on the bench Laura saw a tiny dot off the coast of Lewis marked, Gealach. The island was on the map. Her new home was on this map. What a thrill that gave Laura.

Impatient she wished the bus would come. At the end of this day she would be only a short distance from her new home. Taking a pen she drew the bus route on the map so Jim could see where they were going. The bus traveled around Loch Lomond them through the Highlands to Fort William. After Fort William it climbed into the rugged mountains of Glencoe National Park. The most exciting attraction after Glencoe was the "Candy Box" castle, Eilean Donan. They would cross to the island of Skye via a new bridge. Laura regretted that the old ferry ride across to Skye was gone but the bridge was faster. They traveled across Skye to Uig where they would board the ferry to Harris. Jim asked so many questions Laura had not even noticed the blue Skyeways bus had arrived.   The announcement of its departure surprised her so they made a mad dash to get on board.

Being December and off-season there were only three other passengers. Jim picked a seat with a full window. Laura took the one across the aisle from him. The first hour of the trip involved getting through the city of Glasgow and the suburbs. The physical differences in the houses and the shops fascinated Jim.   Jim was constantly pointing something out to Laura. Having made this trip so many times before, Laura enjoyed Jim's drawing attention to areas she may have seen and forgotten or never even noticed.

Directly after Glasgow they began following the shores of a huge lake with the steel blue water backed up by hills covered with snow. Loch Lomond was one of the most famous lochs in Scotland because of a popular song about it.

"Laura, will we be going above the snow line?" Jim asked as he saw the white hills.

"Yes, we will probably experience snow sometime on the trip. Let's hope since it is raining now it isn't snowing in the higher hills. That could slow us up. We wouldn't want to miss the ferry." Laura responded.

Over hearing their conversation the driver announced the weather was suppose to be dicey between Fort William and Skye but should not slow them down. Laura was glad the driver was so confident. She looked at all the small houses and kept thinking there was a small house with a light on top waiting for her at the end of this trip. Maybe she should have flown to Stornoway instead of taking the bus but flights inside Britain were expensive. Besides, she wanted to see Scotland not just get there. It would not be any fun for Jim if they flew. Patience was not one of Laura's virtues but she knew her new home would wait for her.

After a short stop in Fort William the bus began the climb into high mountains. It took only fifteen minutes until the rain turned to snow. Laura found her lack of sleep began to catch up with her, as the slush-slush of the buses big windshield wipers became a lullaby. The road looked like a black snake curving through the white fields. Laura was jerked to wakefulness as she felt the bus slide a little going around one corner. She looked over at Jim and saw he had fallen asleep. Wanting to wake him to see Glencoe she decided there was no good reason he shouldn't sleep now. Laura tried to not sleep until early evening on the day of her arrival in Scotland. It was the easiest way for her to adjust to the six-hour time difference. If she stayed awake until about 8:00 p.m. she would wake up the next morning on local time. Jim may have a problem sleeping tonight but since she had not warned him she felt it was unfair to wake him up now to tell him. To keep herself a wake Laura drank a can of "Fanta." She really liked this soda and had not been able to get in the US. The bus continued to slip a little on the corners and she noticed the bus was moving slower. The snow was heavy enough you could only see a few feet in the headlights. It was obvious they were climbing into the mountains though. Laura was unable to tell exactly where they were.

"Where are we?" Jim asked. "I must have fallen to sleep. Did I miss much?"

"I don' t know exactly where we are?" Laura answered. "It has been snowing hard. I can't see anything. All you missed was snow. I hope it lets up soon because I want you to see Glencoe."

"I see clearing ahead." Jim answered.

"Maybe, but because we are close to the ocean the weather can really be funny in this sector."

"I definitely see sun peeking through the clouds ahead." Jim insisted.

Laura found she must agree. The sun appeared as a large white globe behind the dark snow laden clouds. As they began a steeper climb the clouds moved just enough to let a few weak rays of sunshine through. Ahead of them were two perfect rainbows arching over the hills.

"Look, Jim. Two rainbows." Laura shouted. "What a great omen of good luck for my new home."

"I don't know about omen but they are incredibly beautiful." Jim answered.

With the increasing light Laura was able to identify where they were. In a few minutes they would reach Glencoe. As she got the map to show Jim the bus began to slow down even more. Looking up Laura saw flashing lights ahead.

"It looks like an accident." The driver announced.

"Darn it", Laura declared. "Will it slow us down?"

"I don't know. I do not see many taillights so there is not a huge backup." The driver answered.

Laura sat on the edge of her seat as the bus crawled up to the flashing lights. A lorry's was on its side off the road. Its wheels were still blocking one lane of their road. The driver stopped the bus and got out to check. To Laura it seemed like he was gone forever. Laura remembered it was common for bus drivers here to spend time blithering and forget about schedules. After ten minutes the driver stuck his head in the door and informed them the truck was too far out on the road for the bus to pass. They were expecting a wrecker to arrive in a few minutes to move it and they should be on there way shortly.

Delays kept slowing up Laura's trip to Gealach. First, the fuel leak on the airplane and now a lorry across the road on an almost deserted snow covered Highland road. Every time some thing went wrong Laura worried more and more about whether she would be able to cope with so many changes. As the doubts crept in Jim drew her attention to a beautiful sunset that was breaking through the gray clouds over the white mountain in front of them.

"It is only four o'clock. What time does the sun go

down here? Jim inquired.

"We are very far north. If I remember correctly it will be completely dark by 4:30 p.m. and the sun will not rise until 9:00 am. The very short days are frustrating but it is made up for in the summer when the days are long. Sometimes the sun sets in the summer after 11:00 p.m. and rises before 4:00 in the morning. This delay will mean we will more than likely miss the Harris ferry." Laura admitted.

"Will there be places to stay at Uig?"

"I believe Skyeways has to make sure we find a Bed & Breakfast. There is nothing to worry about except I need to telephone Larry Macdonald to tell him not to expect us until later. It frustrates me all of these delays. I want to get to the island and begin to get settled." Laura was exhausted and a little depressed. All the interruption of the trip had finally gotten to her. If she could she would run back to Granton right this second but the bus was not going anywhere now. She would just have to stay put.

Jim seeing how unhappy Laura was started asking questions about Glencoe. Why was the area so famous? Where they actually in Glencoe? Always before he had been able to get Laura to stop doubting her decision to come to Scotland by tapping into her love for the country, this time Laura just stared out the window and watched the sunset.

"Laura did you hear me?" Jim queried.

"Jim, please leave me alone. I want to think. Just watch the sunset. There are no more splendid sunsets anywhere."

Jim recognized he was failing to distract Laura and for the first time he wondered whether he was succeeding in his mission. Knowing he should let Laura work through her feelings, he turned his attention to the sunset. He decided to get off the bus and look around. As he stepped off the bus he was hit by cold icy mountain air. Walking a few feet to a small rise he got a panoramic view of the area without the artificial flashing lights of the police cars. To the side were huge treeless hills covered with snow. In front were many tall white mountains. The absence of trees gave the mountains a peaceful appearance. The snow had covered all the rocks and made the sides look perfectly smooth. The sun was slipping into the valley between two of the tallest mountains. When the large orange ball attained a point level with the mountain tops the rays began to reach out into the valley. Orange beacons that finally get lost behind the nearest hills cut the gathering darkness. Within minutes the ball had disappeared leaving only a peach glow in the surrounding mountains. It all happened so fast Jim could not fetch Laura to watch. As the sky turned from peach to deeper and deeper shades of lavender someone touched his arm. He turned to find Laura standing beside him with tears in her eyes. Jim sensed she was not crying from frustration but from the magic of the moment.

"Isn't it beautiful?" She declared.

"I have never seen anything like it. This is my first Scottish sunset. Are they all so beautiful." Jim asked.

"I believe the sunsets on the West Coast of Scotland can not be equaled anywhere in the world. The sun has all sorts of backgrounds to set into. There is ocean and mountains. Best of all, there are combinations of both. Many times mist adds interesting shades of color. It is one of the reasons I want so badly to live here. A sunset over the ocean with mountain covered islands in the distance is the most spectacular sight I can think of." She answered.

Jim was relieved when he realized Laura was over her dejection. He was scared she would not snap out of it this time. As if it was planned the final shades of pink faded from the sky when the driver called them back to the bus. The lorry was out of the way and they could be on their way.

The ride through Glencoe was dark so Jim found himself getting sleepy again. Laura reminded him to schedule his return trip so he went through Glencoe in the early morning. She wanted him to see this beautiful mountainous area. Laughing she realized the rest of the way they would be seeing mountains and ocean. This was Scotland.

As they began their descent they could see a gigantic loch on their left. This was a good sign since they would soon be crossing a bridge at the end of the loch that would take them on to the Isle of Skye. As they reached the flat lands Jim became aware of a lighted building on the left.

"What is that? He asked Laura.

"That is Eilean Donan Castle. Isn't it gorgeous? This is one place you want to see at night. The floodlights make the castle standout against the black of the surrounding lochs and the shapeless mountains in the background. It is a small gold jewel surrounded by black velvet. Most of all it means we will soon be at Kyleakin where we cross the bridge to Skye."

"Laura, please remind me to get a post card of this castle. It is one of the most beautiful things I have seen yet." Jim stated.

Within a few minutes the bus stopped and paid the toll on the bridge to Skye. It was much easier than it was when Laura had taken the ferry to Skye. Laura felt it was too easy. The ferry ride had been like the official entrance to the islands. Skye is a Hebridean Island but it felt more like part of the mainland with the bridge. It did not feel like you were in islands until you rode a Caledonian MacBrayne ferry.

They quickly crossed Skye. The island was dark except for a few cottages with lights still on. Even when they went through Portree, the main town, the streets were lifeless. It was an empty town colored gold by the streetlights. About an hour later they reached Uig that was just a few houses plus a ferry terminal. Jim and Laura both had fallen asleep so when the driver announced Uig they awoke to find they were the only two people on the bus.

The driver explained they had missed the last ferry but there was one at 8:00 the next morning. He has notified one of the local B & Bs and she was expecting them. He dropped them off at the front door of the only cottage with lights on. They knocked but no one answered so they tried the door. It was open. Walking into the entryway they found a note saying they would find two rooms at the top of the stairs and breakfast was at 7:00 am. Jim could not believe it. You just do not leave the door open and let strangers walk into your house. He was learning the islands people trust each other. Too tired to meet his first island resident he was glad. All he wanted to do was sleep if only for a few hours. Laura smiled at Jim's reaction and led him upstairs. Most island cottages are set up the same with the bath at the top of the stairs and the bedrooms on each side so she needed no guide. Tomorrow she would see Gealach.

CHAPTER TWELVE

"Breakfast is ready." A gentle Scottish voice called.

Laura roused to the smell of bacon and coffee. It took her a few minutes to remember where she was. Finally awake she remembered she was at a Bed & Breakfast in Uig where she would catch the early morning ferry to Lewis. "I'll be there in ten minutes. Did you wake the other person?" She asked the friendly voice.

"He is up and gone for a walk."

When Laura got downstairs she found Jim eating a typical Scottish breakfast of eggs, sausage, bacon, mushrooms, grilled tomatoes, and toast. He had his toast piled high with a thick orange Marmalade.

"Try the jam. It is out of this world." Jim suggested. "Every thing is great. I hadn't noticed we didn't have a full meal yesterday but after my walk I found I was starved."

"Where did you go?" Laura asked as she spread her toast with the marmalade.

"I walked over to see the ferry. It was still dark and floodlights illuminated the boat. I can hardly wait until we get on. Mrs. Murphy, our B & B hostess, said it suppose to be a calm day with no clouds. The sunrise over the water should be super."

"Good, I don't want any bad weather to cause any more delays." Laura commanded.

As Mrs. Murphy placed Laura's breakfast in front of her she gave Laura a curious look at her abrupt comment. Laura felt she must defend herself from that curious look.

"I am moving to the Isle of Gealach and I am anxious to see my new home."

Mrs. Murphy smiled but still seemed skeptical. "I know your friend told me. Did you know they believe there is smuggling going on that island?"

"No! What have you heard?"

"All I know is one of our guests two days ago said the Stornoway police were investigating a report of drugs being brought in by boat out near Gealach Head. Isn't that where the lighthouse is located?"

"Yes but I am sure it was just a rumor. Did the people have any facts?"

"No, only that he had heard about it while eating lunch in Stornoway. Speaking of Stornoway we had better settle up and get you on your way. The ferry leaves in twenty minutes and it is always on time."

After Jim and Laura paid Mrs. Murphy they walked down the hill where cars were lined beside a small stone building. Sitting at the end of a long dock was a large ship with a black hull trimmed in white. Caledonian MacBrayne was written in large white letters on the black sides and a bright red smokestack had a large yellow circle contained a red rearing lion. This fierce lion rampant was sometimes known as the symbol of Scotland Laura explained to Jim. As they bought their tickets in the terminal Laura began to hum the song "Over the Sea to Skye." She felt the line "speed bonny boat like the bird on the wing over the sea " was appropriate except she would change the destination from Skye to Gealach.

Jim was so enthused Laura found it hard to keep up with him as they walked the long pier to the boat's gangway. He kept asking Laura question after question about the boat. Some of which she could answer but most she could not. Not wanting to give Jim the wrong answers she suggested after they got on board he buy a little booklet they sold about the ferries. As they gave their tickets to the attendant Jim asked where he could get the information book about the boat. The attendant laughed and asked if it was his first sailing. Knowing Jim did not want to be treated like a kid, Laura told the man it was the first time for both of them slyly winking at Jim

Laura led the way to the cafeteria where they got a table beside a huge window with no obstructions looking out over the deck. After they were settled she suggested Jim go watch the loading of the cars while she had a cup of tea. Without a moment hesitation Jim dug out his camera and was off. Drinking her tea Laura wondered if the story of drug running on her island was true. She knew there was no way she could find out until she got there. As she thought about Gealach she realized she had not called Larry Macdonald last night to tell him she would be late. She asked one of the crew if there was a telephone on board. He said no but if she wanted to get off and walk back to the terminal they had one there. Looking at her watch Laura realized there was not time to get to the terminal and back. As soon as they docked at Tarbet she would call him so he could meet them.

A blast of the boat's horn indicated their departure. Laura hand holding her cup of tea started to shake. Putting her cup immediately down on the table, she realizes she was the one shaking not the ship. As the boat gently glided out of the harbor, she knew she was almost to her new life. How she wished for Peter to share this wonderful moment. Being alone made her sad.

"Laura, they really pack the cars in here." Jim interrupted her thoughts and reminded her she was not totally alone. "It is amazing how many they can get on. If you are the driver it must be frightening since you have to park so close to the other cars."

Laura responded. "Peter always drove on to the ferries. I was afraid to try. I will have to get over that since I may be going back and forth a lot."

"Do you have a car over here? Jim wondered.

"Yes, there is a Land Rover that came with the lighthouse but I do not know how often I will take it to Stornoway since cars cost a lot on ferries. Can you imagine I bought property on an island and did not ask how much it cost to take the car back and forth?"

"I'll bet it doesn't cost that much to take the car on the Gealach ferry or someone would have said something. When do you suppose the sun will come up? I want to be on the deck to take pictures?

"I would guess we have another 30 minutes before that happens so why don't you get a cup of tea then we will go out on the deck."

Jim got a cup of tea and they found a bench on the deck sheltered by a lifeboat where they could see to the east and were sheltered from the wind. As they drink their tea they saw a lighthouse off in the distance. "Is that yours?"

Jim asked.

"No, that is Neist Point. It is one of the first lighthouses Peter and I looked at. It does not have access by car. The trail out to it is a difficult climb. We were worried as we got older we might not be able to get back and forth. The lighthouse is perched on top of a huge head and it has magnificent views. Take my binoculars so you can get a good look. Can you see it?"

"Yes, but not very well. It does sit beautifully on the top of the high cliffs. I can barely imagine what your lighthouse will look like."

"Even though I have seen pictures I can't either." Laura answered.

They sat quietly watching the red orange globe of the sun peeking slowly over the gray blue glass of the quiet sea. A long trail of orange coasted toward the boat. As the sun got higher the orange trail spread out in a golden glow. When the sunshine hit Laura and Jim they felt instant warmness. As the sun climbed higher they watched the glass sea become alive with million of sparkling dots. The ferry continued to push forward cutting through the sparkles. Laura and Jim were struck by the beauty of the moment and felt no conversation was necessary. It would be an intrusion on the moment. They just sit and watched daylight take over the sea and themselves.

In the distance they could see an island. "That must be Lewis and to the south is Harris." Laura whispered. Gealach must be just south of here. I can't see it but maybe we are not close enough." She said as she leaned over the side trying to see her new home.

"Is that it? Jim said as he pointed to a lighthouse coming into view on the right.

"No, that is Eilean Glas which is located on the island of Scalpay just off of Harris. Don't you just love the red and white stripes? Not many Scottish lighthouses have that type of decoration. Eilean Glas is now being rented out weekly for people to take their holiday. That is called self-catering here. Peter and I considered doing that with our lighthouse until we could retire over here. The lighthouse means we soon will enter the harbor and arrive at Tarbet where we catch the bus to Stornoway where we grab the ferry for Gealach."

Laura and Jim stood at the front of the boat and watched as the harbor town of Tarbet came into view. The excitement Laura felt was mixed with a strange type of fear. Will she like living here? What about this smuggling rumor? Since they were late how would she find Larry Macdonald to get the key to the property? She felt short of breath from her excitement and anxiety.

"Are you alright?" Jim asked.

"To be honest, Jim, I am a little bit scared. No, that is not true I am not a little bit scared I am terrified. When I started this it all seemed like a dream but it isn't. It is real and I am about to start a new life in a foreign land. Right now it wouldn't take much for me to turn around and go home to the US."

"I can understand that. We are here so lets check it all out. You can always change your mind latter when you have seen the place and found out all the details."

Laura was thankful for this young man who had only been a part of her life for less than 36 hours. In that short time she had come to rely on him. It was so much easier when you were not alone. She knew she could have handled it alone but to be able to share her thoughts with someone kept things from overwhelming her.

As the ferry pulled into the port Laura and Jim gathered up their belongings. Laura noticed her little box containing the rose cuttings from Peter's garden. It would only be a few days until she would be able to put them in the glass house at the lighthouse. Grabbing the box she hurried down the gangplank with Jim to find a telephone to call Larry Macdonald right away. There was no answer at the Macdonald's. Laura was disappointed but would try again when they reached Stornoway.

As they arrived in Stornoway Laura remembered she had to go grocery shopping before she caught the ferry. Laura asked Jim if we wanted to go the grocery with her but he declined. He wanted to see the town and would meet her at the ferry. After her trip to the grocery Laura headed for the ferry.

Jim met her with a bottle of wine in one hand and a bouquet of flowers in the other. "We definitely must bless the new house so I got some things to do it with." Jim said as he raised the wine and flowers. Laura was so excited Jim had to steer her in the right direction. As she reached the end of the gangplank she saw a short dark man with a big cardboard sign that said "Laura File" on it. She hurried over to the man. "I am Laura File."

"Welcome to the Hebrides. I am Larry Macdonald, the attendant at Gealach Head Lighthouse." The man replied in a strong Scottish accent.

"How did you know to meet this boat?

"I figured since you didn't make it last night you would be on this boat. If you did not make this one you'd be on the next one for sure. I brought a lunch and was just going to sit in the park and enjoy the beautiful day.

"I really appreciate your doing that. I was concerned about finding you since you have the keys to the house. How long is it until the small ferry leaves for Gealach?" Laura asked.

"We have about a two-hour wait. Why don't we go have tea at the hotel? They really have great fish and that means neither of us would have to cook tonight. We do not have any real good restaurants on Gealach. In fact, we have none so we had better eat here. I thought you would probably want to stay at the lighthouse tonight"

"I want to stay at the lighthouse but wasn't sure whether there would be anything to sleep on. Oh, dear, I forgot to introduce Jim. Larry, I would like you to meet Jim Greene, a friend I met on the plane who was kind enough to accompany to the island. He also has volunteered to help me get settled."

"Pleased to meet you, Jim." Larry said. "The keeper's left two plain wooden beds and a couple of chairs. The electricity is on and I brought you some peat for a fire. We can stop at the store and get you come groceries. If you would be more comfortable I made a tentative reservation at "The Black Gull", the island's only Bed and Breakfast, but since I didn't know about Mr. Greene I did not make a reservation for him. I am sure Margaret MacDougal has another empty room since it winter and very few tourist are on the island in the winter."

"Thank you, Larry, for being so helpful. I believe we will stay at the lighthouse and I have already picked up a few groceries. Jim can either stay there or take my room in town. Why don't we discuss this over tea."

Larry led them to a nice hotel with a view over the sea. They ordered the haddock special and drank tea while they waited on the food to arrive. Laura had so many questions she wanted to ask Larry she didn't know where to begin. She decided to start with the biggest worry and get it over with first.

"We heard in Uig that there has been smuggling on Gealach. Is that true?"

Larry was quiet and hesitated before he answered. "A couple of people have reported seeing lights out by the lighthouse. Ian Mitchell, our local police constable, has investigated the reports and found no evidence of boats landing or anything unusual. He felt it might be kids out there fooling around since the lighthouse is empty. He said tomorrow he was coming out to see you and explain. He instructed me to tell you not to worry. One thing you will learn quickly about these islands is gossip and rumors are abundant. Related to that, you should not be surprised that people are very curious about you. They know an American computer expert bought the lighthouse and that you are a widow. The island has talked of nothing else since you bought the "Head." I would not be surprised to see lots of people at the dock just sitting or in the store buying a little something just so they can see you."

"I must admit I am relieved to hear there was no evidence of smuggling. Related to the gossip a widow I am but a computer expert I am not. I am a graphic designer who works with computers that means I do know a little about them. How did they find out about my working with computers?

"You are going to be working with The Western Isles IT Project, aren't you? One of the island residents is working in that project and he heard about it."

"It will take some getting use to this gossip. What

did you call the lighthouse, The Head? Tell me about it."

"The locals call the lighthouse "The Head" because the buildings sit on a giant head with steep cliffs to the sea. It is easier to say "The Head" then Gealach Head. It is a beautiful place and you are a very lucky lady to be able to live there. I value every minute of my time there. I am required to come out once every two weeks to check on the light but usually visit once a week. While it has been empty I have been going every day. Your nearest neighbor is Jill McGiver about two miles away. She lives in the croft just before the entrance road starts around the mountain to the lighthouse. You cannot see her place but you pass it each time you go and come from the lighthouse. Everyone wonders why she stays out there alone. Seventy-two and totally blind she is a tough old lady. She has a seeing-eye dog and a nephew helps her once and awhile. It has got to be hard for her. I don't want to spoil your impression of the lighthouse so I won't try to describe it. I will drive you out today so you can spend all your time just looking. The Land Rover is in the garage. I put gas in it and made sure all was in working order."

"That reminds me of a question I forgot to ask anyone. Will the Gealach ferry take cars the size of the Land Rover?

"Being very small it can take five cars each trip but if a large vehicle is involved the number of cars drops. Most of us take the ferry on foot and then the bus into Stornoway because of the cost for the car on the ferry. Lewis and Harris have good bus services so it is no problem to get around. Speaking of the ferry we had better go."

CHAPTER THIRTEEN

Watching as a small ferry pulled up to the dock, Laura could not contain her excitement. The "Moon Isle" was no larger than a small fishing boat. Laura had expected a bigger boat. Two people disembarked and no cars rolled off.

Larry told them they could purchase their tickets on board. Waiting on the dock they watched the crew load a petrol lorry and groceries. "Mostly the ferry carries groceries and supplies needed by the islanders. I forgot to mention if you do bring your car off the island be sure and fill it with gas. Petrol is expensive on the island. The store is the only place you can buy it. The purchase of petrol is getting to be a problem for all remote areas of Scotland. There are fewer and fewer gas stations and the prices are very high. It is not uncommon for a local station to run out of petrol until the next ferry trip."

"It sounds like we are going to the end of the world." Jim declared.

"No, when you live on an island you have to plan ahead and be prepared." Larry answered. "They are motioning for passengers to get on. We had better move fast since they have a tendency when they are done loading to take off immediately."

Larry, Laura, and Jim were the only passengers on the trip to Gealach Island. Laura stood at the front of the boat so she could see the island as soon as it came into sight. She knew it had some small hills but was mostly flat. Larry explained the ferry ride would take about 20 minutes. Laura searched for the outline of the island.

"Is that it?" She asked Larry.

"That is Gealach. Doesn't look like much from here but having a little bit of everything it makes a perfect place to live. The highest parts of the island are on the south end where the lighthouse is. Most of the people who stay full time on the island stay near the store and the dock in the middle of the island. We have no real town but everyone calls the place where the store and the B & B are located "Mid Point" It is the closest thing we have like a town. The people who live around "Mid Point" are mostly fisherman. The north end has a few hill farmers. Fishing and agriculture is about it."

"What do you do Larry?" Laura asked. "The lighthouse job is not full time?

"I am a hill farmer. I raise Hebridean sheep on my croft. You may have never seen any since they are quite rare. They are black and the perfect breed for an island like this. I live on the same side of the island as the lighthouse but on the other side of the Geata Bay. The bay was named many years ago when it was the "gate" for whisky into the island. It has a beautiful protected beach with easy landing for boats. Look you can see the dock and the small building behind it is the store, post office and petrol station. My brother, Paul Macdonald, is the proprietor. Look at all the people on the dock. Word must be out you are on the boat."

"How would they know?" Laura asked

"I telephoned Ian Mitchell, the local police constable and asked him to meet us at the dock. You seemed worried about the smuggling so I wanted him to explain. The big guy standing on the end of the dock is Ian. Ian and I are good friends. He went to college and studied agriculture. His plan was to come back and farm his father's croft on Gealach. His father died while he was at college. His brother ran the farm after his death. His brother knew nothing about agriculture and soon was in serious financial trouble. To make a long story short, they had to sell the farm but were able to keep the house. The brother moved to Glasgow. Ian preferred to come back to the island to live. He changed his field of study in college and became a policeman. He has been here for over ten years and turned down many promotions. He would be required to move to Stornoway if he took any of the advancements. Ian wants to live on Gealach."

Laura began to feel weak with excitement as the small ferry pulled up to the dock. Tears came to her eyes as she stepped off the boat and put her feet on "her island". Ian Mitchell helped her off the boat. Big was the best word Laura could use to describe him. He was over six feet tall and weighed at least 200 pounds. He had short brown hair but his deep green eyes were like the color of the sea. His eyes were so bright and cheerful Laura immediately felt at ease with him.

"Welcome to Gealach. I am Ian Mitchell, the local police constable. Larry said you were concerned about the reports of smuggling near "The Head". I staked out the area for about a week and saw nothing. I think some locals may have had a few pints out there since the lighthouse was not occupied. The only two houses out that way are Jill McGiver's, who is blind, and the empty lighthouse. It would be a perfect place to party. If you see anything strange in the future just let me know." He said as he handed her his card.

Thanking Constable Mitchell, Laura and Jim climbed into the car with Larry. There were many people standing around staring at them. Laura did not want to start meeting people until after she had seen the lighthouse. Impatient to see her new home, she decided to come back for anything they needed. Larry understood her desire to get there as rapidly as possible so he didn't take any time to talk to Ian. As he opened the car door he told Ian he would call him tonight.

The road was a flat one lane for the first few miles. As soon as they were out of sight of the "Mid Point" the road began to curve as it climbed into the hills. A few tiny white croft houses nestled among the rising hills could be seen on side roads. After two miles the main road turned south and a side road had a sign "MacDonald's." "That is where I live." Larry said.

Just like a little kid Laura asked, "How much farther? It seems like I have been waiting forever."

"You can see Geata Bay on the right coming into view. You will not be able to see the lighthouse until we pass the McGiver croft and travel around that big hill ahead."

The area was mostly gently rolling landscape but he hills ahead were lofty. You could call them mountains but they probably were only 700 to 1000 feet above the sea. They resembled most of the Highland mountains smooth with very few trees and lots of rocks. As they came closer to the water a small yellow house could be seen sitting almost on the beach. It was neat but had no flowers or decoration.

"That is Jill McGiver's croft." Larry said as he pointed to the lone house. "You should call on her as soon as you are settled. She is a friendly soul. She has a few animals and they are her whole world. Each sheep as well as dog has a name."

"It will be wonderful to have a neighbor so close." Laura replied.

"You can not see her house from the lighthouse but she is not very far away. A little further on you will get a better view of the bay that is quiet today. The rocky coastline gives way to a smooth beach covered with smooth gray sand. People swim there and many fishermen use it to put their boats in the water. It was just on the other side of the beach where the land starts to curve back out to the sea that the strange lights were observed."

Suddenly the road rose sharply and the sea began to fall quickly away from them. The sea was off to their left but as the road turned and twisted it was often hard to see.

"Does this road get dangerous during bad weather?" Laura tentatively asked. She had never once considered the road to the lighthouse would be a problem. One of the main reasons in her decision to buy was the property had been a good access road.

"It can be a little tricky when we have gales and heavy rain. We get so little snow you will not have a lot of trouble with that. Ice might be a problem. Because the lighthouse sits down near the sea you should always check by walking up the road until you reach the first flat spot. If the road is going to be slippery it will start there. Don't fret about it. You will be able to interpret the weather after a short while. Besides you have a complete weather station at the lighthouse with barometer and wind gage. It wasn't taken out when we automated. I pick up the information once a week but you can look at it on a daily basis." Larry replied.

As they reached the top of the hill Laura strained to see her new home. It still was not visible as the road continued to curve down hill this time. It took another five minutes until she could see the black cap of a lighthouse protruding above a hill. Laura felt weak like she was trapped in a dream. Excitement overwhelmed her. Larry's Land Rover rounded the curve of the hill. At the end of the winding road a small complex of white buildings with a white tower at one end could be seen. A broad line distinctly outlined the complex, which must be the rock wall. Most Scottish lighthouses had a walled garden. It was a reminder of the time when the keeper's were given a cow as a part of their pay. Gealach Head looked so clean and neat sitting on the end of the world with the sea behind it. Laura stared at the upcoming buildings. Larry stopped the car as they rounded a curve so Laura could see clearly the dazzling white compound of buildings. Laura thought it was exquisite. Noticing a few sheep grazing on the surrounding hills Laura asked Larry, "Whom do the sheep belong to?"

"They are Jill McGiver's. She rents land from you. You will have to sort all of that out later. Jill has only a few sheep so they should not bother you. The lighthouse is surrounded completely by the wall so there is no problem with sheep being able to bother your garden. Are you ready to see your home up close?"

"Wait a second." Jim said as he got out of the car. "It is such a beautiful day. I want to capture this first sighting on film. Laura, get out so I can take a picture of you with the lighthouse in the background. You can give it to your friends back in the states."

Laura had forgotten all about the people back in the USA. The Madisons and of course Gary were the main ones. Oh, how she wished Gary was here. Shaking her head in an attempt to make the hurt go away she jumped out of the car to stand in the foreground of Jim's picture. Outside of the car she smelled the fresh sea air for the first time. It was cool with the breeze stirring just a little. Being a calm day there was not a wind but just a puff of air once and awhile. It smelled like she knew it would. She still couldn't believe this wasn't a vacation where she would have to leave in two weeks. She could stay forevermore in this wonderful place. "Hurry up Jim, we can always come back and take pictures. I want to see my new home."

"I'm done. Lets go." He replied as he jumped back in the car.

The rest of the drive was down a hill that was not nearly as steep as the first part of the drive. The station buildings looked like they had been newly painted. They stopped at the gate for Larry to unlock it. He handed the huge key ring to Laura when he got back in the car. As he drove up to the house he said, "Welcome Home, Mrs. File."

"Thanks" Laura replied as she quickly got out of the car and looked around. They had stopped at the garage. Off to the left was a walled vegetable garden with a small glass house in need of repair. She could see rhubarb and a few turnips in the garden among weeds and debris. The garden needed a lot of work. Heading up the driveway she found three different buildings in front of her. Larry said. "The center one attached to the lighthouse is where all of the equipment to operate the light is located. It is locked and my area of concern. I will give you a key in case of fire or you ever need to turn on the back up generator. On the right is a small bothy with a kitchen, bath, and two very tiny bedrooms. Jim might want to sleep out there. On the left is the main house. It is pretty exposed with three sides facing the sea but all of the windows have been double-glazed and have wonderful views. Want to go and have a look."

Laura walked up five stone steps to a simple wood door and tried a key. It took three tries before she found the right one. The door opened onto a tiny entranceway. Straight ahead a door opened into a short hall with a door on the left and another door at the end before the hall turned right. Fantastic, she thought most of the rooms would have windows on the sea.

The door on the left led to a small room with a Rayburn cooker and one rather old battered chair. There was one window looking toward the mainland and the hills. The other window looked out on the sea. Off of the dining room was a door to the kitchen. On the counter in the kitchen Laura found a small bottle of scotch whiskey with a card saying, "Welcome to Gealach Head" and signed Larry Macdonald.

"My wife wanted to welcome you and wasn't sure whether you were a scotch drinker but it seemed appropriate. The scotch is Talisker made on Skye. If you look closely you can see Skye in the distance." Larry explained

"Thank you for the whisky, what a thoughtful thing to do. Jim and I will drink some tonight to celebrate our arrival."

A laundry room and a bathroom were located behind the kitchen. Off of the main hall were two small bedrooms that were well lighted by large windows looking out on the sea. Across from the bedrooms was a good size sitting room with fireplace.

Laura hadn't even noticed she had picked up her rose cuttings until now. She went back to the kitchen and placed them gently on the ledge above the kitchen window. She felt like Peter was with her in her new home and she smiled.

CHAPTER FOURTEEN

"Before I leave you to your new home I need to show you the Land Rover and explain some of its quirks. It is a good machine but it sometimes needs coaching to get started. If you'd follow me to the garage I will demonstrate." Larry explained.

They left their belongings in the house and followed Larry to the garage. Like everything else in the complex the garage was neat and clean. Parked in the middle was a Land Rover that looked like it was brand new.

"I thought the Land Rover was five years old. This looks brand new." Laura commented.

"It is five years old. The Board had it repainted to cover up their emblem. I washed it yesterday in preparation for your arrival." Larry answered.

"You have been so good to us I need to repay you somehow."

"Just part of an island welcome for you and no repayment is necessary." Larry said as he lifted the Rover's hood to explain when it doesn't want to start you wiggled the wires to the distributor cap and it would take right off. "I must get going since my wife is expecting me for tea. Here is my telephone number. If you need any help getting settled be sure to call. It looks like you brought your own help in this nice young man but if you need another hand, let me know. If not, after you are settled give me a call. I will come over and give you a tour of the light tower complex. Regulations forbid me giving you a key to the tower."

"Thanks again Larry. As soon as I do get established I will have you and your wife over for tea."

With that Larry drove away and Laura looked at Jim and wondered where they should begin. She had many things, which needed to be done, but all she really wanted to do was sit, watch the sea, and stare at the tower surrounded by the clear blue sky. Jim sensing Laura's need to be alone walked around the property taking pictures from all angles. Returning to Laura he asked her whether she was going into town to buy any more groceries. If so, he would take his film in for processing. Jim's question brought Laura back to the present.

"Let's inventory what we have in the house first. Then we can make a list what we need from town or maybe I should say "Mid Point" since by most definitions it isn't a town. We will get what we need immediately here on the island. Tomorrow we will make a trip to Stornoway. My computer should be in by now. I could have had it delivered but since we had to go into to town to get furniture and supplies anyway I told them I would pick it up."

"Sounds good to me. Maybe in Stornoway they will have a one-hour photo-developing store. That way I won't have to leave the pictures in 'Mid Point' after all. I should pick up some more film. This place makes for some great pictures and I am really burning film." Jim said as they went back into the house and started looking through the rooms.

Laura picked up the telephone to find it had a dial tone. She decided to call the Madisons and tell them she had arrived alive and well. When she only got the answering machine she was disappointed. Thinking of home, made her think of King so she called the kennel to see how her dog was getting along. The news on that front was good. King was doing well. The vet had come and done all the necessary tests. The people were warm and so reassuring Laura felt very positive when she hung up. Jim had made a list of the contents of the house. It included two single beds, three rather old chairs, the telephone, and that was it. At least the kitchen had a refrigerator and stove and all were in working order

"First, we will make a short list of items to buy at Midpoint for supper tonight and breakfast tomorrow. Then we will decide what staples and groceries we need from Stornoway. We will also need to go furniture shopping in Stornoway. Hopefully, it can be delivered quickly. It would be nice if we could have the house all set up by the end of the week. Jim, why don't you get the car out and we will be on our way to "town?"

"Laura, I have never driven on the other side of the road." Jim answered in a panic.

"This is a great place to learn since we have no

traffic on the lighthouse road. I will drive when we get in town. Getting the car out will help you get the feel of a car with the steering wheel on the opposite side from the US." Laura answered.

Laura got cleaned up as best she could while Jim moved the Rover out of the garage. When Laura arrived in 'Mid Point' she felt people would be giving here the once over. Laughing to herself she thought, "I am the biggest thing that has happened to this island in a long time."

Jim had had no trouble getting the Rover out of the garage. He was proud of his accomplishment. He drove to just outside 'Mid Point' and Laura drove them into town without any difficulty. When they went by the McGiver place no one was outside but a car had arrived since they had gone by earlier in the day. Arriving in town they went to the store, which was deserted when they entered. The aisles were barely wide enough for a person to walk. Every square inch of the area except the narrow aisles was covered with merchandise. Standing behind the counter was a very large man, who was easy to identify as Larry Macdonald's brother. They looked a great deal alike.

"Welcome, Mrs. File and Mr. Greene. Is there something I can help you with? I am Paul Macdonald the owner of this establishment." He cheerfully said with a huge smile.

Laura and Jim looked at each other. It definitely was a small island. Larry had been talking to Paul because Paul knew about Jim along with his name. Accepting that everyone knew them Laura handed the storekeeper the list of items they need. Quickly Paul Macdonald went about the business of finding all of the items. Laura was thankful for his help because the store was so packed she would never be able to find anything. Thinking of the possibility of a cold night ahead Laura asks if he sold sheets and blankets.

"No, I am sorry I don't but my Mrs. though of that and I have some blankets we will lend you for the night. You probably will be going to Stornoway tomorrow to pick up your own." He said as he brought a bundle from a tiny room behind the counter. Again Laura felt touched by the kindness of the people on the island. As they were waiting for Mr. Macdonald to finish filling the order the store suddenly became extremely busy. The customers seemed more interested in the new neighbor than buying anything. She was polite and wished everyone a good day. No one stopped to talk but she could feel their friendliness. One of the people was Ian Mitchell. Ian was a large man but his face was kind and gentle with sparkling eyes. Not at all like what Laura expected a police constable to look like. He picked up his paper and tipped his hat to Laura as he went outside. His "Isn't all this attention fun" smile communicated to Laura a type of sympathy. Laura nodded her head and laughed in response. Collecting all of their purchases they went out to the Land Rover. Standing beside the Land Rover was a stooped gray hair lady with a seeing-eye dog. Knowing this must be Mrs. McGiver Laura introduced her.

"Mrs. McGiver, I am Laura File."

"Pleased to meet you, dear. My nephew came and picked me up so I could get a few things at the store. I would like for you to meet Roger who provides my eyes." Mrs. McGiver indicated the big golden retriever sitting obediently at her feet.

Leaning down to pat the beautiful animal Laura replied, "He is beautiful. I have a dog named King. He will be joining me in six months after his quarantine period is over. I'll bet Roger and King will get along famously. As soon as I get my house together you, Roger and your nephew are invited over for tea."

"Just let us know. Roger and I are always available but I cannot promise Steve will be there. His job is off the island. If he happens to be home I am sure he will be glad to come. Would you and Mr. Greene like to come over tomorrow night for a simple meal? I imagine you will be going into Stornoway for supplies and coming back on the late boat. It is a tiring trip and you won't want to cook. I make a delicious shepherd pie."

Laura was again astonished at how fast the grapevine worked on this island. She had not introduced Jim to Mrs. McGiver but she definitely knew all about him. "Actually not having to cook dinner would be nice. We would be glad to come. Can I pick up something in Stornoway or bring a bottle of wine?"

"I only have a little sherry so wine would be delightful."

As they were talking a rather short young man with bright red curly hair joined them. "I am Steve McGiver. Welcome to our island. If you need any help moving furniture or repairs I often work as a handy man for the locals."

"Thank you Steve, I'll remember that. Well, we had better go. It is getting near sunset and I don't want to drive the road to the lighthouse in the dark. At least not until I know it better."

Laura and Jim chattered most of the way home about how everyone knew them and how it seemed necessary for almost the entire village to make a trip to the store. When they started down the road to the lighthouse the sun was just starting to slip behind a few scattered clouds that had developed while they were gone. "Laura, could we stop at the passing area so I could get some pictures. This is going to be a beautiful sunset."

They stopped. While Jim scrambled over the surrounding hills looking for the best angels for his photos Laura sat on the hood of the car hypnotized by the smell of fresh salt air, the breeze on her face and the developing scarlet beauty in front of her. The sun was already turning a bright scarlet orange as it descended towards the sharp line of the gray ocean. As it got near and near to the water line it spread a column of glittering gold across the water toward the mainland. The streak of intense color glittered with ridges of varying colors. When the sun finally did slip behind the ocean horizon, the sky filled with cloud images started to change colors. It went through every shade of blue, orange, and then to the purples. Laura felt no concept of time or space she was so involved in the event. When the colors started to change to the dark of night she became aware that Jim has joined her sitting on the hood. No words were necessary between them. The beauty was gone for now. They both climb down and got in the Land Rover to drive the rest of the way down the hill.

"Jim, look." Laura called out. "The light! The lighthouse has turned on." Laura is beside herself. She jumps out of the car and ran to the highest spot in the area. Standing there she watched as "her" light revolved in the growing dusk. "Isn't it the most amazing thing you have ever seen?" Laura asked Jim. All Jim could do was nod.

"Lets go down and watch it close up." Jim suggested.

"Good idea." Laura answered as she jumped back in the car.

Reaching the lighthouse they unload the Land Rover stopping periodically to watch the light. They were so fascinated with the light they paid no attention to the rapidly dropping temperature.

"Laura, it is getting cold out here. There will be many nights to watch the light. We had better go inside for awhile."

Jim was right Laura realized as she felt the cold creeping through her thin shirt. "Once the sun is gone the moisture and the chill seem to take over." She replied.

"Why don't I start the fire and make up the beds while you put something together for us to eat."

Laura shook her head in agreement and took the grocery bags into the kitchen. As she made the dinner she looked out the window and could see the white tops of the waves as they broke against the coastline. The sound of the waves was so soothing she opened the window so she can hear it better. All of sudden big clouds of smoke were coming from the living room. Filling a dishpan full of water, she rushed into the living room to find Jim down on his hands and knees blowing into the fireplace but all that was happening were big clouds of dark smoke rolled into the room. "Jim, have you ever started a coal fired before?" Laura asked trying to control her laughter.

"No but it should not be any harder than starting a wood fire. I rolled up some newspapers and put it under the coal to get it started. I checked the chimneys flew and it is definitely open. The blasted thing just doesn't want to start." He answered.

Laura left him and returned to the kitchen where she

had seen just what they needed. Returning she showed Jim a square block. "This is a fire starter for coal. It takes a higher temperature and longer period of applied heat to start coal than wood. Put this under the coal and you should have no problem."

It took Laura a few more minutes to finish dinner. After she sat the table she went to the sitting room to find Jim sitting in front of his brightly burning coal fire. "Nothing to it when you have the right tools." He said.

"It feels good. We will need those blankets tonight. The Rayburn in the kitchen will warm this place up but having set so long empty and being a little damp it will probably take awhile. I have dinner on the table. Should we have Larry's scotch now or later? We could take our drinks and walk up the hill and watch the light if you are up to it." Laura suggested.

"That is exactly what I was thinking." Jim answered.

After they had eaten and done the dishes they poured their drinks, put on their coats and went outside. The weather was still good and the sky above them was full of a million stars interrupted every five seconds by the rotation of a large beam of white light. They climbed the hill and looked back at the lighthouse. To Laura it reminded her of a miniature Christmas ornament she had back in the states. It was hard to believe it was the real thing.

"Laura, look." Jim interrupted her thoughts as he pointed away from the lighthouse. "Am I seeing things or are there two small lights moving down near the Geata Bay?"

Turning Laura followed where Jim was pointing and saw two tiny lights moving around one small spot on the beach. "I see it too."

CHAPTER FIFTEEN

"Laura do you want me to go see if I can find out what is going on." Jim volunteered.

"Absolutely not. You don't know the countryside and in this dark you could fall and hurt yourself. Lets just watch and keep tract of the exact time and how long the lights are visible." Laura replied. Sitting at the top of the hill the lights seemed to be clustering around a small area or object. In about twenty minutes the lights disappeared but then could be seen periodically. Someone was climbing up the hills away from the beach. Suddenly the light disappeared completely. Since neither Jim nor Laura knew the landscape they had no idea exactly where the lights were coming from. The first sighting with the longest activity probably was the beach. From their location it was hard to tell for sure.

"Let's go back. I want to write down all we have seen for Ian Mitchell. Do you think we should call him tonight? I really need to get some sleep." Laura said as she sets off for the lighthouse below them.

"Someone is bringing something in by boat. I don't know if they are smuggling but why else would they do it at night? If we had arrived sooner we could have seen whether the lights came down from the hill or if they originated at the lower elevation. But, my guess is someone is bringing illegal contraband in from a boat off shore. Isn't it exciting?" Jim told Laura.

"Not exciting, terrifying. It scares me. Remember I am going be living out here all by myself until King comes. I am not sure King would make a very good watch dog." Laura answered. Jim was sorry he had said what he did. He could hear fright in his new friend's voice.

"It probably is just someone fooling around on the beach. I am sure Ian will be able to figure it all out. We can wait until morning to call him since who ever it was would be long gone by the time he got here." Jim said in a reassuring tone.

First thing the next morning Laura called Ian Mitchell but got an answering machine. She left a short message.   After they had eaten their breakfast Laura suggested they walk along the bay's beach toward where they saw the lights.   They might just find something Ian might find useful.   The exercise would do them good, and help Laura get to know the "lay of the land" so to speak.

"Sounds good to me but you had better dress warm there is a very strong wind out there. I went out to get some pictures of the sunrise and it was blowing so hard I could hardly hold the camera still." Jim told her.

Once outside they found it is necessary to follow the cliffs a long way until they found a place beside a stream leading to the bay.   The sides of the burn were gently slopped to make it possible to use it as a path to the beach. Most of the streams they had seen were like small cuts made in the rock and dropped sharply to the sea. Laura began to understand how dangerous it would be to wander this area without knowing the topography. She made a mental note to buy an ordinance survey map of the area when she is in Stornoway. Once they reached the beach the cold become more intense and biting with the addition of salt spray in the strong wind. They tucked their heads into their jackets and walked the beach away from the lighthouse. Just to be sure they could get home they placed a marker at the foot of the stream they used to get to the beach from the cliff. As they walked they notice the tide was going out. Last night when they saw the lights must have been high tide. They would be very lucky if there was any evidence of last night's activity. As they wander the beach they saw no indication of anything unusual. The beach was deserted and looked like no one had been around in a good long time. Chilled and getting wet from the sea spray they turned around and went back to find Jim's marker. When they found it they struggled up the hill to the top of the cliff. It was a great deal harder going up than coming down.

"I will make us a cup of tea." Laura offered when they got back to the lighthouse. "We should both take a good hot bath and dress in dry clothes for the trip to Stornoway. It looks like a nice day except for the wind. Sometimes it is less windy in-land away from the sea."

"Sounds good to me. I had no idea how cold a stiff

wind off of the ocean could be."

As they were having their cup of tea a car could be heard coming down the hill. Considering last night's events it gave Laura a feeling of security to know when a car approached the lighthouse by the road she could hear it. Looking out the window she could see a white and orange police car.

"It must be Ian. Where did we leave those notes we made last night?" She asked Jim. She found the notes and met the handsome police constable at the door. "Come in Constable Mitchell we were just having a cup of tea. Would you like to join us?"

"That sounds mighty fine. It is very fresh out there this morning." He answered. I got your message on my answering machine and tried to call you back. There was no answer so I thought I would drive on out and see what was up."

"Last night Jim and I saw lights in the hills near the bay. We didn't know the countryside well enough to go out and investigate. We did make detailed notes with times and what we saw. Jim do you want to go over the notes with Ian?"

"It was a wise decision to not go out in these hills at night. They can be very dangerous in the day time and night is even worse." Ian replied as he went over to the counter where Jim had put three cups of tea and some biscuits. "Now tell me all about last night."

As Jim read the notes Laura filled in details. Ian took his own notes and asked each of them questions as they went along. "I am beginning to think there is more to this than just some kids out on the beach to have a good time. There have been too many sightings. Every time I go out to investigate I find no sign of any thing on the beach. If it were kids there should be some sign of their presence. Maybe it is a ghost." Ian replied.

"Jim and I hiked this morning to the general area where we thought we saw the lights and found nothing. The beach was clean with no sign of anything. I had thought there should have been some physical proof of someone being there last night. I don't believe in ghosts so maybe someone really wants to cover up being there. Have you ever had smuggling on Gealach before?"

"We have had no problems with it since I have been the constable. We did have a few problems back during prohibition when they were bringing whisky in by the boatloads. The days of Whisky Galore you know."

"What ever they are bringing in it is not whisky." Jim replied.

"I think I will go along and check the beach since you are not sure exactly where you saw the lights. I will contact the main police station in Stornoway to see what they think. I would suggest both of you stay near the house at night. Let me know immediately if you see anything unusual." Ian said as he started out the door. Looking back, he smiled, "Oh, and thank you for the cup of tea."

Laura returned the smile and realized Ian was the first guest from the island in her new home. "You are welcome and come again. You were the first islander to visit my new home and I hope the next time you will come not on official business."

"You can be sure I will return when it is not official business." He shyly answered.

As Ian drove up the hill Laura thought he might just become one of her first friends on the island. Looking at her watch she realized if they were to catch the ferry to Stornoway they better get going. Getting use to relying on the ferry to get them back and forth to the big island was something she would have to pay more attention to. "Jim, get the list of things we want in Stornoway and lets be off before we miss the ferry."

"Got it. Lets go." Jim replied.

As they drove to the ferry they passed Ian police car parked on the side of the road. There was no sign of the tall policeman so he must be down on the beach checking for some sign of what was making the mysterious lights. Laura felt a chill and wrapped her sweater tighter around her.

They arrived in time to be the last car allowed on the morning ferry. "I will have to learn exactly the time it takes to drive from the lighthouse or I will never get back and forth to Lewis. We almost missed this one."

Once on board they sat down with a cup of tea and went over the list. If they were to get everything today they would have to split up the items. She took the furniture items and picking up the computer while Jim agreed to go to the dry goods store, get the film developed and go to the grocery. Laura was to meet him at the grocery at three. As they approached Stornoway seemed rather bleak even on this fine sunny day. They found a parking place for the Land Rover behind the tourist board. Laura gave Jim the extra set of keys and they went their separate ways to try and get everything done.

First Laura went to the furniture store. She wanted simple but comfortable pieces. The furniture was quite a culture shock. Styles were not the same as in the US. The names for things were also different. The owner was helpful and soon she had picked out everything on the list. He agreed to get the haulage company to deliver it to the lighthouse tomorrow if there was room on the ferry. If a lorry went on the ferry only one other car could make the trip. Laura was beginning to see that living on an small island does have its challenges.

Noticing he did not have any electrical appliances she asked him where she should go to get those. There was only one store in town where she could get what she had on the list. The same place she was to pick up the computer. Laura was anxious to see if her computer had arrived.

Finding the appliance store Laura was relieved when the owner of the electrical appliance store assured her the computer arrived yesterday. It was in the back room still in its boxes. He showed her a computer very similar to the one she ordered. Laura was excited at the prospect of putting the new computer together and getting online so she could contact her friends back home including her son. The appliance store did not have a large selection so choosing the washing machine and dryer was easy. When she had the shopping completed she decided to drop in on the computer organization she would be working for on the design of home pages. She found the office location easily but Mark FitzSimmons, the person she was supposed to see, was at a meeting. She went next door to have a bit of tea and biscuits. It was fascinating sitting in the window of the restaurant watching the people go by. Island people are a hardy group. She had always noticed how the weather gave them ruddy complexions with pink cheeks. They moved a little slower than the bustling Americans did. The pace of life was one of the things that had made her want to live here. As she was finishing up she saw Jim go into a green and yellow telephone booth. Once again she wondered whom he could be calling that he couldn't call from the house. She has no reason not to trust him but something wasn't quite right. He was allowed to have secrets. Maybe he had a girlfriend. She decided she was just being paranoid and took out her list to see if there she had missed anything. Not seeing anything she decided to go and see Tom Morrison, the estate agent. She wanted to thank him for everything he had done for her during the purchase of the lighthouse. She needed to pick up the plat map of the property he said dated back to the building of the lighthouse.

Once she found the estate agent's office the girl at the desk asked her to have a chair while she located Mr. Morrison. A rather heavy bald man came to the door, introduced himself as Thomas Morrison, and invited her in for a cup of coffee. Laura suspected the wait was not so much to find Mr. Morrison but to get a cup of coffee prepared. She really didn't want a cup of coffee but felt they would be insulted if she refused. Mr. Morrison turned out to be a rather grumpy person full of lots of complaints. He went on and on about how bad the weather had been since winter had arrived. Laura wondered how this pessimistic person could sell real estate with such a negative attitude about the world. He complained so much she found herself not listening to him. She was caught up short when he asked her a direct question. "Laura, have you seen any evidence of smuggling around the lighthouse? We have heard all about the mysterious lights out there."

Laura was reminded one more time how effective the gossip links on the islands were. She felt she didn't want to add to the gossip by mentioning last night's incident. She politely told Mr. Morrison she had to leave for an appointment with Mark FitzSimmons who supervised the computer grant.

When she arrived at the IHP office Mark FitzSimmons was back. They had a long conversation about how she was to work with the various participants in the grant to develop their home pages. Mark was a tall handsome Highland born computer genius who went to college at St. Andrews. He had brown straight hair and lots of freckles that Laura found appealing in someone that age. Laura noticed how his eyes flashed with mischief and how when he laughed his nose wiggled. She decided she liked this handsome young man. Working with him would be a pleasure. She wished she could talk longer but it was time to meet Jim or they would miss the ferry. The ferry was beginning to irritate her. Your whole life rotated around the ferry. She told Mark good-by and ran to meet Jim at the Land Rover. Jim was sitting on the running board eating a scone when she got there. Proudly he announced he gotten everything on his list plus some things he added like the scones. Laura laughed at him because he was so proud of his accomplishments. After they picked up the computer and were safely aboard the ferry, they compared notes about all the things they had heard in town. Jim kidded her about Mark FitzSimmons because she blushed every time she talked about him. Jim's kidding did not seem particularly funny to Laura. She was too old and widowed too recently to be interested in anyone. Trying to change the subject she told Jim about Mr. Morrison and the gossip about the smuggling. Jim became serious because he had become more worried about the smuggling issue since many of the people he met when he mentioned where he was staying wanted to know if that was near where the smuggling was reported.

"I am beginning to think there is more to this than just a few kids out there playing around and Ian Mitchell has not told us everything." Jim said.

"I agree. I think we should stop and see Police Constable Mitchell as soon as we get off this boat." Laura replied.

CHAPTER SIXTEEN

As soon as the ferry landed Jim and Laura headed for Ian Mitchell's office. Laura was becoming more and more worried about the smuggling. She felt the constable was not being totally candid with her. Especially after what happened last night. The policeman's car was out side his office so without hesitation she rushed in and blared at him. "You have not been honest with me. Tell me the truth about this smuggling. As hard as she tried she could not keep the desperation she felt from showing in her voice.

Ian looked at her for a long time before he answered. His handsome face showed neither anger nor amusement at Laura's out burst. "How was your trip to Stornoway?" He asked.

"Don't you avoid my question by asking about Stornoway. What is going on down on the beach near the lighthouse? Everyone in Stornoway is talking about it. I do not think it is just rumor or a bunch of kids fooling around. I have a right to know since I live there and will soon be alone." Laura sobbed.

"Wait a minute, Laura. No one says I am leaving you yet." Jim interrupted.

"Okay, you two I will tell you what I can but you must keep it confidential. As you found out rumors get going pretty fast on these islands. Let me make a cup of tea and we will talk about it." Ian replied in a soothing tone.

"We started getting rumors about lights on the beach approximately four months ago. I think it was just a few weeks after the keepers moved out of the lighthouse. A few nights I staked out the area and nothing happened. If something was going on it was like someone knew when I was there. About ten days ago I decided to tell no one what I was doing and I borrowed a car from one of my neighbors and took it down to the beach early in the morning like I was someone going fishing. I hid the car behind the lighthouse and set up a lookout on top of the hill just about the same place you two reported seeing the light. I stayed most of the day and watched the activities through my binoculars. Nothing happened during daylight. The beach was empty and there were not even any fisherman. About midnight I saw a light near the water. Just like you did last night. As soon as I saw it I started walking in the direction of the light. It was slow going because it was a dark night and you know how treacherous those hills can be. The contour of the landscape makes it very difficult to keep focused on any one specific area. One thing I was sure of was someone had gone to the beach from the road. As I got closer I could hear the sound of boat motor and the muffled voices of people. I could not understand exactly what they were saying but I was pretty sure there were three of them. I only had a couple of more hills to climb when I heard the roar of the boat motor as it took off. I tried to go faster but the rocky footing and not knowing exactly where I was slowed me up. As I rounded the last hill near where the lights had been I could see the light moving above me almost at the road. Then it disappeared. I was disappointed that I hadn't been able to get closer. I waited in a small crevice of rocks to protect me from the cold winds that has started to blow. As soon as it was daylight I went down to the beach to see if there were any tracks. There weren't. It was obvious someone had raked the sand to remove any signs of activity. I could still see the rake marks the tide had not removed. I looked for a trail back up the hill. There was a path that was only obvious because someone had brushed the area with a broom. I followed it up to the road. It lead to the lay by just before you turn to go down the hill to your house. Of course that is a popular spot so it was difficult to tell if any of the tracks were new. The wind was blowing even harder there so a lot of the tracks were only partial. There have been no more sightings since that night until you saw them last night. I have come out every night since I saw the light except last night. I didn't want to scare you on your first night here so I stayed away. I don't know what is going on but my guess someone is bringing in something illegally by boat. Whether it is drugs or what I do not know? My best guess would be drugs because there is the most profit involved in that but it could be people who do not have a visa, guns or jewels. I wanted to tell you yesterday but I felt with someone living down there now no one would try anything. I was wrong.

The custom and excise people have been notified and they will be sending someone from the main office to assist in the investigation. I know this is very frightening for you but I guarantee we will protect you as best we can."

"As best you can." Laura screamed. "That's not good enough. I am in danger out there in that isolated location. I don't know what ever possessed me to believe I could come to Scotland and live at a lighthouse alone." All the frustration and fears Laura had since she made the decision to buy the keeper's accommodations overwhelmed her and she started to sob uncontrollably. Jim tried to console her. He just didn't know what to say that would help. It was true she could be in danger. He had not planned to stay more than a week to help her get settled and now he was afraid to leave her. Ian watched Laura carefully. He felt sympathy and understood how she felt.

"Mrs. File, I promise we will do every thing we can to find out what is going on. It might be a good idea for you to stay in Stornoway for a few days until we can get it all sorted out."

"I'll be darned if I will let you or those lights run me out of my new home." Laura defiantly answered. "I will get a gun and learn to shoot so I can defend myself. No one will run me out." With this firm statement Laura regained control of her emotions and the tears stopped

Ian Mitchell once again studied Laura carefully before he spoke. "That is the worse thing you can do. If you have a gun you are not only in danger from what ever is going on at the beach but you are in danger of shooting yourself. Besides, in this country it is not easy for foreigners to purchase guns."

Ian's statement enraged Laura and without another word she stormed out of the police constable office and got in the Land Rover slamming the door. Jim not knowing what to do thanked Ian for the tea and apologized for Laura's bad behavior. Ian just shook his head and said nothing. It had become obvious to Jim as he watched the interchange between Ian and Laura that Ian was a quiet thoughtful man who was very careful before he spoke. Laura on the other hand had a quick temper and could be very emotional. Jim hoped they get over this disagreement because he felt Laura was going to need Ian Mitchell in the upcoming weeks.

When Jim got in the car Laura was crying and pounding the steering wheel. She kept muttering, "What a fool, what a fool, what a fool." Jim decided not to ask her whether she is talking about herself or about the police constable. Trying to settle her down and change the subject he asked if she thought they should stop at the store on the island for anything they forgot in town. This seemed to get through to Laura because she shook her head no and started the car. Both of them were silent as they drove home. Jim could see Laura struggling with her fears as they drove the windy road toward the Head.

"As soon as we get home we will unload everything and may even have time to get the computer set up before dinner. I want to go online and find out from the US embassy what it takes to get a gun permit. It will also make me feel more secure if I have a computer link with my friends' back home. Not that I will tell them what is going on. It will just be someone to talk to especially next week after you are gone." Laura explained.

"Laura, I was serious I will not leave here until this activity at the beach is all figured out. I would feel awful if something happened to you after I left."

"Jim, I have to learn to live here alone some time. You cannot protect me from all the things, which might happen. It is just not possible. If it wasn't the strange activities on the beach it could be a frightful storm. No, if this is going to work I have to be able to stand on my own two feet. Lets just forget about that now and get busy setting up my house. Why don't you take the responsibility of putting the groceries away and making up the beds with the new sheets and blankets while I put the computer together? We don't have to cook because we are invited to our neighbors for dinner."

Recognizing the determination Laura was showing to keeping going Jim agreed to Laura's suggestion. As they went by the McGiver's there was no sign of activity. Jim wished Laura nearest and only neighbor was not blind. She could be a big help to Laura. As they came over a rise the sun was just setting behind the lighthouse and Jim noticed Laura smile at the beautiful sight. He thought to himself this is one very strong and determined lady. No matter what the danger she is not going to let anyone disturb her in her new home.

Once they reached the lighthouse they unloaded the car and for the next few hours they were busy putting the house together. Tomorrow when the furniture arrived it will really look like a home. Jim started a fire in the fireplace while Laura finished putting the computer together. He heard Laura calling for him to come to her office. He rushed to join her thinking something was wrong. What office was she talking about he wondered?

Standing in front of the computer which she indicated was her 'office," Laura announced she was about to turn it on and E-mail the US. Since it was such an important event they ought to toast it. Jim agreed and went to get the bottle of Monach Castle White Birch wine they bought in Stornoway. He poured it in the new wine glasses. After he handed Laura a glass she turned the power on to the computer and they stood like two children at the circus watching as the computer sprang to life. When the program manager came up Laura raised her glass saying, "To modern technology which makes miles and oceans disappear." After one sip of wine she sat down and dialed into her online server. With just a few mouse clicks she had sent a message off to her friends the Madisons in the USA. "Now lets go to Jill McGiver's and get a real Scottish meal."

Laura and Jim enjoyed their dinner with Jill. Her nephew was not at home so the three new friends chatted and Laura made friends with Jill's dog. They found Jill was a big advocate of an independent Scotland. You could almost call her a fanatic about that issue. Driving home they looked for signs of the lights on the beach. As they came to the top of the hill they saw a car was parked half way down the hill to the lighthouse. Laura grabbed Jim's arm to stop him from going any farther. "What should we do?" She whispered to Jim.

"I think we should go back to the house and call Ian Mitchell." Jim whispered back.

"No, lets sneak up a little closer so we can see at least the license plate." Laura answered.

Jim thought Laura was crazy and would be putting them both in danger by going closer to the car with no weapons and no idea what they would find. How could he convince her not to do it was the big question because this was one very stubborn lady.

Just as Laura started farther up the hill a voice came from behind a rock. "Stop."

Laura and Jim froze. Both of them terrified as a shadowy figure all dressed in black approached them. "I think it is a very unwise for you to be out running around in the dark considering the circumstances." A calm and forceful voice said. Jim immediately recognized the voice of the police constable.

"Laura it is Ian Mitchell." Jim said with a sigh of relief.

"What are you doing on my land?" Laura demanded.

"Just doing my job, Mrs. File. It seems the owner of this accommodation thinks someone is prowling around on the beach and my job as the police constable is to protect her and her property." Ian replied with a serious tone.

For a minute Laura was taken back and then she decided it really was true. Ian was out here to protect her. "Oh, Constable Mitchell, I am sorry I got so upset in your office today and sounded so hostile. Will you accept my apology?"

"No apology needed but I could sure use a cup of tea. It is really damp and cold." He replied.

"Why don't you move your car down and hide it in our other garage and then we can have a cup of tea. Someone might spot the car from one of the higher hills if the moon comes out." Laura suggested.

"That is a good idea. You drive ahead of me so I will not need to turn on my headlights as we can drive down the hill. Then we can have a quick cup of tea before I go back up the hill to watch for the light."

As soon as they had Ian's car in the garage they went inside and Laura made a cup of tea and put out some biscuits. It was obvious that Ian was cold and hungry as he took his tea and five biscuits over to stand by the fire. He indicated he had been up on the hill since just after Laura and Jim got home and had forgot to pack a sandwich. Laura offered him some stew. Thinking only for a minute he said yes if it could be quick. Jim volunteered to go into the kitchen to heat it.

Laura and Ian talked about her plans for the inside of the keeper's accommodations. Laura noticed that Ian was looking at his watch. She excused herself and went into the kitchen to see what Jim was doing and she found him on the telephone. As soon as he sees her he hangs up and begins to dish up the stew. This was the third time she had caught Jim making secretive telephone calls and not offering any explanation. She made a mental note to ask him about this as soon as Ian was gone.

CHAPTER SEVENTEEN

As soon as Ian went back to watch for lights, Laura asked Jim to set down by the fire for a few minutes. They sipped their tea and Laura wondered how she could bring up the subject of the strange telephone conversations with Jim. She did not want him to think she had been spying on him and yet she was curious about whom he was calling. The use of her telephone did not bother her so much as his wanting to hide making the calls.

"Jim, I want to ask you something. When I came out to get Ian's dinner you were on the telephone. I do not mind you using the telephone but am curious about why it seemed to be such a big secret. Is there something you want to tell me?" Laura asked quietly and with a great deal of warmth. Laura's new young friend stared at her for a few minutes without saying a word his face showing some kind of conflict deep inside him.

"Laura, I have not been totally honest with you. I did not come up here to only help but also to write a story. I am a law student but in addition a freelance writer. After I heard what you were trying to do I felt it would make a good story. The telephone calls are to various editors to see if they would be interested in a feature on your endeavors to settle in a deserted lighthouse without any assistance. I felt you might throw me out if I told you the truth about what I was doing. Your welfare is important to me and I care more about that then writing the story. I need the money for school so the story seemed like a natural way to get a little. I am sorry I wasn't honest with you from the very beginning."

Anger boiled up in Laura. Someone she had come to almost trust completely had been dishonest with her. The hand holding her tea mug started to shake so she put it down before she broke it. Knowing her temper she decided the best thing she could do was to say nothing and go to bed and think about it. "Jim, we are both tired and I need to think about all of this. Why don't we go to bed and we can discuss it in the morning?"

Jim nodded his head and took the remains of the tea into the kitchen and went to bed without another word.

Laura stared at the fire and wondered what she should do. She was frightened with all the strange activities going on around the lighthouse but she felt there was something more that Jim was not telling her. She would like him to stay a few more days but eventually he would have to go. The big problem was "who does she trust?" To survive in such isolation she felt she needed to have someone to talk to and to contact in case of an emergency. Jill McGiver will be the most logical choice but she was blind and could really not be much of help in the case of an emergency. She was somebody Laura could talk to when she needed a listening ear. Ian Webster seemed okay and would be a good place to turn in the case of an emergency. She could not tell underneath that policeman manner what sort of man he really was. He seemed cold and distant at times. The one person she had met who she liked and who seemed he could be trusted was Mark FitzSimmons at the programming company. He seemed warm and supportive. His living in Stornoway didn't help the immediate problems. Thinking about this just depressed Laura more and made her sad. If only Peter was here. She kept thinking about Peter. Laura knew she should stop doing that. It was not going to be. Shaking her head as if to clear away all the bad thoughts, she walked outside to see what the weather was like. The moon was full and it was piercing cold. Thinking about Ian up on the hill she hoped he was dressed in plenty of layers of warm wool. As she looked at the hills, she became aware of the lighthouse beacon twirling above her head and she realized that one thing was constant. The light turned on every night and would always be there to keep her company. It was reassuring. Laura felt calmer. Just the light and herself at Gealach Head maybe that was enough? Turning without even being aware of what she was doing she patted the cold stone tower like a long lost friend and went inside.

The next morning Laura awakened to the smell of coffee and frying bacon. It was still dark so it must be early. Looking at her clock she realized it was 8:20. It will be hard to get use to the short days here. It was not cold in the Wisconsin sense because somewhere out in the ocean the Gulf Stream warmed the ocean. Yet if you looked at a map you would see the island was as far north as Alaska so they had long days in the summer and short ones in the winter. Getting quickly dressed she went into the kitchen where Jim was putting plates on the table.

"Good morning, did you sleep well?" He asked.

Surprising Laura realized she had sleep well and felt rested and ready to take on anything this morning. "I am fine. The coffee and bacon smell good." She stated as she poured herself a cup of coffee. "Is there anything I could do to help with breakfast?"

"Nope, it's ready. Just sit and I'll give the scrambled eggs a couple of more stirs and put them on the plate. I bought some local smoked salmon and scrambled a few bits in with the eggs. I hope you like that? Scottish you know." Jim said with a twinkle in his eyes.

"That will be fine. Jim, I thought a lot about our conversation last night and I would like to ask you not to write a story about my moving here. You can write about the island and the people but my story is private and I still do not know how it will turn out. I am not angry with you but I am a little disappointed you could not trust me. You can stay a while but I believe you should leave before Christmas. I must make the transition to living alone and find local resources which I can rely on."

"Thanks Laura for being so forgiving and I promise I will not write a story about you. I may write about this island and the people. I disagree about my leaving before Christmas but can understand how you feel about getting on with your life. I will be out of here before Santa comes. Okay? But, until then what's up next?"

"Jim, the eggs are wonderful." Laura exclaimed as she ate. "Today we clean the house and make it spic and span so when the furniture arrives we can put it all in place. I also thought I would put a leg of lamb on to roast so we could have a normal meal and evening in a fully settled house. I have a couple of telephone calls to make. One to the kennel to see how King is doing and one to my contact at the computer company to get that all started. How does that sound for a plan for the day?"

"Sounds good to me. I will start on the cleaning

and if the mist clears I will get a few more pictures. Would you mind if I took the Land Rover and drove to other parts of the island while you work on the computer?"

Having agreed on the activities for the day each began their work. Laura started cleaning the kitchen by washing up the dishes from breakfast. Just as she was finishing the telephone rang. It was Ian Webster letting her know he saw no activity on the beach last night. It was friendly and considerate of him to call. Laura once again wondered about this man. His call reminded her she was going to call Mark FitzSimmons.

Mark wasn't in when she first called. Laura began to wonder if carefully screened whom he saw since yesterday he wasn't in when she went to see him. He did call her back in a matter of minutes.

"Mark, before we get into the business part I have a favor to ask." Laura stammered out. "Do you know where I can get a hand gun?"

"Laura, it will takes month's to get a hand gun permit for you. I know why you are asking but it is very difficult. Do you know how to shoot one?"

"Actually I do. I learned from Peter a long time ago. If I could just get one, I would practice to make sure I could hit what I am aiming at."

"Sorry, Laura. I have no suggestions except to borrow one from someone and I do not even know of anyone who has one. If I hear of anyone who has one I will let you know. Now, are you ready to go to work next week?" The conversation fell into a business mode as Laura got the first order to design a page for a local business.

The mist cleared and Jim having finished cleaning his part of his house by late morning took the Land Rover to search for the perfect photo. Laura checked the computer and found two messages from her neighbors in Wisconsin. It was good to hear from home. Then all of sudden Laura realized Wisconsin was not home but Gealach Head was home. Just as she started to set her Windows configurations, she heard a car pull in. Thinking it was Jim she continued working on the computer until the pounding on the door made her realize it was someone else. Answering the door, she found two men standing there staring up at the light tower.

"Excuse me, a ma'am, would you be Mrs. File? We have some furniture to deliver to a Mrs. File. Is this a real lighthouse? I have never been this close to one." The older man asked.

"Yes to both questions. I am Mrs. File and that is a really working light tower. If you bring the furniture in, I will show you where to put it."

For the next 30 minutes the two men brought in pieces of furniture and boxes while Laura instructed them. The two men asked for permission to look around the lighthouse station before they left. Laura knowing the entrance to the tower was locked told them they could look around as much as they would like. Laura wondered how many people would show up at her door wanting to look at the lighthouse. Lighthouses are very popular tourist attractions but of course Gealach Head was not a very big tourist area.

After the two men left Laura set about putting her bedroom in order. She was busy opening up a box with lamps in it when Jim got back. He immediately went to work helping her take things from boxes and move the furniture. It took them a good two hours when Laura realized they had not even stopped for lunch.

"Jim, enough. Lets stop for a bite of lunch. I also need to put the lamb in the Rayburn for tonight."

"I thought you would never ask." Jim answered.

After Laura put the lamb in she and Jim enjoyed their gourmet meal of toasted cheese sandwiches with pickle. "Jim how was the picturing taking?" Laura asked.

"It was great. I found the rest of the island a little flatter and not as remote as this side but it was beautiful. Actually this was as good as time as any to give you a present I got today for you. Wait here." He said running out to the Land Rover and returned with a small box. "I was against this at first but now I think it might be a good idea."

Taking the box Laura opened it and saw a small handgun and a box of bullets. "Where did you get this? Is it legal?" She asked.

"Legal, no. I asked Phil McDonald if he knew of anyone on the island who might have a handgun I could borrow to kills some "rats" that had moved in while the house was empty. Of course, Phil knew a man who had a gun left over from the war. Phil knows everything. I went to see the man. He had a standard British forces issue .38 Webley revolver in working order. It was not an antique or souvenir. It had been fired at least once a month and cleaned so it was in good shape. He had no problem lending it to me for a couple of months to keep down the "rat" infestation. After we get the house settled, we will go to that secluded cove which is far away from everything and see if you can use it. You do understand you can tell no one you have a gun. When you practice it must be secret and the wind in the right directions so no can hear you. If I am not positive, you know how to use this thing properly by the time I leave I will take it back to the man who gave it to me. The last thing I want is to have you shoot yourself."

"Oh, Jim, thank you. I asked Mark FitzSimmons about getting one this morning but he wouldn't help me since it is illegal. Lets get the house settled as best we can and then go try the gun out. We can finish the house after dark. I feel safer already."

Later in the afternoon Laura and Jim went to a hidden cove behind a big hill where Laura tried the pistol. The location was perfect as sound from the firing would be stopped by the huge mountain in one direction and travel straight out to sea in the other. Laura found the gun light and even though she did not hit the center of the target she at least got on the target they had constructed from the furniture boxes. Even though the gun was hard to manage and she ached from the effort of firing it Laura felt a little more secure.

CHAPTER EIGHTEEN

Jim and Laura had made the house at Gealach Head into a home in the last days. All of the new furniture was located in just the right spot making the little cottage resemble a home of long time standing. The last few days had been so busy for the two keepers in residence they spent very little time worrying about the lights on the beach. The act of getting settled had brought a kind of satisfaction to Laura. She went to the beach to practice her shooting and found hitting the target was getting easier. This morning as Jim and Laura sat with a cup of tea watching the sunrise over the vast ocean outside the window Laura realized Jim would be at Gealach Head for only another week, as he wanted to be with his cousin in Paris for Christmas.

"Jim, since you will soon be leaving don't you think we ought to have some of the neighbors in to see our beautiful little cottage and give you a chance to say "Good-by"? Laura asked.

"Laura I think that is a wonderful idea and since Christmas is so close we could decorate the lighthouse and make it festive." He answered.

"I am not sure that is a good idea. I wasn't going to celebrate Christmas. This will be the first one without Peter. It has only been a short time since he was killed. Would her neighbors think it wrong for a new widow carrying out such joyful things?"

"Oh, come on Laura. Would Peter want you to have a dull sad holiday just sitting around the house brooding? Or would he want you to enjoy your first Christmas in your new house with your neighbors? From everything you have told me Peter would want you to have a cheerful Christmas. I doubt if anything you can do will make it jolly but you need to go on with your life and do what Peter would want."

"I suppose you are right but it just seems so strange to think of a holiday without Peter and Gary. To share it with my new neighbors would be a good beginning on the life here. I have no idea what the Gealach Christmas holidays are like but since I am American I guess we could do an American thing. They actually might enjoy seeing what an American would do at this time of year. I have no decorations so we will have to go to Stornoway. Besides we will need food and invitations if we are going to have a party. Shall we go this morning and begin the preparations tomorrow?"

Without any more discussion Laura and Jim made a list of the things they wanted to get in Stornoway. After completing the list they dressed in their warmest clothes. Even thought the sun was shinning in a deep blue sky the thermometer said it was below freezing outside. As they put on various layers of winter clothes they began to feel in a Christmas spirit. Cold weather and Christmas go together in the places where they both grew up.

As they drove to the ferry they discussed one of the first big issues to be resolved. Where do you get a Christmas tree at this time of year on an island that had hardly any type of vegetation taller than two feet? The trees that they had seen were so blown by the wind they did not resemble Christmas tree but tortured skeletons. After much thought, they decided to go to a nursery in Stornoway and buy a live tree in a pot to use for Christmas. The tree would have to be small. The cottage was tiny. Toy size would be perfect for their needs. As soon as they arrived they went to the nursery to see what type of trees were available. The nursery had no true pine trees but they did have a small Norfolk Island pine. It sort of looked like a Christmas tree so they chose the one with the longest and fullest needles. Once the tree was safely placed in the back of the Land Rover they set off for the store to buy decorations. The first decision was easy. They purchased one string of 100 miniature white lights. That should make the little tree blaze. As they looked around at all the decorations and tinsel they did not see anything that fit the image of the lighthouse keepers cottage.

"Jim, I do not see anything I really like here. Somehow it all seems a little too.... garish. I had more in mind something simple and peaceful like the cottage. The last few weeks I have been very careful not to over decorate the cottage. The keeper's who lived there in the past had very simple lives and I want mine to be like that also."

"I agree with you Laura. Why don't we decorate the tree like the keepers would have? They used what they had around and what they could make." Jim responded.

Laura's mind begins to whirl as she thought of what they could use. "We could use the shells I have been collecting on the beach. We could buy some ribbons to tie little bows on the tree. How about stringing popcorn? No, we don't need popcorn. Shells and bows would be enough. Except, we need something special for the top of the tree. Do you have any ideas?"

"Well, the tree has a nautical theme so either a boat or lighthouse would be the perfect answer."

They asked the lady at the store if she has any tiny boats or lighthouses. She led them to the children's toy section where they found a box of six tiny ships. Jim suggested the ships would be best on the tree with the shells so they still needed something to go on top. They looked all through the children's section and found nothing, which would suit. Discouraged Laura went to pay for her purchases. Passing the lamp section she saw a small night light in the shape of a lighthouse.

"That's it." She shouted. "We will put that night light at the top of our tree. A lighthouse should have a tree with the friendly light of another lighthouse at the top. Do you think we can use it? It is made to plug into the wall not to be on top of tree?"

"No, problem we need an small extension cord and I can fix it right up." Jim volunteered.

After leaving the hardware store they went to a stationary store to get invitations for their party. Once again the selection did not suit them. Now, that the Christmas tree had a nautical theme they wanted to stay with that for the invitations.

"Laura, do you remember the little star fish you found on the beach last week? The tiny one, which you said, was a baby? Before we hang it on the tree as an ornament why don't we use it as a model and splatter paint around it. We could entitle the invitations "The Star of Gealach Head" invites you." On the inside we could put all of the details about who, what, when and where. They would be beautiful and be exactly what you wanted. All we need is the right type of paper." The lady behind the counter heard their discussion and suggested they use a simple rough textured paper and splatter it with silver ink.

"Yes, that would perfect." Laura replied with tears in her eyes because it really was perfect.

The next stop was the grocery store to get the supplies for the party. Being here only a short time she had no idea what Scottish people expect for Christmas so she asked the lady behind the meat counter what she should get.

"Do you want a full meal or do you want to just have sweets? The lady inquired.

"Since I do not know how many are coming I think I will just have sweets. Do you have any suggestions?"

"You definitely need a Christmas cake with lots of currants, sultanas and treacle. It must have marzipan on top. Actually the store carries a very good one and it would be perfect. You could have biscuits also but I would suggest the Christmas cake with coffee and tea."

"You have been so kind thank you. We will have a Christmas cake and coffee and tea."

"Don't forget the whisky? That would be nice if it was a cold day to add to the festivities."

"Another good suggestion. Thank you." Laura said with warmth. People in Scotland were so friendly. She and Jim wanted to get home so they could decorate. They hurried through the task of buying the rest of their groceries so they could catch the next ferry. They talked about their tree all during the ferry ride.

As they drove down the hill to the lighthouse Laura found she was looking at it differently. She saw a Christmas scene and considered how perfect the lighthouse looked. Being from a northern climate the only thing, which would make it more perfect, was snow. It did snow on the island once and a while but it is doubtful they would have a white Christmas.

After everything was unloaded Laura put the teapot on. Over tea they began to make a list of people who would attend their Christmas open house. They put everyone they had met on the island including the McDonalds, McGivers,

Ian Webster and Mark FitzSimmons from Stornoway. It didn't seem like a very big list and Laura felt a little sad and depressed. If she had been making a list for an open house back home in Wisconsin she would have pages and pages. Trying to cheer herself up she remembered she had only been here for a few weeks. The list had quite a few names for such a short time.

Jim sensing Laura's sadness suggested, "Let's ask the store keeper for suggestions of any others on the island we should invite."

"That's a splendid idea." Laura said half heartily. "I have a headache so I think I will lay down for a few minutes to see if it gets any better before I start our evening meal."

"You just rest I will cook up something for us to eat and then after supper we can begin decorating the Christmas tree. How does that sound?" Jim asked. Laura didn't reply because she was already half way through the door to her bedroom.

Jim wondered what was up with Laura. She never was rude. Maybe she did just have a headache and didn't feel up to dealing with Christmas right now. He went about making a beef stew for supper and stirred up a cake mix. Maybe if he made a nice dinner Laura would feel better and be more in the mood for Christmas tree decorating. While the cake was baking he went to find a container big enough to set the little pine tree on. He placed the tree in front of the window where people would see it coming down the hill toward the lighthouse. Then he put the small string of lights on the little tree transforming it into a sparkling wonder. Just as he was finishing the timer went off for his cake. Jim felt very domestic and content. For the first time he didn't feel guilty about what he was doing. Determined to stay in a holiday spirit he looked for some green food coloring to add to the can of frosting he was using on the cake after it was cool.

Laura came out of the bedroom at the same time Jim finished setting the table for dinner. He could tell she had been crying, as her eyes were swollen and puffy. She smiled at the table with the bright green cake in the center.

"It sure smells good in here. Your cake is lovely. Did you make stew? " She asked.

"Stew it is. As for the cake, well I guess I got a little too much food coloring in the frosting mix. I wanted us to have a Christmas cake on the night we decorated our tree. Dinner should be on the table in a few minutes why don't you go into the living room. I put a bottle of wine on the table and there is a nice fire burning. The weather has really turned foul. There is a stiff gale and it is raining hard. I will check on the vegetables and come join you for wine."

In the living room Laura curled up on the couch and poured two glasses of wine. Staring into the fire and listening to the wind the tears that had plagued her started again. She missed Peter and Gary. She physically hurt all over. Trying to keep from crying she went to the window and looked at the weather. As she got up she noticed for the first time the tiny tree in the corner sparkling with little white star like lights. First more tears started but then all of a sudden she felt peaceful. The little keeper's house wrapped itself around her with its warm fire, the spicy smell of stew and the twinkling little tree. Gealach Head seemed to be filling her emptiness. It gave her a feeling of history and a kinship with the keeper's families who had celebrated in this room in the preceding years. She began to wonder about those Christmas celebrations in years gone by and whether they had a tree. Were there children? Did they have a green cake? What did they use to decorate the tree? Oh, how wonderful it felt to be a part of something so special. Just like magic her sadness disappeared and she felt excited about the upcoming holiday. After supper she would go find her shells and hang them on the tree. Then she would tie all the wee bows on the branches. Laura remembered a Christmas card she saw a few years ago of a lighthouse with a big Christmas wreath adorning the tower. She could ask the Northern Lighthouse Board if it was okay to put a large wreath on the tower above the door. Then she laughed. How ridicules! A wreath would blow off the tower. Suddenly, she had a wonderful idea. "Jim, do you thing we can make a wreath or some type of decoration to put on the gate at the top of the hill so people can know Gealach Head is celebrating Christmas?

CHAPTER NINETEEN

As soon as Laura and Jim finished the supper dishes they set about decorating the little tree. Jim carefully attached strings to each shell that Laura had found on the beach. Laura placed them on the branches. After each was hung, Laura would stand back from the tree to resolve whether this was the correct place for that particular shell. All of this brought memories of the Christmases in the past when she, Peter and Gary had done the tree. They always made it a big deal and everyone was home the night of tree decorating. Laura seemed comfortable with these recollections now. There would always be memories she could treasure. Memories would not go away. She knew in the future there would be many times when her heart would cry out for the loss of those two people. Life must go on and she was determined it would. It seemed funny to her that she kept putting Gary in the same category as Peter. He was very much alive in the United States going to school and living with his new friend. Maybe she would send a letter to him inviting him over for Christmas and telling of the events on Gealach Head. Completing the shells she tied ribbons carefully to the branches to fill in the empty spots. It looked good for a scraggly plant with homemade ornaments.

"It looks beautiful." Jim exclaimed.

"Yes, it is splendid and I thought it might look dull with none of those shiny ornaments we used in the US. I think because Gealach Head is a simple place we don't need the fancy stuff I am use to. We have one task left and that is to put the wee lighthouse at the top of the tree. Do you think it will work? I am worried it is too heavy and will bend the branches or maybe even break them."

"I have it ready." Jim explained. "While you were resting, I put the cord on it and attached some wires to the back so it could stand at the top without a problem." Jim placed the miniature lighthouse night light at the very top of the tree. "Are you ready?" He asked Laura. Laura shook her head yes and Jim plugged in the night-light.

"It is perfect. It looks like it was made for a Christmas tree. You did a wonderful job securing it. I think it has stopped raining. Let's go outside and see if the tree is visible from the top of the hill?" Jim and Laura bundled up in their warm clothes and went outside to see the tree.

The rain had stopped but the wind was still blowing. They tucked their heads down and walked a few feet up the hill and turned to see if they could see the tree. Yes, it was a tiny bunch of lights in comparison to the large revolving light above but definitely there. Excited about how nice it looked they continued up the hill to see how far they would have to go before it disappeared. Not noticing the distance, they found themselves at the lay by. The little tree had faded to a microscopic dot but could still be seen in the window. They felt very proud of their efforts.

"Look, Laura. The lights again." Jim shouted over the wind. Laura looked around and saw the lights on the beach. This time they seemed closer to the lighthouse.

"Lets hurry back and call Ian. Maybe he can get out here before they leave." Laura suggested.

When they reach the house, they called the police constable but there was no answer. "Do you think we should investigate?" Laura asked.

"Yes, lets go. I would like to have this resolved before I leave here. Do you think you are ready to use that gun? Or would it be safer to leave it here?" Asked Jim.

"I will bring it. I have been doing pretty well with my practice and feel comfortable with it. I doubt if we will get close enough to use it but I will feel safer if I have it" Laura answered as she put the gun in the inside pocket of her parka.

Jim and Laura quickly climbed to the top of the hill and looked for the strange lights again. They had decided instead of going down to the beach they would follow the road. Every time the lights had been seen they were going up the hill toward the road. Ian felt something was being transported from the beach to the road. More than likely there would be a car or truck waiting depending on what was coming up from the beach. It was easier to follow the road than to try and get down to the beach in the dark. After walking a half-mile Jim and Laura stopped to look down at the beach to see if the lights were still visible. This time they were much closer and they could see one light coming up the hill only a few yards ahead of them. Motioning to Laura by placing his fingers to his lips Jim indicated they should be quiet. Laura nodded her head and pulled out her gun. They slowly walk along the side of the road toward the bobbing light. It was only a couple of minute until they saw a white Vauxhall parked on the side of the road. A figure in a dark parka with a hood appeared. The person was carrying a large torch and it was obvious this was the light they had seen coming up the hill. The person also had two large sacks flung over his back like Santa Claus. Laura thought this was no Santa Claus and found her heart racing with fear. The figure opened the trunk or boot as the Scots call it and put the two bags in. He quickly got into the car and started the engine.

Jim grabbed Laura's arm and dragged her to a place where they would not be seen from the road. Hiding behind the hill they watched the car drive toward the lighthouse and then disappear.

"Do you think the person is going to the lighthouse?" Laura stuttered.

"No, I think we will see it again. It probably went as far as the lay by at the top of the lighthouse road and turned around. When the car comes back you memorize the first part of the number on the license plate and I will do the second. We will then be able to tell Ian so he can look up the number. Also try to see the driver since this time he is on our side of the road."

Laura nodded, as the two headlights appeared coming toward them. The car was moving slowly on the curvy mountain one track. As it passed they both looked at the driver but it was still difficult to tell anything since the parka hood was still up. There were no lights inside the car. The one thing they could see was the driver was smoking. As the car rushed by each of them memorized their part of the license plate. It was difficult to do it quickly. Laura felt she had hers but wished she had brought a pencil with her.

"Did you get yours? I think I have mine?" Jim asked.

"I hope so. I wish we could have a better view of

the driver. It would be helpful if we had a face to identify." Laura whispered.

"No need for whispering. No one else seems to be around but lets go back a few yards where we can see the beach and check if we can catch sight of a boat. I would be willing to bet a boat will be out in the bay heading toward the open sea. They may have turned on their running lights by now." Jim said as he began to walk quickly back the way they came.

When they reached the overlook they saw no sign of a boat but sometimes in the roar of the wind they could hear what sounded like a motor running very slowly. Seeing no boat they head down the hill and just as they reached the lighthouse the lights of a boat appear way out in the bay.

"They have turned on lights but they are too far out to distinguish what type of a boat it is. I wish I had brought my binoculars. I am not very good at this detective stuff. We at least can tell Ian there was a boat and we have the license plate. Lets go in and call him right now." Laura uttered as she ran for the house.

Even before taking off their coats, Laura and Jim sat and wrote out the license plate number. That done Laura called Ian. Again there was no answer but this time she left a detailed message on his answering machine. Taking off her coat, she headed for the glowing coal fire to warm up. Standing in front of the fire she continued to shake. She realized she was more frightened than cold. Her mind raced with thoughts of what would have happened if that car had come to the lighthouse and she was alone. Then she would have to use her gun. Tomorrow she would definitely practice shooting some more. Before it seemed like a game but after tonight and seeing a real person on the mountain it was no longer play. Jim appeared with a glass of scotch for Laura.

"I thought you might need this." He said as he handed it to her.

"You better believe it. I am terribly frightened. I wish Ian had been home. We will have to call him again tomorrow if he does not get back to us early in the morning." Laura stuttered.

Suddenly Laura noticed the small Christmas tree by the window and thought of the contrast between the peace and fun of decorating the tree and the horror of the activities on the beach.

"Jim, did that person look like a black Santa Claus coming up the hill with his bags over his back?"

"I was just thinking that. He definitely did but I'll bet those bags did not have presents or a lump of coal in them. It was probably some kind of drugs. What a strange night this has been. I guess we should get some sleep because it is only a few hours until morning. We wanted to get the invitations to the party out tomorrow. I want you to know I am not very keen on going off and leaving you with all of the night activity."

"Jim that has been settled. I let you stay some extra days but you are leaving in a few days. We will have the party next Friday. That gives us exactly five days to get the everything done. So I am off to bed so we can begin addressing them early tomorrow. I do believe I will add just a few more wee drops of a scotch to my glass. I am going to need help to get me to sleep. See you in the morning."

After Laura went to bed Jim sat by the fire and thought. When he was sure Laura was asleep he made a telephone call praying the person he was calling was home. Luck was with him and he reached him. When he had finished the telephone call he felt a little better and decided maybe he should get some sleep.

The next morning before light there was a knock on the door that woke Jim and Laura.

"I'll get it, Laura." Jim said as he put on his pants while he ran for the door. "Ian, come in." Jim said welcoming the police constable.

"Sorry it is so early but when I got Laura's message late last night I felt I should get out here right away. Is she okay? I am worried she will be able to tolerate all of these goings on."

"She seems to be determined to make this work but she is scared. Who wouldn't be? Laura, it is Ian. I am making tea and we are in the kitchen."

Just as the water boiled, Laura joined Ian and Jim at

the kitchen table. It is obvious she had not slept much by the bags under her eyes and yet she was smiling and relatively cheerful. "Ian, did you get our message and did you have a chance to check out the license plate?" Laura asked.

"I got the message and did check out the license plate. Do you want to have breakfast before we get into all of this? I think we can all think better after a good breakfast."

Laura sat with a cup of tea as Jim made porridge for them. When breakfast was served Laura played with her food. "I can't stand it. What did you find out? Whom does that car belong to?"

The police constable hesitated but knew he had to tell her sooner or later. "The car is registered to Steve McGiver. It was a real shock to me. Jill McGiver depends on Steve and it will destroy her if he is involved. I am going to check with them as soon as I leave here. Maybe someone stole his car or borrowed it, which happens a lot on the island. We must not jump to conclusions until we know all the facts. How large were the sacks you saw the person carrying? " Ian asked trying to get Laura and Jim's mind off of the idea that their nearest neighbor might be involved in what was going on.

The tactic didn't work. Laura's commented. "What am I going to do out here all by myself if my nearest neighbor is a smuggler?"

CHAPTER TWENTY

"Laura, I will let you know right away what I find out from the McGivers. I do not want you to worry about this until I have more information. Why, don't you and Jim come over to my house tonight for dinner and I can bring you up to date on what I uncover. Besides seeing your little Christmas tree reminds me I have done nothing for Christmas. I am a pretty fair cook and we could sit by the fire and compare the Christmas customs of our two countries." Ian offered.

"Thanks, Ian we would like that. We need advice about who we should invite to the little Christmas get together we have planned for next week before Jim leaves. What time would be good?" Laura responded with relief in her voice.

After setting the time Ian took off for the McGivers. Jim and Laura started making the invitations and discussing who should be invited and who shouldn't. They both tried to avoid the issue of the McGivers. The invitations turned out to be more beautiful than anything you could buy in a store. They would begin addressing them tonight after they had dinner at Ian's.

Jim asked Laura if he could borrow the Land Rover and go into Stornoway to do some Christmas shopping. Laura knew she should stay home and become familiar with her new computer but going into Stornoway sounded likes a lot more fun. They could catch the late boat back and be back in plenty of time to go to Ian's.

"Can I come with you?" She asked.

"Of course, besides it is your car. I will need a few minutes by myself. I cannot buy you a Christmas present if you are with me. Santa has to have some secrets."

"Well, I was thinking the same thing. I need to talk to Santa about you and can also have a conference with Mark FitzSimmons related to the contract work I will be beginning after the first of the year. I will give him a call and see if he can meet me for lunch." Laura added.

Jim noticed the thought of meeting Mark FitzSimmons cheered Laura immensely.

They soon were on their way to the ferry and Stornoway. After passing the McGiver's house and seeing Ian's car was not there the terror of last night's events seemed to fade. Laura was in a festive mood and Jim noticed she even has a small candy cane pin on here sweater. Most of the way to Stornoway they chattered about their past Christmases and what kind of presents they should buy their family. Laura appeared sad when she talked about sending Gary something from Scotland for Christmas. Jim tried to change the subject but Laura's grief and anger at Gary spilled out. The violence of Laura's rage and hurt surprised Jim. She got so upset she was screaming as loud as she could while tears poured down her face. Jim sat and listened as he could think of nothing to say.

As they got off the ferry at Stornoway Laura's emotions were drained and she seemed to be more in control. "Jim, I am sorry. I had no idea that was going to happen or how mad and hurt I was. I guess it is not a good idea to keep things like that bottled up inside you. It must be all this Christmas stuff. Anyway, lets split up as soon as we get into Stornoway and do our shopping. I will go see Mark and we will meet at the car around two. Does that sound like a good approach to you?

"Fine, Laura. After I get all my shopping out of the way I want to look through the Castle. Would you like to join me?" Jim asked.

"No, you do that while I see Mark. I just realized I did not even call him so he might not be available. If he isn't I will come looking for you at the castle and we can have lunch together."

"It a deal." Jim said as he jumped out of the car and headed for the main street.

After parking the car, Laura proceeded to Mark's office. The receptionist said he was in and she would ask him if he had time to see her. Laura was delighted when Mark walked through the door and called her name. "Thanks for seeing me Mark. Jim and I had a sudden itch to come to Stornoway to do our Christmas shopping. I felt if you had a few minutes I would show you the draft of the Web page I have on this disk. Since we have not worked together before I thought it a good idea to show you what I have come up with to see if this was what you had in mind. Do you use Hot Dog for HTML?"

"We use three or four programs but we do have Hot Dog so lets take a look." He responded.

As they set at the computer Laura found Mark's closeness unsettling. She was very much aware of the cologne he was wearing. They went over the Web page. Mark was generally pleased with the work. He did offer some suggestions that Laura felt showed in-depth knowledge of the field. It was a relief to have a knowledgeable person to work with.

"Would you like a cup of tea?" Mark asked.

"Thanks, I would love one." Laura answered looking forward to a few non-work moments with this handsome man.

Sitting in Mark's office with its view of the water with a warm cup of tea in her hand Laura relaxed for the first time since last night's events. Mark asked a lot of questions about the lighthouse so Laura just naturally ended up telling him about the horror of the prior evening events.

"I do not believe any of the McGiver's would be involved in anything like this. They have lived on Gealach for many generations and are well liked. I hate to do this Laura, but I have another appointment and I must go. Could you have lunch with me sometime next week so we can discuss the final draft of the web page? Also, there is a staff meeting slash Christmas party coming up in two weeks and I would like for you to attend. Can you do that?" Mark asked.

Laura made note of all the dates but wondered why all of sudden Mark was in such a rush now when all morning he had been so relaxed. She thought to herself maybe it is the island way. Laura knew she had much to learn about the customs in the Western Isles.

After leaving Mark Laura went the bookstore and bought a book for Jim about the Western Isles. It included a picture of Gealach Head. Laura stared at the beautiful photograph of her new home and felt the warmth of ownership and pride. In a rebellious mood Laura decided to have the store send Gary the same book. She wrote a short note and inscribed the book to her son. She directed his attention to the picture of the lighthouse and once again invited him for the Christmas holiday. She knew the book would arrive too late for him to come for Christmas but it was the thought that counts. While she was waiting for them to wrap Jim's present she saw Steve McGiver go into the building where Mark FitzSimmons office was located. As soon as the book was wrapped, she went to a restaurant where she could see Mark's building and ordered a cup of tea hoping to see Steve came out. Sitting there for ten minutes with no sign of Steve she realized she was late meeting Jim. Still curious Laura went by Mark's office building to see what other businesses were in the building. All the other listings were medical related services. Laura decided maybe Steve was just picking something for his aunt.

When she arrived at the restaurant to meet Jim he was waiting surrounded by many packages. Laura wondered if she should have gotten more him than the book. "Sorry, I am late, Jim, but it took longer than I thought to get the presents wrapped. Have you been waiting long?" "No, Laura I just arrived. I saw Steve McGiver come roaring into town and thought it might be a good idea to see where he went. He went into the same building as Mark FitzSimmon's office so I got worried he might be after you. I watched but he never came out. Concerned I would be late to meet you if watched any longer I left."

"That is exactly what I have been doing. I saw Steve go into the building and decided to watch for him to come out. I never saw him exit. There may be a back door that he could use. I think we should tell Ian about Steve's visit as soon as we get back to Gealach. Now, what should we have for lunch?" Laura asked trying to change the subject.

Both Laura and Jim were silent on the ferry ride back to the island. They stood on the deck and watched the gray rolling sea as the ferry made its trip to the island. As soon as the ferry landed they headed for the lighthouse since Ian car was not in Mid Point. They were really glad they were having dinner with Ian that night. Both really wanted to talk to him about what he found out and what they had seen in Stornoway. As they passed the McGiver's they saw Steve's car was in the driveway.

"How did he get home before we did? He must have been on the ferry with us and we just didn't see him." Jim asked.

Laura just shook her head. She was very confused by the whole situation. As they drove on to the lighthouse they saw a car in the car park at the top of the hill. They slowed because it was unusual to see any one at the car park in December. Even more strange was the window on the driver's side seems to be open.

"Jim lets stop." Laura said. "Something is not right here."

"Laura, I think we should go to the lighthouse and call Ian."

"No, lets stop." Laura repeated and pulled as far to the side on the one lane road as she could and brought the Land Rover to a stop.

"You stay in the car with the motor running. I will go see what is in that car. If there is trouble you can make a run for it and call Ian." Jim directed her.

As Jim walked slowly to the car he looked in every direction. The hills were quite and all he heard was the soft sound of the wind and the surf. When he reached the car he began to smell something slightly sweet. An odor vaguely familiar but which he just could not place. He carefully walked up to the open window of the car. Slumped in the seat was what was left of a human being. The top of his head was gone. Glass, blood and brains were all over the car. The familiar smell was fresh blood.

"Laura!" he screamed as he ran for the Land Rover. "There is a dead man in that car with his head blown off with blood and tissue all over the place. Oh my God it looks like he has been murdered. Lets get to the lighthouse and call Ian."

Jumping into the car they roared down the hill to the lighthouse. As they approached the beautiful building they noticed the front door was slightly ajar. "Jim, didn't we lock the lighthouse when we left?"

"I thought so." Jim replied. "You had better let me

go in first. I will take a tire iron from the trunk just in case I need it." Laura who was in a state of shock just shook her head.

Jim got his weapon from the trunk and cautiously advanced into the house. As soon as he was in the door it was obvious someone or a group of people had searched the place. Everything was turned over or out of place. Whoever had not been gentle in how they looked either. Chairs were broken. The little Christmas tree lay on the floor with all of its decorations spread around it.

With great caution Jim searched each room looking for the perpetrators who had done this but always hoping he would not find them.

When he returned to the living room Laura was standing in the middle of the room with a look of alarm and disbelief on her face. She was not crying but Jim could see fear in her eyes.

"Laura, it is okay. They have not done much permanent damage. We can have it straightened up in no time." Jim said in a soothing voice.

"No, it is not the damage I am worried about," she whispered as if the intruders were still there. "It is the whole situation. Up on the hill we find a dead body. My home has been vandalized. It is just getting worse and worse." She spoke as if she was in a hypnotic state as she all of sudden hurried to the bedroom.

Within a minute she reappeared with her gun in hand. "I will get those bastards yet." She screamed.

"Laura, settle down. Lets call Ian and let him do his job. Why don't you start straightening up and I will call Ian." Jim directed her hoping she would snap back to a rational attitude.

Laura stared at him for a few seconds and then the tears started. With the tears seemed to come reason. She laid the gun on the kitchen counter and began carefully to pick up things and put them back. The Christmas tree was the first priority and she breathed a sigh of relief to see the little lighthouse on the top of the tree was not damaged.

Jim picked up the telephone and called Ian hoping he would be there. Ian answered on the first ring.

"Jim, I was just beginning to get dinner ready I hope there has not been a change of plans." Ian asked.

"Yes, I believe there has been a change of plans." Jim replied. "Please get over here immediately."

CHAPTER TWENTY-ONE

"Laura, I was wrong I think we should leave things pretty much the way we found them until Ian gets here." Jim suggested as he gently raised Laura from beside the Christmas tree. "Why don't I make us a cup of tea and we go out to watch the ocean for awhile? Laura looked at him with a blank empty stare but was easily led to the kitchen where Jim prepared two big mugs of tea. Considering Laura's state of mind Jim added a little drop of whisky to the mugs and put them with some biscuits on a plate and carried them outside. Laura followed him like a dog on a leash. She seemed devoid of all emotions now except the desire to retreat back to the USA.

"I am going home Jim. I can't take any more mystery especially a murder. It is so awful!" she said in a broken voice.

Jim wondered what he could say if anything to help calm her. "Laura, how can you make King go through quarantine and then have to go back to the USA without even seeing his new home. He would not get to romp on the beach or listen to the surf with his one ear cocked in that funny way you keep talking about? The mention of King seemed to get through. Laura looked out at the slate blue sea under the gray clouds and seemed to be picturing King running in the surf as the beginnings of smile appeared on her pale face.

"Thanks Jim, you are right. I can't give up after all I have put King through. I have to stick it out be brave and get better with my gun. No one is going to trash my home at Gealach Head again. When they come the next time I will shoot them. I will keep practicing so I can't miss." A determined Laura responded.

Jim and Laura sat without conversation and listened to the sound of the waves. Neither knew what to say so they treasured the peace of the moment. Their solitude was broken by the faraway screech of a siren.

"Ian must be going." Jim said. "I was so shook I forgot to tell him to look in the car at the car park. Do you suppose he will stop?"

"No, I think he will come right here since you only told him to get over here and not why."

As Laura projected Ian's car appeared at the top of the hill with lights flashing and siren blaring. He drove the curves of the hill like a Grand Prix driver and came to a screeching halt in front of the lighthouse. Jumping out he ran up to the area where Jim and Laura sat.

"What is wrong?" he said looking directly into Laura's tear swollen eyes. Seeing the terror and anger flashing there he reached out to touch her gently on the shoulder.

"Ian." is all Laura could say before the tears started again. In total frustration Ian looked to Jim for an answer to his question. Jim explained as quickly as he could about the body in the car at the top of the hill and the condition of the lighthouse when they arrived. Without another word Ian went inside and carefully walked from room to room not touching anything. As he returned to the two people huddled at the foot of the tower he asked.

"Did you touch or move anything?" Once again Laura could not bring herself to respond. Jim explained about the Christmas tree and making tea. Ian nods his head and runs down to the car to use the radio. When he is finished he returns to Laura and Jim. "I am going up to investigate the car." In about twenty minutes a helicopter will arrive from Stornoway with chief inspector, William Wallace. And no, he is not related to the famous Scottish hero. He will want to ask you some questions. I will stay up the hill with the car. If you do not mind could you lend him your Land Rover so he can come up and meet me. After we are done I will take you both over to my house for that dinner I have been working on. Please, do not touch anything until Bill arrives. As soon as they are done taking pictures, fingerprints and investigating the crime scene I am sure he will tell you can put the house back in order. That is exactly what I suggest you do until I come back. Laura, it will be all right? I promise." Without another word or a backward glance Ian ran to his car and drove up the hill.

Laura and Jim waited for what seemed like hours until the helicopter arrived. Two men got out of the helicopter before it lifted off with the pilot and one other person. They found William Wallace to be a short man of approximately 50 years with a cheerful smile and dark piercing eyes dressed in a neat suit and tie. He was friendly, kind and seemed to know the right questions to ask. As he questioned Jim and Laura a man in a uniform covered by a white suit who was not introduced went directly into the house with a bag and a camera around his neck. Inspector William Wallace finished quite quickly with his questions then he went inside to begin looking around. Laura and Jim were amazed how relaxed William Wallace had made them feel and how compassionate he was. Having been the first time Jim had been questioned by a detective he was pleasantly surprised. As William Wallace disappeared through the door Laura turned white. "Jim, my gun. Where is it?" Laura asked in a panicked whisper.

Jim did not answer but lifted his shirt and Laura could see the handle of the gun sticking out of his belt. "I think I will go out to the garage and see if I can find a box or some kind of container to put anything we find inside that is broken. Laura you stay here if Inspector Wallace has any more questions until I get back." Relieved Laura smiled for the first time since they had found the man in the car. Jim winked at her and hurried out to the garage.

The inspector and his officer took about 30 minutes to search the premise. They asked Laura and Jim to go through each room with them to see if anything was missing. After a complete examination it seemed nothing was missing. "Either this was just vandalism or it was a message from someone who wants you out of here. From what Ian has been telling me it is probably the latter."

Laura fully recovered from her fright announced with determination, "Well, the message is not accepted. This is my new home and my dog is coming in a few months to run on the beach so I am not changing any of my plans."

Inspector Wallace looked at her for a minute and answered, "I admire your determination but I feel you may need to reconsider since we also have a homicide up in the car park. This is no longer just smuggling it includes murder. The danger is real and definitely should not be taken lightly. I am very glad there are two of you here instead of just you Mrs. File. I must meet Ian up the hill. He said you had a vehicle I can use." Laura not wanting to talk about Jim's upcoming departure just motioned toward the Land Rover and handed the keys to the inspector. Remembering what Ian had said Laura asked, "Can we begin to put the place back in order?" The inspector nods his head in the affirmative as he and the uniformed officer head for the Land Rover.

Jim and Laura went into the house to begin the painful task of cleaning up. Laura finished putting the Christmas tree back together. Knowing that there was an unspoken question between them Laura said to Jim. "We will need to get this place cleaned up spic and span with the combination Christmas and farewell party coming up so soon. We had better put the groceries away since they are still sitting outside the front door where we dropped them when we came in."

"Laura, I feel..." Jim began but was sharply interrupted by Laura. "No, Jim you must leave. If I am going to make it here I must learn to live alone. I will be alone all of the time. You must finish your trip and see what you can before it is time to go back to school. I appreciate your concern but there is no discussion, the subject is closed." Jim looked at her and wanted to say something more but realized it just might upset her and she did not need any more of that.

It took them a good two hours to straighten just the living room. They wondered what they should do about the invitation to Ian's house for dinner when the telephone rang.

Laura answered and it was Ian. "Laura, I just got home. I will have dinner ready in about an hour. I will pick you up in 45 minutes as they are still using your Land Rover. When we get back here we can have a drink and talk. I know you have all kinds of questions but we can discuss those when you get here."

"That sounds fine Ian. Can I bring anything?" Laura asked out of politeness. Ian hesitated before he said "No."

Ian arrived to pick them up about 50 minutes later.

It took a while to make themselves presentable after cleaning the lighthouse so he had to wait for a few minutes. Arriving at the house they found Ian's house a surprise. His walls were covered with soft Scottish impressionists pictures. There were the soft strains of Vaughan Williams music in the background, which seemed strange since Ian did not seem like the classical music type. An even bigger shock was when the big policeman put on a ruffled apron.

"Okay, I know the apron is a little much, but it was my Mother's and I am very fond of it." Ian told them before they had a chance to ask. "Have a seat in the living room and I will be right there. I have to put the veg on to cook. You will find whisky and red wine on the coffee table. Help yourself." He said as he hurried off toward the kitchen. Laura and Jim fixed themselves a drink and sat down by the glowing fire. The room was warm and pleasant with its smell of peat. The furnishings were simple and there was a bouquet of flowers sitting in the window. Laura was taken back because the house seemed to have a woman's touch but she knew there were no women in Ian's life.

Ian returned minus the apron and fixed a drink and went to stand by the fireplace. Laura noticed Ian was an extremely handsome man and the soft touches of the sitting room seem to fit his image.

"I thought I would get all of this discussion about what happened today out of the way so we could lay it aside for a few hours and enjoy the meal. The dead man in the car was a tax and excise man who was watching the area for smugglers. He was one of three each taking an 8 hours shift watching the beach. We believe he must have been killed not too long after he arrived. Bill Wallace was of the opinion the searching of your house was done for two reasons. To scare you off and to make us think it was robbery. If it was a robbery than the man on the hill was killed because he could have seen the robbers escaping. The problem is they did not take anything of value from the lighthouse. The most valuable thing you have is your computer and they did not touch it. My theory is the stake out saw something and was killed because of that. The best explanation is they thought they could try and cover what ever they were doing with a robbery that also might scare you. I think I am responsible for them knowing about the stake out. Last night when I went to see Jill McGiver to find out where Steve was I was afraid I had scared her so I mentioned we were going to watch the area much more closely. She must have told Steve. Steve was not at home last night but had gone to a party at Mark FitzSimmons house. It seems Steve has been going out with Mark's secretary. In fact Mrs. McGiver says he spends many nights with her. I have not had time to check the girl out yet."

"That is why we saw Steve going into Mark's building today." Jim added.

"What time did you see him?" Ian asked.

"A little before lunch since it was before I was to meet Jim." Laura answered.

"Well, that means he could have not been involved in the murder because he would have to take the ferry back and the medical examiner says the man died a about two forty five. The ferry does not get in until three thirty." Ian pondered.

"That is the funny part, Ian. We were on that ferry and we did not see Steve and when we drove by the McGiver's his car was there. It seemed very strange to me. We decided we could have just missed seeing him on the ferry but it is so small that is unlikely."

Ian stood and looked at the fire. "We are dealing with smugglers who use boats. Maybe Steve came back by private boat. If so he could have arrived in time to do the murder and be sitting at home with cup of tea by the time you got back to the island. The part that does not make any sense to me is Jill McGiver. If Steve did it then the only way he would know about the stack out is if she told him. I have known Jill all my life. She was a close friend of my mother's. She has always been warm and friendly. Even after her eyesight went she stayed positive and up beat. I cannot believe she would be involved in something like this. It is baffling. Tomorrow I will check with the Stornoway harbormaster to see what boats left the harbor this afternoon. Laura, I want you to know we are going to continue to watch the area around the lighthouse but we are going have who ever contact you by telephone and tell you exactly where they are. Any one who calls or who you meet will say to you. 'Good day Mrs. File, when is your dog King coming home? I hear he is a Sheltie?' If you meet someone in the area that does not say that call for help immediately. You should not try to do anything else. This is a very dangerous situation. Now, how would you two like to sample my cooking?"

CHAPTER TWENTY-TWO

Ian convinced Jim and Laura to stay the night. He felt a good night's sleep would do them both a world of good. When Laura awoke it was still dark in Ian's little cottage. She could hear Ian in the kitchen and could smell coffee. Laura went into the living room to find Ian dressed in his uniform. He said. "I'll bet you would like to take a shower. You'll find everything you'll need through there. Are you hungry? I will make us some porridge. When you get done with your shower I'll be in the kitchen." Not waiting for an answer Ian left.

Laura was impressed how comfortable this big man was in the kitchen and yet there seemed always to be a strong slightly military presence about him. When he walked it was like a drill sergeant with everything totally under control. "I wonder why I never noticed how handsome and kind Ian was before? Maybe it relates to my fear of policeman." Laura thought. Maybe she was just thankful someone was watching over her. They had a big bowl of porridge after which they took a cup of coffee with them as they sat down beside the small warm peat fire. Laura wanted to talk about something other than what was happening around here so she felt compelled to ask Ian more about his life. The policeman was relaxed and shared how he had come back to the island. It was obvious Ian loved the island and was happy just being a police constable in this small place. The more he talked the more Laura respected this quiet strong man. The conversation could have gone on all morning.

"Laura do you still want to have a few of the islanders for a Christmas party?" Ian asked

"Yes, I do?" Laura answered. "We have already made the invitations. Jim and I were so excited about the Christmas party. I do not know if it is right to have it immediately after someone was murdered?" Laura pondered.

Not knowing how to answer Laura's question, Ian replied. "The people of Gealach would like to come to your house. They would like to get to know you better and of course they are curious about the house. But from now on you can stay here. You can go over to the lighthouse for the party. It is not a good idea for you to be at The Head alone right now. After the party I would suggest you stay some where in Stornoway until we can get this smuggling all sorted out."

"No, Ian I will stay at the lighthouse. It is my home and I cannot run from life. If life at Gealach Head includes some danger then I must learn to live with it. I will cooperate with you in any way I can and will be very careful but I am staying." Laura stated flatly.

"Laura, you are being foolish going back there but I know it will not do any good to argue with you. I will make sure the word gets out that you are having a small gathering. I do not think you should mention Jim leaving. I also think it is a bad idea to let Jill McGiver and Mark FitzSimmons know about the party."

Surprised, Laura asked slightly blushing, "Why Mark FitzSimmons? I really want him to come."

"Mark's secretary is dating Steve McGiver and that just might lead to Steve knowing about the party even if you did not invite his aunt." Ian replied.

Getting visibly upset Laura declared, "I think it is time for me to go home. Ian, I appreciate your concern but I am inviting Mark FitzSimmons to MY party. I will ask him not to tell his secretary. After all he is my boss."

Ian tried reasoning with Laura about going home but nothing he could say would change her mind. He got her coat. As he helped Laura on with her coat his hand rested lightly on her shoulder for a little longer than necessary. "You are one stubborn woman and I did not know Mark attending the party meant so much to you. I am sorry if I upset you more. Most of all I just want you to stay safe."

"Mark is my boss and nothing more." Laura said maybe more to convince her than Ian.

As they drove to the Lighthouse Laura reflected on what Ian had said. She tried to evaluate why she wanted Mark FitzSimmons to attend so badly. There was no doubt she was attracted to him and he had been more than kind to her. It was still too soon after Peter's death for her to be looking at other men but still she was attracted to Mark. As they passed the McGiver house Laura looked at Ian. He was such a kind gentle person to be a policeman. She found his some times dictatorial manner made her angry but he always seemed to have her best interests in mind.

As they drove into the yard of the beautiful little lighthouse Ian told Laura and Jim to wait in the car while he checked everything out. He got out of the car with his gun in hand. Seeing the gun frightened Laura. She tried to draw deeper into her coat and hide. Ian checked all of the buildings. After a few minutes he came back and helped Laura out of the car.

Entering the house she found the whole house had been straightened and there was some food on the kitchen counter. "Where did that come from?" Laura asked.

"Who has a key?"

"Only Larry Macdonald."

"I would guess it was Larry then. More people will be dropping by with food. They want to let you know they care."

Laura thought a moment. "The people of Gealach are not so different from the people of Granton when it comes to carrying for their neighbors."

Ian seemed reluctant to leave Laura but once the officer on duty in the area had checked in and asked Laura the appropriate question he could not think of an excuse to stay. "Laura, call me if you need anything. I will be checking on you two or three times before the party."

After Ian left Laura and Jim wandered around the little house. Who ever had cleaned up the house had done a good job. Laura remembered the gun and started out to the generator house to get it. Jim saw her putting her coat on and stopped her. "Is this what you are looking for?" He said as he took the gun out of a drawer.

Laura nodded. Some how the gun's presence made her feel safer but also brought back memories of the dead man they had found seen last night. She decided she needed a large dram of whisky. Jim and Laura sat down by the peat fire. Laura saw the little Christmas tree that she and Jim had so lovingly decorated. "Oh, Jim I am so sorry you decided to come visit Gealach Head. If I had not asked you to visit you might not be involved in all this." Laura told him.

"I have to admit it did not turn out the way I thought it would but I am still glad I came." Jim responded.

……………………………………………...

The weather the day of the party was violent and stormy. Laura was not the least bit excited. As the time for Jim to leave drew closer Laura began to dread it. The excise men had been checking in regularly and that was some comfort. The activities of getting ready for the party had kept them busy. She was not looking forward to spending time with people she did not know well. She just wanted to hide in her little house with her gun for comfort. Suddenly she remembered how Gary said he felt at Peter's funeral. Dealing with anguish and meeting new people was difficult. Now she understood a little better how her son must have felt.

Shaking her head to clear her thoughts she made a last minute check on everything. The little house was sparkling clean and the little tree twinkling. Laura had debated and debated about whether to keep the tree up but they had put so much effort into it she decided she would. Besides if she took it down those criminals were ruining more of her life. She made the Christmas cookies that Jim had requested and they were artfully arranged on the small table along with the Christmas cake and sweets from some of Gealach residents. The house smelled spicy from the mulled wine simmering in the kitchen. She had soft music playing on the stereo. The little house was festive but simple. All of a sudden Laura thought of past Christmases. The hurt of thinking about the tragedies in the last year was more than she could bear. She sat down as if someone had kicked her in the stomach. The people she loved the most were gone. Peter was dead. Gary was still alive but had chosen to abandon her. She had not heard from him since she arrived in Scotland. His absence was the most severe torment she felt. Death had taken Peter but Gary was claimed by stupidity or misunderstanding. She wasn't sure which.

Laura heard the postman drop the mail through the door. As she picked up the mail she opened the door to look outside. "It is raining so hard you can't see more than a few feet. Hard pellets of sleet were mixed in with the rain. Putting her hand out the little ice crystals felt like needle injections or jags as they were called in Scotland. I hope people still come." Laura said to Jim as closed the door and picked up the mail. There was a package addressed to Mrs. L. File. It was the size of videotape. She dropped the package on the kitchen counter realizing it was time to get dressed.

After changing her clothes she stared in the mirror to see how she looked. Surprising she looked quite nice in a dark blue wool dress. "Some how it seems wrong to look so nice when all the people she loved were dead or missing. I should look like a old hag." Laura depressingly said.

Returning to the living room she saw the return address on the package. Tearing it open she squealed with delight. "It is from the kennel. Maybe it is a video tape of King." She put the tape in the video player and there in front of her eyes was her beautiful black dog running and playing in a fenced field. He seemed healthy and happy. Someone not seen on the tape called him. King ran right up to the camera so his face completely filled the lens. All Laura could see was a big black nose and a pink tongue. With the assistance of someone else off camera he was made to sit. He looked marvelous. The person behind the camera slipped a sign in front of the camera. "Happy Christmas, Laura. I love you, King." Laura pushed the pause button and the screen was filled with King's happy face and the wonderful sign.

"Jim, come see. It's King." Laura squealed. "I am not alone. I have King and soon he will be with me. What a wonderful gift. Do I have time to call the Johnson's?" Laura asked but the doorbell rang and she knew the answer to her question.

Laura opened the door to find Larry Macdonald standing with hat in one hand and his wife beside him. "Come in Larry. You are soaked." As she took Larry's coat Laura realized this was the first time she had ever seen Larry in suit coat and tie. "Larry, you look handsome all dressed up. Would you like a glass of wine?" Blushing Larry nodded yes.

The next to arrive was Mark FitzSimmons who had taken the ferry. Laura was delighted he could make it. The weather being so turbulent she was wondering whether the ferry would make the crossing. Mark explained the ferry ride wasn't too bad but there might be a problem with the later ferry. If it got worse he might have to stay on the island. Laura informed him he was welcome to stay at the lighthouse if that happened. Mark mentioned he had seen Ian picking up someone at the boat. Ian had wanted Mark to tell Laura he might be a few minutes late since he needed to go home and change clothes. Laura made no comment as she made Mark a drink. From then on Laura was busy as many people arrived that she had not met yet. Jim and Larry made sure she was never alone and helped her cope with the new people. The final people to arrive were Ronnie Macdonald and his wife. They brought Laura a small basket of citrus fruit that was a delicacy on the island. After everyone was settled the conversation revolved around the weather, the price of lambs and Christmas until all of sudden Mark changed the subject and asked if there was new information on the murder. Silence filled the room, as no one seemed to know how to answer him.

Laura seeing the discomfort of everyone told everyone they would have to wait for Ian to find out the latest on the recent events so why didn't we leave the subject until then. Mark acted a little hurt but agreed and went on to tell about the newest things happening with the computer project. Laura began to wonder if Ian was ever going to get there. It was not like him to be late. When an hour passed and Ian still wasn't there she decided to go ahead and serve the soup and homemade bread. Just as everyone sat down to the table to eat Laura heard a car arrive. She went to the door to greet Ian. The rain had turned to snow and the tops of the hills around the lighthouse were beginning to be dusted lightly with white. The flakes were so big and feathery she could not see Ian but could hear the car doors open. It did definitely sound like two doors. "Maybe he has brought another neighbor." Laura thought.

"Ian, hurry the soup is on the table and you will catch your death out there." She called.

"I am coming I just have to get something out of the boot." He answered.

Laura getting cold standing in the doorway decided to shut the door and wait until she heard steps outside the door before she opened it again. When she opened the door standing in front of her was not Ian but Gary. At first Laura could not believe her eyes. She stammered, "Is that you Gary?"

"Yes, Mom, Merry Christmas." Laura's handsome son answered.

"Oh, my God," Laura whispered as she enclosed her son in her arms for a big hug. "What are you doing here?"

"I came to see you but I can explain all of that later right now can I come in since Ian is standing behind me freezing."

CHAPTER TWENTY-THREE

"Of course, I 'm sorry. It is such a shock to see you. Please come in." Laura stammered.

Ian struggled in loaded down with all kinds of packages plus what must have been Gary's luggage. "Where do you want Gary's luggage?" he asked.

"Just put it in with Jim in the spare bedroom. I have no other rooms except the living room ready but he could sleep on the couch. I can not deal with making any decisions right now." She answered.

"Would you like a wee dram or some punch?" She asked her son so rattled she did not what else to say.

"I will take the punch. I am afraid if I drink the whisky that I will fall asleep right in the middle of everything."

"Oh, my guests." I almost forgot. "Everyone I would like for you to meet my son, Gary who just arrived from the United States." She said leading him around the room to meet everyone.

The gathering went well and turned out to be a joyful event with Gary even seeming to enjoy himself. Laura got to know more about her new neighbors and enjoyed the conversation. It was obvious to everyone she was nervous and kept looking at her son with an odd expression. Ian noticed Laura's strange behavior but decided it was not the time to ask about it. Besides, Mark FitzSimmons was constantly by Laura's side so Ian did not have a chance to ask her anything. The snow was coming down harder. It might be difficult to get up the hill so people began to leave early. Mark FitzSimmons called the ferry and found the storm had cancelled the night boat.

"What am I going to do?" Mark thought out loud.

"You can stay here if you would like Mark but it will mean sleeping on blankets on the floor. You are more than welcome if that doesn't bother you."

Mark answered immediately. "I would love that Laura. Why don't Jim and I straighten up and you can talk to Gary for awhile."

Ian was the last to leave wanting to make sure

everyone got up the hill as he was afraid he might have to push some of the other cars with his Range Rover. Laura stood on the porch and watched all of her new friends leave. She hardly even noticed Gary standing beside her. Waving at Ian as he finally went up the hill and out of sight Gary interrupted her thoughts by saying. "Its cold out here lets go in and have a hot toddy and talk."

Dazed Laura followed her son inside. She set by the little coal fire while Gary got the drinks. Mark and Jim could be heard banging around in the kitchen so they thought this might be a good time for a private conversation.

"Gary, what are you doing here?" Laura asked for the second time but more forcefully as if she really wanted an answer.

"It is a long story but I will try and summarize it. Jim is an old friend I met in law school. When I realized you were actually going to do this insane thing of moving to Scotland I asked his help. He was going to visit his family in Paris and so we planned for him to bump into you. You told me what plane you were taking and we arranged for Jim to get a seat beside you. The rest you know except that he was keeping me updated on everything that happened over here. When he called and told me about the murder I decided it was time I came in person. Mom, you have to give up this foolishness of living alone at this remote lighthouse especially now with smuggling and a murder. With Jim gone you will be totally alone and the smugglers know it. I thought we could spend the holidays here and fly back to the States around January 12th. I have talked to the people at the kennel and we can get King out and bring him back to the States. What do you think?"

Laura just stared at him. Her face reflected a cold hardness as if she was made of ice. Instead of answering she put her coat on and went to the door. Stopping she turned to him and said, "I want to be alone so I am going to walk to the top of the hill and watch the light in the snow. We can talk about this in the morning." With that statement she slipped out the door.

"Mom? Wait? Gary shouted.

"Leave her alone, Gary," Jim said as he entered the

room. "She has had a shock and she needs to work through it. She will be back soon. It is too cold to stay out very long."

"Shouldn't I go and see if she is alright?" Gary asked.

"No, I think the best thing we can do is go to bed and see how she feels in the morning. You take the couch and I will make a bed on the floor for Mark.

"Jim, we should have told her the truth sooner. I am terrified of what she might do. I will go get changed and hit that couch. I didn't sleep much on the plane last night and am really bushed." Gary commented as he went into the bedroom.

Outside Laura climbed slowly up the hill with the heavy wet flakes falling on her face to mix with the hot tears, streaming down her face. She wanted to scream but some how the silence of the beautiful snow kept her from making any noise. Gary's arrival had really complicated things. Laura was glad to see him but when he told her why he was there she felt betrayed. Showing up unannounced on her doorstep on the day of her party took some nerve. And Jim – what a fool she had been about Jim. Jim and Gary had deceived her. Laura felt the worse about Jim because she really thought Jim was her friend. Jim had lied. She had come to like and trust him. It was all a performance. He was a spy and had betrayed her. Deep inside her she knew he hadn't meant to harm her. He probably was really trying to help. Why hadn't he just told her?

Laura was infuriated at both her son and his friend. Now, Gary expected her to go home with him. Reaching her favorite lookout, Laura turned to look at the lighthouse. The beacon was creating beautiful long rays of light in the snowflakes that resembled the propellers of a helicopter. It was one of the most awe-inspiring sights she had ever seen. "How could she leave this?" She thought as she sat on a rock and watched the snow settle quietly around her. The only sound she heard was the roaring of the waves in the distance. This was what she had always wanted. She would not give it up. Tomorrow she would tell Gary she would not go back with him. He would be furious with her but she had found over the last few months she could live without her son. If he did not want to accept her new life then that was his choice. Somehow reaching that decision made the tears stop and Laura once again felt at peace with the world.

All of sudden out of the darkness dotted with snowflakes a figure appeared. Laura was terrified. She remembered the murder and her promise to Ian not to go out alone at night.

"Laura? Laura?" a male voiced asked.

Laura held her breath and did not answer waiting to see what would happen next. In a few seconds Mark appeared in front of her covered with snow.

"Mark! You scared me to death. What are you doing up here?"

"Looking for you. I figured I might be the only one you would talk to since I am not involved directly with Gary and Jim. You should not be out here alone so I came to escort you back home."

"I appreciate it Mark. I just now realized what a foolish risk this walk was. If it had been one of the smugglers instead of you I would have been in jeopardy."

"Well, it is only me so you are safe. You look cold. Come here."

Laura moved slowly toward Mark. When she reached him he put both arms around her and held her very tight. "Is that better?" he asked.

"Yes." Laura answered.

"I know it is way to soon for me to say this. You are not in a holiday spirit right now but I would like to get you under the mistletoe. Lets pretend the mistletoe is hanging on one of the cloud above us."

"Mark I hardly know you." Laura whispered.

"Laura I have been attracted to you since we first exchanged emails. It sometimes happens like that on the internet." Mark said as he kissed Laura gently and continued to hold her. "Laura I do not know what you are going to do about the future but if you stay here I would like to see more of you. Maybe you could come into Stornoway more often and I will come out here as much as I can. I know you have lots of things to work out so we can talk about all this later when you decide what you want to do about going back to the States."

"Mark, I am sorry but my mind is full of so many other things. Too much has happened tonight. Maybe in the future but I am not capable of any kind of romantic relationship right now. Laura said as diplomatically as she could since Mark was her boss.

Laura did feel a kind of relief in what Mark said. When Gary and Jim left she would have Mark and of course, Ian was always around. "Let's go back inside. It is getting awfully cold and we are both soaked. I will talk to you in the next few days when I have settled every thing related to Gary and Jim."

Mark and Laura walked down the hill arm in arm watching the beautiful beams of the lighthouse beacon play on the snow and clouds.

When they reached the house the only light was Laura's precious little Christmas tree with its friendly light on the top. Gary had laid bedding on the floor for Mark and was snoring loudly on the couch.

"Mark, I suggest you build up the fire since you do not have an electric blanket like the rest of us. It might get really cold in here by morning." Laura advised.

"Will do." Mark answered as he watched Laura walk to her bedroom and close the door.

The next morning when Laura looked out the window the hills were covered with white but there was a bright sun shining. That meant within a few hours the snow would disappear and things would go back to normal. When she went to the kitchen she found Jim, Gary and Mark drinking coffee and eating Christmas cookies left from yesterday.

"Can't you cook yourselves a decent breakfast or are you waiting on me to do it?" She kidded them.

"Nope," Gary answered. "We just decided with all the snow outside the Christmas cookies were the best choice."

"Well, I am going to cook some porridge and while I am doing that I have some things I want to say." Laura said as she put a pan of water on the stove and poured in some oatmeal.

"Maybe, I better leave." Mark interjected. "I am sure the ferry will be leaving this morning. If I do not get off the island before Christmas Day I will be stuck, as there is no ferry on Christmas. As much as I would like to spend Christmas here my Mother is counting on me being home. Laura if you would like you could join us."

"You had better catch that ferry and thank you for the kind invitation. We will talk later." Laura answered.

After Mark had left Laura turned to Gary and Jim. "Sit down both of you. I have a few things I want to say. First, I want you to know I recognize what you did was because you cared. I understand how you feel. But, I cannot support your methods. I am angry and disappointed in both of you. You have lied and tricked me. I do not approve of what you have done. Why didn't you tell me, Jim?

"I wanted to but I had promised Gary that I wouldn't't. Jim replied sheepishly.

"Mom, to be honest, I was afraid you would turn Jim away and by then I was really worried with all the smuggling." Gary said interrupting Jim.

"I guess I can understand that but not telling me just made it worse. If you had told the truth I would have still gladly accepted Jim's help. As for the rest of your behavior I find it despicable. You did not answer my calls or letters. Then you show up here and lay down an ultimatum that I leave with you. Well, the answer is no. I am not leaving but you and Jim are. I want you out of here before the day is over. You can take the afternoon ferry. As Mark mentioned if you do not get off the island before Christmas you will be stuck for three days. And I want both of you gone. Do you understand?"

Gary was angry and started to argue. "Mom, you are being ridiculous. You cannot stay here alone with smuggling and the murder going on. Be sensible!"

"I can and will stay here. This is my home. I will work with the local authorities, and we will catch the smugglers. Gary you just don't understand. I love this place. Maybe if you had been here with me you would understand. You did not come here to find out about Gealach but to take me away. I do not want you to stay and find out how wonderful it is. I want you gone as soon as you have had your breakfast. I will take you to the ferry. Do you understand?"

Gary turned his back and walked into the bedroom with out a word.

Laura set down to eat her porridge and realized she was glad she had said what she did. Yet, deep inside she felt puzzled. Why?

CHAPTER TWENTY-FOUR

Gary and Jim were packed before lunch. They all set down to eat as if nothing had happened. Just to keep busy and make the minutes go faster Laura had made a big pot of stew. She wasn't sure whether she wanted time to go fast or slow. As she cut up the potatoes and carrots she thought about what it was going to be like here by herself. She would have to get to know her neighbors better, see more of Mark, and be more careful about what she did. When she remembered going to the lookout last night without even thinking it made her shudder. If Mark had been a smuggler she could have been kidnapped or even worse killed. From now on Laura would not go alone anywhere on the island at night.

Gary and Jim had tried a couple of times to get Laura to talk to them. But she would not discuss it any more. When they brought up the subject she stopped them in mid sentence or pretended not to hear. After four or five unsuccessful attempts Gary and Jim just quit trying. Laura made one effort to lighten the mood by serving them a another piece of her first Scottish Christmas cake. Gary raved how good it was and this made Laura feel a little better. After lunch with their tea Gary made one more try at getting Laura to discuss the situation and this time she did respond.

"Eventually we will put all of this behind us but right now I am angry and hurt. Even if I weren't angry with you I would want to stay here. Gealach Head has become my home. I love it. I do recognize I am in danger but I will deal with that. Ian will find the crooks. Eventually it will be over and I can enjoy my home without worrying about crime. I promise you I will not do anything stupid. If it becomes necessary I will even go into Stornoway for a short period of time until this is settled."

"Mom, I am glad to hear you say you might go into town because I think the situation might get more dangerous before it ends. You are safer there." Gary answered as he stared out into space. It was obvious he didn't understand his mother. "When is the ferry?"

"It leaves in about an hour and a half so we will need to depart within the hour. I called Ian to check on the roads and he said the snow was gone on most of the island's roads. The early morning ferry that Mark took went right on time."

"I will pack the car." Jim volunteered in an attempt to leave Gary with his mother.

"Fine." Laura answered just as the telephone rang. "Hello. Oh, Mark you made it back okay? Did Lewis get the snow? Well, I guess we were just lucky. Gary and Jim are taking the afternoon ferry so I have got to run. I appreciate the offer to have Christmas dinner with your family. I want to stay here and have Christmas at the lighthouse. No, Mark, I will be perfectly safe. I imagine smugglers celebrate the Christmas holidays also. Yes, I would be glad to accompany you to the Hogmanay party on New Year's Eve. Give me a call after Christmas and we can make the final arrangements. No, I have not opened the presents yet. I am glad you liked the tweed. I purchased it when I first arrived. I did not know if you had a clan so I thought the plain would be best. Got to run but I will talk to you later."

As soon as she hung up the phone she could hear the car idling. She ran and got her coat. As she closed the door and locked it she felt a shiver run down her back. Laura dismissed it as the cold air outside and yet she could not deny she felt anxious. "Did you lock the windows?" Laura asked Gary and Jim in an attempt to make the trembling go away.

"Yes, we went all through the house checked to make sure everything was locked." Gary answered.

As they drove by the McGiver's house it was deserted. Laura gave a sigh of relief. She really did not like the thought that Steve McGiver was in the area. Laura was so relieved she hummed Christmas Carols.

"Mom, cut it out. How can you be so callous? I came all this way and you are kicking me out. There is no reason for a Ho Ho spirit." Gary screamed at her.

"Gary, you did not come all this way to celebrate Christmas with me. You came to drag me back to the US and I am not going. I am happy to spend Christmas in my new home and I will sing carols if I want too." Laura replied angrily.

When they got to the jetty it was packed with people waiting on the ferry. "I guess everyone is going somewhere for Christmas. A quiet peaceful holiday in my new lighthouse home will be the best Christmas I could have." Laura thought.

The boat arrived and Laura gave Gary and Jim a hug. Gary started to say something but changed his mind and walked quickly onto the boat. Laura stood and watched the boat pull out. Feeling depressed she turned away before the boat was out of sight and headed for the car. Standing beside the car was Ian, holding a rather large package.

"Ian what have you got? It is huge." Laura proclaimed.

"It is your Christmas present. I couldn't bring it last night because I had Gary in the car. Do you think it will fit into you trunk or should I follow you home and deliver it."

"I am sure it will not fit and it would be really nice if you followed me home. I just put Gary and Jim on the boat and a little company would be nice." Laura answered.

"Laura, Why? I guess it is none of my business but I really do not like the idea of you being at the lighthouse alone. I will bring the present over and we can have a cup of tea. But, I warn you I am going to try to convince you to stay in Stornoway until we catch the smugglers."

Laura smiled as she got into her car. "We will see about that, Ian." She said as she started her engine and drove off toward home.

Laura thought she would find the keeper's house depressing when she got home. Instead the little house was warm and friendly with its funny little Christmas tree. It helped that Ian was right behind her. She sat listening to the waves out side, and thought about how much she liked her little lighthouse home. She heard a car coming down the hill. A little frightened she ran to the window only to see Ian's police car.

As she came to the door Ian was unloading the big Christmas present. "Laura, come out here. I think you will have to open this outside. I do not think it will go through the door."

"What in the world is it? "Laura asked.

"Open it and see."

Laura tore a hole in the paper and she could see wood painted yellow just like the trimming on the lighthouse. As she removed more of the paper she realized it was a doghouse. A very distinct one because just above the door was painted a lighthouse with the name King under it. "Oh, Ian it is wonderful. Did you make it?"

"Yes, I made it. It isn't perfect because I am not very good with a paintbrush. I wanted it to be special for King. You can always paint over the trimming.

"Ian, it is perfect." Laura replied.

"I know how much you are looking forward to having King back so it had to have his name on it. I think it turned out okay. Do you know where you want it or do you want to think about it for awhile?"

"I really want to think about it since it must be in just the right spot. Why don't you put it beside garage where I can see it from my bedroom window? It will remind me that King soon will be home. I do not know how to thank you. It is perfect and just what I needed to make it easier to face Christmas."

"Laura, what happened? Why are Gary and Jim gone? I thought for sure they would stay through Christmas." Ian asked.

"Come in and I will explain."

While she made them tea Laura told Ian the story about how Jim had deceived her and how Gary had tried to make her go back to the US. Ian listened in silence. He could see how hurt she was and how close to panic. "Well, I am not sure I agree with your decision but I can understand. What's done is done. What I want to know is when are you going into Stornoway to stay? It is just too dangerous for you to be out here alone."

"Tomorrow is Christmas Eve and there will be no ferry again for two days. I promise you I will go to Stornoway on the first ferry after Christmas." Laura responded.

"Laura, I really think you should go before Christmas but I can see I will not be able to talk you into that. I know how badly you want to spend Christmas day here. The surveillance teams will not be on duty on Christmas so I will have to cover the area. I will stop by many times each day and check on you. Here is my mobile phone number. It is suppose to be used only for official police business but I think if you need me that is official police business."

"Thank you for being so understanding and I really will appreciate your stopping by but won't it interfere with your Christmas?" Laura asked.

"No, as I said I am officially on duty over the holiday. I have to make the rounds any way." Ian lied. Laura being new to the area was not aware that everything stopped over Christmas including a lot of police work. Ian hoped the smugglers stopped so Laura would be safe. He felt the smugglers just might take the lack of police activity as an opportunity to move.

"Well, I guess I had better be on my way but I will stop by tomorrow." Ian said.

Laura watched him drive away and the dread she had felt earlier returned. She locked the doors, put some more coal on the fire, and decided to open the presents under the tree. Not knowing which was which she grabbed a small box and read the tag. It was from Mark FitzSimmons. She slowly removed the paper trying to make it last as long as possible. Inside nestled in box of velvet was a gold lighthouse pin. It was beautiful in the light of the fire. Laura rushed to the telephone and dialed Mark's home number but there was no response except his answer phone.

CHAPTER TWENTY-FIVE

As the beautiful pin sparkled in the glow of the fire Laura felt herself losing her way in a maze of doubt and fear. Christmas Eve was tomorrow. She was totally alone in this house. "Was a home in a lighthouse worth this? Why had she sent Gary and Jim away? They could have stayed until after the holidays. Why didn't Gary love her enough to understand why she wanted to stay here? Would they catch the smugglers or would she die alone beneath the light of her new home? Mark FitzSimmons - how did she really feel about him? Thinking about Mark brought her back to reality. She glanced down at the little pin still glittering in her lap. Maybe Mark represented a new beginning. All she had to do was to get through the Christmas holiday. Then she would work hard making a life here. Besides King would be home in a few months. He now had special quarters, the beautiful doghouse that Ian had made. Thinking about King finally brought a healing glimmer to Laura's eyes. Her little house seemed to sparkle and shine, as houses should at Christmas. In the corner the little tree with the lighthouse on the top reminded her she didn't need others to make Christmas a holiday. All she needed was the courage and the faith to make it special. Shaking her head as if this would drive all the sadness and fears away she got up and started a list of groceries she would need to cook a Christmas dinner. After she completed the list she straightened up the little house and started to turn off the lights on the little tree. Just as she stooped to pull the plug she decided the little tree being her only company should be left on. Forcing herself to whistle a Christmas Carol she went to bed.

Laura left early the next morning for the store since she was not sure what time they would close. As she drove into the store car park Ian was backing out. Ian rolled his window down and hollered at her. "Laura, wait."

"Ian, Happy holiday." Laura shouted back.

Ian got out of the car and walked over to the window. "How are you this morning?" he asked with deep concern.

Laura knowing she shouldn't lie to Ian answered truthfully. "I am determined to make this a happy Christmas even though it hasn't been great up to this point. I am going to buy a chicken and cook an exquisite dinner tomorrow. Maybe tonight I will make myself so many hot toddies I won't mind being alone on Christmas Eve." She responded.

"I have a better idea. Why don't I pick you up and we go to the Christmas Eve service at the local church? That is if you do not mind my being in uniform, as I will be on duty. Afterwards I will take you home and we can have a coffee. The church service is a real part of the island festivities." Ian explained.

"Ian, that's perfect and no I would be honored to be accompanied by a handsome constable in uniform to the service. Will the people on the island think I am under arrest when we come into the church? Later when we get back we can have some of my Christmas cake with coffee to make it even more festive." Laura responded not able to hide the relief and joy in her voice.

"It's a date. They won't think you are under arrest but they might think we are becoming a "thing." They are always trying to get me married off. I will pick you up at 7:00 since the service starts at 7:30, see you then." He said as he walked back to the police car.

After buying her groceries Laura sang Christmas Carols as she drove home and thought about what she would wear to the church service. When she got home she found a message from Mark FitzSimmons on her answer phone. She immediately called him back and thanked him for the beautiful pin.

"Laura, what are you doing tonight? I know you said no to my invitation once but I wish you would reconsider. I could come to Gealach on my boat and we could have dinner on board on our way back to Stornoway. In Stornoway we could go to the midnight service. Christmas day you could come with me to my family's house for dinner before I bring you back to the island. The weather forecast is a good one and sailing would be calm and beautiful." Mark asked.

Laura thought of all of her plans for a Christmas alone and realized she would rather be with Mark. "I would love to but are you sure your family will want me intruding?"

"My mother will be delighted to finally have me bring a beautiful lady home as she has never given up hope that I will marry and settle down." He laughingly answered. "I will pick you up around 5:00 at the jetty in town. Okay?"

"I'll be there." Laura answered.

It was only after she had hung up she remembered her promise to Ian. She dialed Ian and was relieved she got the answer phone. "Ian, I am not feeling very well and have decided to just stay in tonight. I really appreciate your offer and have a great holiday. After she hung up Laura wondered why she had lied to Ian. She could have just told him the truth. Feeling a bit guilty she put the groceries away and began planning what she would wear on the boat and in Stornoway. She needed warm clothes on the boat and a good dress for church. All of sudden she realized Mark had said nothing about where she was going to be staying all night. Did he expect her to sleep at his house? She hoped not since she knew she was not ready for any kind of intimate relationship with Mark. She barely knew him.

Having put the groceries away she sat down at the computer and sent the beautiful multimedia Christmas cards she had made to all her friends in the States. Each friend would also receive a long letter relating all the positive things about living on an island in the Hebrides. As soon as she got offline the telephone rang. "Laura, its Ian. I just got your message. I'm sorry you are not feeling well. I can drop in later tonight and check on you and at least we can have that coffee."

"Thanks Ian, but I feel rotten and think I will just go to bed with a good book. Are you having Christmas dinner with your brother's family? She asked trying to change the subject.

"Yep, sure am. Even the police get an hour for lunch on Christmas day. I will give you a call or maybe even stop by tomorrow as I do my rounds." He answered.

"If I do not answer don't get concerned. I am one of those people who need to be alone when I am sick. I will hang a red bow on the door to let you know I am fine and if it isn't there you'll know something is wrong." She answered and hung up.

Laura felt like a heel. Why did she lie to that nice man? Was she ashamed of meeting Mark or just too big a coward to tell a nice guy she was standing him up for another? Some how Laura's meeting with Mark was becoming not so much fun after all.

Laura decided to forget Ian and started to get her clothes together for the trip to Stornoway. After that was accomplished she took a shower and spent a good bit of time on her hair. She laughed out loud when she realized after sailing to Stornoway on a small boat her hair would be a wreck. She quit fussing and laid down with a book only to drift off into a deep sleep.

Laura woke in a cold sweat. What ever she had dreamed had frightened her. Looking at the clock she realized she only had an hour until she had to meet Mark. She fixed some leftovers and put on the clothes she had chosen to wear on the boat. Grabbing her bag she put it into her car and looked back at her little house with lights glowing in every window. She had left them on so if Ian came by he would think she was inside. She had also attached a red bow to the door to indicate she was all right.

Quickly driving to town, she did not see Ian's car hidden behind a hill but he saw her. His first reaction was Laura must have been going to see the doctor so he decided to follow her. She did not turn down the doctor's road but headed straight for the pier. Now, Ian was really curious. He continued to follow but kept far enough back so she could not see him.

When she arrived at the pier a big motorboat was waiting. Ian could see Mark FitzSimmons getting off the boat in the dock's lights. Laura hurried on board clutching a small suitcase. Ian was totally perplexed. He did not feel that Laura was the type of person to lie to him. He did not know her that well so maybe she had. He ached inside thinking that Laura had intentionally deceived him. The other thought that crossed his mind was he knew almost nothing about Mark FitzSimmons except that the smugglers had visited his office. The most frightening thought was could Laura be in danger?"

CHAPTER TWENTY-SIX

It was a picture perfect evening as the boat left the Gealach jetty for Stornoway. Laura stood on the deck and watched the lights of her island home fade in the night. "How she had come to adore the island and the people who had become her friends." She thought.

"Well, at least for Christmas Eve you can get away from those dreary people. Most of them have lived on the island all of their lives and that is all they know." Mark said almost as if he could see what Laura was thinking. Laura was shocked at Mark's comment. How could he put down the wonderful people in her chosen home?

"Mark, how can you say that? The people of Gealach are warm and generous. Some might think they are not modern but maybe that is what makes them so special. I have come to love the island and most of all, its people. Maybe we think differently and tonight is a mistake. We are only a short distance from the jetty, would you please turn around and take me back to Gealach"

"Laura, I am sorry I did not mean to put the Gealach people down but it is a small place and they really are behind. It is time they joined the real world." Mark said trying to calm Laura down.

"You are entitled to your opinions but I do not agree with you so please take me back." Laura demanded.

"We are not going back." Mark snarled.

"Take me back!" A frustrated Laura demanded.

"I am sorry but I can't do that. My job was to get you off of the island and take you to Stornoway. And that is where we are going." Mark snarled.

"Job!" Laura screamed. "What job? I thought we were going to church and then to your parents."

"We are." Mark answered realizing he has made a big mistake. "Just forget everything I just said. Let's enjoy the trip and Christmas."

"No! Take me back to my island." Laura demanded.

Mark's face became hard and his eyes cold. "Laura, I am taking you to Stornoway and that is that. Just enjoy the trip." He said as he increased the boat's speed.

All of sudden Laura was afraid. She felt like she did not know this man. As she thought about it she really didn't. She had met him first by Internet where you cannot really tell anything about the person on the other end. She had encountered him in person a few times related to work along with a few telephone conversations. He had given a magnificent pin to Laura, which she realized now, had been strange since they did not know each other very well. It was a much too expensive gift for the beginning of a relationship. "Mark, what is going on?" She asked as she tried to keep her voice from shaking.

"You will find out soon enough so I might as well tell you. We have a shipment coming in tonight and it might have been difficult with you at the lighthouse. So, my part of the action was to get you off the island and into Stornoway. I had hoped it would go smoothly and you would never be the wiser. But, now that you know the ending will have to be a little different than planned. Laura, go below or I will have to tie you up." Mark growled.

"Tie me up. You are one of the smugglers, aren't you?" Laura shrieked.

"Not just one. I am the head man." Mark answered with an arrogant smirk. "I am the brains behind the movement that was going so well until you moved into the lighthouse and began to make things more difficult. It became particularly difficult for me because I have taken a strong liking to you."

Even with Mark's statement of affection for her Laura knew she was in real danger. Being only a short distance away from Gealach maybe if she yelled someone would hear her. "Help, Help!" She screamed. "Someone help me!"

Mark shook her so hard she fell to the deck. "Laura shut up, no one can hear you. It is Christmas Eve and all of the simple people of Gealach have gone to church on the other side of the island. Go down stairs like I told you. I don't want to hurt you. I like you too much." Laura realized to resist would get her in more danger so she complied and went down stairs.

Mark was wrong. Ian standing on the jetty heard her faint calls for help. Continuing to listen he heard nothing more. Something has happened to Laura. He rushed back to his car and radioed Stornoway giving them a description of the boat and asking a helicopter to search for the boat and rescue Laura. The man on duty in Stornoway said it be awhile until they could get a helicopter up since almost everyone was off for Christmas but he would start working on it right away.

Ian realized the sergeant was right. The police force was at a bare minimum so as many of the personnel as possible could spend the holiday with their families. Hopefully they could find enough officers in time to rescue Laura. Ian pondered as he sat in the car and watched the boat lights disappearing. "Why would Mark want to kidnap Laura? She worked for him. He had observed the way he looked at her and knew that Mark wanted more than friendship. Why would Mark want to take Laura away and even more important why would she go with him? Laura probably went with Mark because she was lonely. Mark was a handsome man. Ian had never had delusions of being a charming and handsome fellow like Mark FitzSimmons. He was just an ordinary looking police constable on a small island. It was no surprise Laura would chose to spend time with Mark tonight instead of with him. The even more perplexing problem was what happened on that boat to make Laura scream. Had Laura found out something from the work they had been doing together that Mark was trying to hide? Laura had not been working with him that long so it was probably not that. Could Mark be involved in the smuggling and Laura knew something about it she had not told Ian? One of the smugglers did visit Mark's office. All of a sudden Ian knew. The smugglers wanted Laura away from the lighthouse and Mark was taking her. Something was going down tonight. Knowing there was no way for Ian to catch Mark's powerful boat and help Laura, Ian must do what he could to protect the island from more smuggling. He would have to leave Laura's rescue to the officers in Stornoway. He radioed Stornoway, told them his theory, and asked for back up.

"Are you nuts, Mitchell? I am having enough trouble trying to find some one to chase the boat your girlfriend is on. I found the helicopter pilot now I am looking for some men to ride with him. Now you want a smuggling team! Ian, it is Christmas. You really do want a miracle."

"She is not my girl friend and yes I want a miracle." Ian answered. "I am going home and get my gun and head for the coast to see if I can stop the smugglers. You had better get me help. Oh, by the way, Merry Christmas."

Ian went home and got his shotgun and headed for the beach. Since they wanted Laura out of the picture what ever was going to happen would probably be around the lighthouse. He decided to park his car in the garage of the lighthouse if it was not locked and then find a place in the hills to observe.

Ian was not surprised to find the garage to the lighthouse unlocked even with the recent break-in. Laura was beginning to think like all of the islanders did. It was not necessary to keep things locked up. He put the police car in the garage and climbed up the hill to the spot were Laura always sat to watch the lighthouse. Curling up in a Harris Tweed blanket he nestled back in the shadows and waited. As he waited he watched the soothing rotation of the lighthouse beacon and thought about how beautiful it was. He could understand why Laura was so determined to stay. The sky had become completely cloud covered. It was black all around him except for the beacon. He could see some shoreline with its faint outline of white as the waves broke against it. His problem was he could not see all of the shore. Where would the smugglers attempt to land? After much thought Ian decided to stay where he was since he still felt the abduction of Laura was the key. They wanted her out of the way so it would be near the lighthouse. He must listen carefully since it would difficult for them to come in without making some noise. In the silence of the night any noise they made would be noticeable.

Ian looked at his watch. It was 3:00 and still no sign of any thing. Maybe he was wrong. Maybe he did not hear Laura scream for help. He decided he would wait another hour and if nothing happened here he would move on to another area. Getting up to stretch his legs which has begun to hurt and were stiff from sitting in one position he saw something tiny move about 50 yards off shore. It might have been a fish jumping but he kept his eye focused on the spot in the inky sea. There it was again. Something was definitely moving. Ian tried his binoculars but it was just too dark for them to help. They only showed dark sky and the lighter ebony of the ocean moving below it. If only the island's namesake moon would come out. Then he could tell if his eyes had fooled him or there really was something out there. Just then the beacon from the lighthouse rotated in the direction he was watching and he could faintly make out the outline of a small boat in the light it cast.

Ian was excited and scared all at the same time. Something was definitely out were and coming toward shore. What could he do to stop them? For sure, there would be more than one of them. He would only be able to observe and hope reinforcements would arrive soon.

The small boat landed and two men jumped out to pull it further up on the shore. As soon as they had the boat safely on land they began unloading what looked like large boxes.

One of the men went up the hill to the road but came back immediately. Evidently who ever they were supposed to meet had not arrived yet. The men sat down on the boxes and one lit what must have been a cigarette. Ian could hear them talking but had no idea what they were saying.

All of a sudden headlights could be seen coming in Ian's direction. In his exposed position there was no place to hide. If he did not get out of the car park he would be seen for sure. Reacting without thinking, he rolled down the hill toward the lighthouse. He finally came to rest with a loud thud against a small standing stone half way down the hill that he had never noticed before. Looking up he could see the lights of the car in the car park. Hoping he had left nothing behind Ian got the shotgun ready just in case they were looking for him. He heard voices but they did not come his direction. Unless he had been knocked senseless in the abrupt meeting with the standing stone the voices were getting farther away rather than closer. "Maybe they are going down to the boat. If I crawled up there now while they are gone I could surprise them." Ian thought.

Deciding to give it a try Ian slowly crept back up the hill. When he reached the car park he found it empty except for a small lorry. Looking around for a good place to hide, he saw a rock just off the road where he could not be seen from the car park. Just as he reached the rock he saw the light of torches coming slowly up from the bay. If each man had a torch there were three people. The lorry driver must have joined the two people from the boat. If they were armed Ian decided he would be better off not trying to intervene. The best thing to do would be to get the license plate of the lorry and their descriptions. They probably would not leave the island with tomorrow being Christmas Day. He had already asked for help from Stornoway. As soon as the Stornoway force arrived they would search the small island until they found the lorry. The only thing he had to do now was stay unnoticed.

The men appeared over the hill carrying three large metal boxes. It was obvious to Ian from the way they were carrying them that they were heavy as well as bulky. What ever was inside must not be drugs. The men were chattering confidently as if they were sure no one was near enough to hear them.

"I am sure glad Mark got that bitch from the lighthouse off of the island. It makes it so much easier not to have to worry about her." One of the men said.

"Mark, will take care of her just the way he took care of the customs man." Replied the other.

"Come on quit talking and get this stuff in the lorry. As soon as Mark has taken care of the girl he will be back to pick us up." A female voice said.

Ian was terrified. Laura was with Mark and he was a killer. He wanted to run down the hill to his car so he could radio Stornoway but the smugglers were between him and the car. Feeling trapped all Ian could do was wait and watch. He did copy down the license number of the truck and realized he knew two of the men. It was Laura's neighbor, Steve McGiver, and his best friend, Hamish Dore, who lived on a croft over on the other side of the island with his wife and two children. The third person Ian could not see but it sounded female when it talked. He tried to scribble on his notepad in the dark a description of each of the men.

After the lorry was loaded Steve and the woman got into the front. Hamish went back down the hill. The lorry turned around and started back up toward Ian's hiding place. Ian carefully moved around the rock as the vehicle came closer so that when it passed just a few feet from him he would still be hidden. The lorry continued down the road without the passengers taking any notice of the police constable behind the rock. As soon as they were far enough away that Ian was sure they could not see him, he stood on the rock to see if he could tell what direction the lorry had gone. It came as no surprise that the van did not go towards town but stopped at Jill McGiver's cottage.

"They are either letting Steve off or that is where they'll hide until Mark arrives to pick them up." Ian thought as he ran down the road to his car. His biggest concern now was Laura's safety and getting the Stornoway police to catch Mark when he landed which he realized looking at his watch would be within the next few minutes.

"Stornoway, this is Gealach. Over." Ian screamed in the radio. There was no answer.

"Stornoway, answer me. This is Gealach and it is a matter of life and death." Ian tried again. There was still no answer.

"God, damn it. This is nonsense. Someone has to be on radio duty even if it is Christmas Eve." Ian screamed as if that would carry all the way to Stornoway.

Grabbing his mobile phone he dialed the Stornoway police station. The phone kept ringing but no one answered.

"Where are they? Why isn't someone answering the telephone or the radio?" Ian said as he looked at his watch and realized Mark was probably just now landing. Once he was on Lewis he could take Laura anywhere and do anything he wanted with her. It would be almost impossible to find her. "Where is the man on duty at the Stornoway Police headquarters?"

Thinking maybe who ever was on duty may have just gone to the bathroom he tried again but the results were the same. No one was answering his calls.

CHAPTER TWENTY-SEVEN

Terrified Laura sat on the chair in the boat's cabin wondering how she could have been so stupid. Mark FitzSimmons was a criminal and she had had no idea. Even worse she had had some silly romantic thoughts about him. She had made some dumb mistakes and Mark FitzSimmons was just one of many. Maybe she should have not sent Gary and Jim away in such a hurry. Lying to Ian was another mistake. He was only trying to be nice and keep her Christmas from being a total disaster. If she could only apologize and tell him how sorry she was. "King, oh, King, I need you so much." she whispered. Asking a dog for help showed just how alone Laura felt. Laura was terrified with nowhere to turn. She was on a boat in the middle of the Minch with a smuggler or maybe even worse, a murderer. Was Mark involved in killing the excise man? If so she was in terrible danger. As Laura's panic began to weaken its hold on her she glanced around. The cabin was beautiful. Laura felt she would be safe down here as long as Mark stayed upstairs steering the boat. She needed something to use to contact shore or to protect herself. Quietly she searched the cabin but found no radio or telephone. There were no communication devices in the cabin at all. She found a life jacket, some cans of food, a coffee maker, paper plates and plastic forks but saw nothing that could be used as weapon.

On the wall was a calendar being held by a big pushpin with a bright yellow top. The spike protruding from the end of the yellow head was about a half inch long, sturdy and sharp. Maybe she could use the pushpin some how, Laura thought. If it was applied in a vulnerable area Laura just might be able to surprise Mark and get away. Laura contemplated what she could use to hang the calendar if she removed the pin. Looking around she focused on the plastic forks. "The tines of the fork might hold up the calendar." Laura thought. After breaking off one of the fork spears she carefully removed the pushpin and inserted the fork's tine. It was too small and the calendar fell to the floor. She broke off another tine and inserted it with the first in the hole. The calendar was still too heavy. Frustrated Laura started to lay the fork down and put the pin back in the hole when she looked at the fork again. "Not the tines but the handle would do it," she thought. Breaking the top part of the fork off so the handle would fit in the hole she prayed as she tried to hang the calendar again. The broken fork held snuggly in the hole and the calendar did not sag but the fork stuck out so far it looked strange. Hearing footsteps approaching Laura hurriedly removed the fork and broke it one more time. This time when she stuck it in the hole it did not look too much different than the pushpin unless you were real close. "Laura, what are you doing down there?" Mark called.

Laura did not answer him but tidied up the cabin making sure no pieces from the plastic fork were evident on the floor. Her next big problem was what to do with the pushpin. The only place private and big enough to hide it was in her bra but it would jab her. Looking around again she saw a box of tissues on the counter. Taking a bunch of tissues she wrapped them around the pointed end of the pushpin and stuck it into her bra just as she heard Mark coming down the cabin steps.

"Laura, dear, I have been calling you." Mark said arrogantly. Laura stared at him and did not answer. She knew there was nothing she could say which would please him so she just said nothing.

"I think you should come on deck to watch the lights of Stornoway as we will soon be landing." Mark ordered.

Laura reluctantly went up the stairs with Mark. The lights of Stornoway were only a short distance away and indeed beautiful. Being Christmas Eve there was no activity evident. If people were out and about going to church it was not near the waterfront. The lack of people was another negative in any escape plan. The pushpin was nestled safely close to her heart but Laura was beginning to doubt if it would be of any help against a big man like Mark.

"As much as I hate it I am going to have to tie you up while I am docking the boat. It will only be for a short time. I will position you so you can look at the beautiful lights and enjoy the night." Mark said as he tied her to a bench near the front of the boat. Laura kept wondering why this man who was kidnapping her was so concerned about her seeing the lights.

While Mark docked the boat, Laura kept trying to figure out how to get near enough to him to use the pushpin. An even bigger problem was if she did use it to get free where would she go. Laura decided her best chance was to wait until they were on land where it would be easier to make a run for it. For now she would be cooperative and see where he was taking her. Mark untied Laura and led her toward a car parked beside one of the warehouses. Laura began to doubt whether she would have any opportunity to get away when Mark got in on the driver's side and automatically locked all the doors. Starting the engine he turned the radio on where Christmas Carols song in Gaelic played softly.

"Ah, such a nice Christmas Eve." Mark commented as he hummed softly to the music.

"How, can you say that? You are kidnapping me and that is not a Christmas Eve activity." Laura shouted.

"Laura, my friend, I am not kidnapping you. I am keeping you out of harm's way. I have an even bigger Christmas surprise when we get where we are going." Marked laughingly answered.

Laura had no doubt that Mark's surprise was to end her life. She was so terrified she started to cry. Pushpin or no pushpin she knew her chances of seeing another Christmas and her beautiful lighthouse home again were slim.

"Stop crying, Laura. That is no way to celebrate Christmas Eve. Besides, it gets on my nerves." Mark snapped.

Knowing that the only way she would have any chance at all of escape was not to anger Mark, Laura started looking out the window for Christmas trees as they hurried through the dark streets of Stornoway. Soon they left Stornoway and Laura noticed the road signs said "Ness" so they must be heading west. She had been out this road a few times going to the Butt of Lewis Lighthouse. Realizing that it might become important later she looked at the clock on the dash in front of her. Laura began to time how long it would take from Stornoway to where they stopped. They traveled through deserted marshy moorland with very few houses along the road. Mark turned off the highway on to a road, which was even narrower than a one track. It was more like a cattle path. Laura took note of the time. After a few minutes they arrived at a deserted croft house with dirty windows and puffs of wool on the building's corners from grazing sheep.

"We have arrived. You will wait here until I can get back from another boat trip to Gealach Head to pick up some 'Christmas presents'. When I get back we will take off in my boat for France and then on to Paris. You will love Paris, Laura."

"You are out of your mind. I am not going anywhere with you." Laura angrily replied.

"Now, Laura you will come to like me and we will have a grand old time in Paris. Just in case I need to convince some body like your friend, Ian, that interfering with my plans is not a good idea I'll take your wedding ring so they'll know that I am taking good care of you. I am sorry I do not have a Christmas tree or any directions for you but the place is warm."

The inside of the house was indeed heated and actually quite comfortable. It was obvious someone lived there at least on a part time basis. The furnishings were not lavish but they were not dilapidated either. "Is this your house, Mark?" Laura asked trying to keep from showing her fear.

"No, a friend of mine who off the island is letting me use this house. She takes our supplies over in small amounts to Skye on the ferry. Being Christmas she went home to Glasgow to visit her parents. She will be back in a few days but I am sure she will not mind your using the house for a few hours. Which reminds me I am afraid I will have to tie you up again as we would not want you wandering off into the marsh and getting lost."

Mark started to tie Laura to a big bed on one side of the main room. "Mark, I need to go to the toilet. Can I go before you tie me up since it may be a long time until you get back?"

"That is a good idea. It is just through that door." He replied.

As soon as Laura got into the bathroom she looked for something beside her precious pushpin she could use as a weapon but there seemed to be nothing of any real merit in the room. She took out her pushpin, put it in her pocket, and hoped that Mark would not feel or see it as he tied her up. After going to the bathroom and washing her face she went back out into the room. Mark was on the telephone and all she could hear was the murmur of his voice. If only she could hear what he was saying she might be able to tell the police something more when she got free. "If she got free?" She thought.

Mark hung up the telephone and invited her to sit on the bed. He then proceeded to tie her hands to the iron headboard with some rope he had brought from the boat. "I wouldn't want you to be uncomfortable so I will not make them too tight. You can't reach the telephone and the bed is much too large for you to drag around. Well, I must be off. Since the next time I see you it will be Christmas. Merry Christmas, Laura." Mark said as he kissed her full on the mouth before he went out the door.

Laura wished she could wipe her mouth and listened for the departure of the car. She waited for what seemed like hours but by her watch was only ten minutes. She then carefully wiggled the pushpin out of her pocket unto her lap. She carefully turned so it was on one of the pillows, which she pushed up so she could grab, the pin by her teeth. Using the spike end she began to dig at the rope that bound her to the bed. She did not force it hard because she was afraid it would break. Gradually Laura cut one fiber after another with the point of the pin. It would be a lot faster if she detached more than one fiber at time but if she broke the pin there was no hope. She examined her watch, as the fibers were broken. A half hour later she was only about three-fourths through the rope. Stopping the digging for a second she tried twisting her hand to see if the weakened rope would break. It still would not split. Her whole body hurt from being in such an awkward position but she could not give up. Back to breaking one fiber after another Laura started to sing Christmas Carols just to keep herself from getting hysterical. After what seemed liked another two hours the last strand on the rope broke and her hands came free.

"Thank you, trusty old push pin." Laura said as she rushed to the telephone to dial the emergency number, which would connect her to the police.

"Stornoway Police Department, Merry Christmas." answered a cheerful female voice.

"Oh, thank God. My name is Laura File and I live on Gealach Island at the lighthouse. I have been kidnapped and brought to Stornoway by one of a group of smugglers. He left me in a house somewhere west of Stornoway. I am not sure exactly where." Laura afraid they would not believe her added, "If you do not believe me please contact Ian Mitchell, the police constable on Gealach."

"There is no need. Ian reported your abduction a few hours ago according to the log. "I have caller ID and it is giving me the telephone number of your location. It will take only a few minutes to find the address that goes with the telephone number. I will send a car immediately but it would be helpful if you would blink a light to make it easier for the officers to find you."

"I kept track of the time when we came out. It is approximately 25 minutes to the turn off if you are going 65 - 70 miles an hour. I will start blinking the light in 15 minutes. Please hurry I do not know when Mark will be back or whether someone else might come. Oh, and could you let Ian know that Mark is on his way back to Gealach to pick up what ever it is that is being smuggled."

"Yes, I will do that and you be careful. If you can, find a place to hide just in case one of the smugglers shows up before we do. It won't be long."

"Thank you, I will start blinking the light in 15 minutes." Laura answered.

After she hung up Laura did not feel safe. Mark had called someone. Maybe that person was coming here. She needed to careful. Laura began to look around for a place to hide. The house was so small there did not seem to be any corners, which would conceal her. Then it occurred to Laura that if she started blinking the lights and one of the smugglers came back they would know something was wrong. Laura needed a torch so she could walk out to the main road to wait. If the police car came she would signal if it was one of the criminals she would hide. She searched the house and could not find a torch anywhere. All she found were some candles and a paraffin lamp. If she found some matches she would take the candles and the lamp out to the road and wait. Finally after much searching she came up with a cigarette lighter. Knowing it was cold outside she rummage around and found some extra clothes and a blanket she would use to help keep warm.

Leaving the light on Laura took her supplies and started walking down the drive to the main road. It had turned out to be a beautiful night with bright stars. The silence was complete and the shuffle of her feet on the road sounded thunderous. It took her about five minutes to reach the main road. Laura had been hoping there would be a rock or something to hide behind until the police got there. But there was nothing. The only place Laura could see where she might hide was a small hillock a few feet down the road toward town. It would be big enough to conceal her if she lay down. Laura burrowed down behind the hill and wrapped the blanket around her shoulders while she waited for the arrival of the police.

It seemed like she had been there forever when she heard a car. Deciding to wait to light the lantern until the car was closer she got the cigarette lighter ready. The car was coming very fast. It dawned on Laura. She had made a mistake. She should have called Stornoway back and told them she would be out on the road instead of blinking the lights at the house. It was too late to go back and tell them now. She would have to hope she could identify the car fast enough to get the lantern ignited. "What a fool she has been." Laura thought.

The fast moving car showed no sign of slowing and had no markings on it so Laura did not light the lantern. She sat and watched it as it sped by. There were two people in the front seat and two smaller people, probably children in the back.   Someone on their way home from church Laura thought as she settled back in her warm blanket to wait.

A few minutes later another car came from the direction of town. It was going much slower and Laura was sure it must be the police so she got ready to light the lantern. She was just about to light it when the car got close enough she could see no markings. Laura was frightened as the car moved slowly toward her. She tried to lie as flat as possible so who ever it was could not see her. The car chugged slowly by and Laura could see one person hunched over the steering wheel. "It is either a pensioner or someone who is not very comfortable driving at night but at least it was not a smuggler," Laura thought thankfully.

Almost immediately she saw another pair of lights coming slowly. After her last disappointment she waited until the car was close enough to see the lights on top before she struck the cigarette lighter and lighted the paraffin lantern. Taking it in her hand she went to the top of the hillock and began to wave it back and forth. The car slowed and finally stopped. Two police constables got out.

"Thank God." Laura said as she rushed to meet them. "What a great Christmas present."

CHAPTER TWENTY-EIGHT

Ian moved up the hill toward the McGiver house and kept trying to reach the Stornoway police station using his mobile phone. Finally after thirty tries a voice answered.

"Stornoway Police, this is Officer Moira McDuff, may I help you." A pleasant voice answered.

"Where the hell, have you been? I have been trying to call for over ten minutes. I am in the midst of a kidnapping and smuggling investigation and no one at Stornoway Police is answering the telephone. I suppose you are going to say it is Christmas Eve and that makes all the difference. Well, if Laura File is found dead, it will not be a very happy Christmas for any of us." Ian ranted.

"I am sorry sir. I just came on duty. Who is calling?" Officer McDuff asked without missing a beat.

"This is police constable, Ian Mitchell of Gealach." Ian screamed back.

"Why are calling on the telephone instead of your radio?" Officer McDuff replied.

"Because no one was answering the bleaking radio and I thought my chances were better on the telephone as the public can always get through even if the police can't."

"P.C. Mitchell, as I said I just came on duty so I do not know what went on during the last shift. It isn't fair for you to scream at me for what someone else did. Now, could you please tell me exactly what has happened and what you want?"

Suddenly it dawned on Ian; he was being irrational and not very professional. "I am sorry Officer McDuff. It has been a difficult night and you are right it is not your fault. When I was able to get someone on the radio earlier, this evening I reported the kidnapping of Laura File by a Mark FitzSimmons in a boat. I also asked for assistance, as there could be potential smuggling activity on Gealach Island. I asked for a helicopter and some men to back me up but with everyone being off for Christmas Eve there was a problem getting help. Well, since then I have watched a boat land on Gealach and three men bring something on the island in the dead of night. I am sure the way it was carried out we had illegal cargo carried ashore." Ian responded.

"Related to Ms. File, she has managed to escape and two officers picked her up just a few minutes ago. I show no sign of a request for a helicopter but I will get one off as soon as I can." Officer McDuff replied

"Thank God Laura is safe." Ian stuttered. "Send the helicopter to the other side of the island from the lighthouse. I will meet it there. If we have the helicopter land anywhere near the smugglers they might be able to hide or destroy evidence. How soon do you think you can get someone out here?"

"We will have to call in some officers and get the copter pilot but I would say they should be at the island within the hour." Officer McDuff replied.

"Okay, I will watch the smuggler's house and let you know if any thing changes before the copter arrives on the island." Ian replied before he broke the connection.

Ian drove slowly by the McGiver house with his lights off. As soon as he had rounded the curve where he could not be seen from the house he parked and walked back to where he could observe the house. The house lights were on and smoke was coming through the chimney but he did not see the lorry. The McGivers had a large steading where a lorry could be hidden but until he had some assistance he would not investigate. Settling in to wait for help from Stornoway he thought about Laura. He was so glad she was safe but what a way for her to spend her first Christmas on Gealach. Maybe this would scare her so much she would give up and leave the island. Ian felt sad at the thought of Laura leaving the island. Without even being aware of it he had become fond of Laura. After this was all over, he would have to get to know that lady a whole lot better. That is if she stayed on the island. The thought of the island made him look into the deep black sky full of very bright stars. They were so stunning. No where was the light as pure as in the Hebrides he once read and tonight was an example of how true that could be. The air was crisp and filled with the sound of gentle waves. "What a beautiful place this little island is. Laura could be very happy here. I will convince her to stay." He whispered to the stars.

Looking at his watch he realized he must take off to meet the helicopter. As he drove to the other side of the island all the houses were ablaze with lights and in some he could even see Christmas trees. Somehow it all seemed very wrong he was chasing smugglers on Christmas Eve but that was the life of a policeman. At least he did not have a family who he had to leave making the Christmas preparations without him. Some of the men coming on the helicopter would have had to leave in the middle of their family celebration.

When Ian arrived at the landing area the helicopter was still not there. He radioed the Stornoway office and friendly Officer McDuff assured him the helicopter was on the way. There was nothing for him to do but wait so he turned on the radio and tried to find something beside Christmas Carols or church services. All of a sudden he resented Christmas taking over the world and everything coming to a screeching halt. Some people did still have to work. Turning the radio off in disgust, he just set in the car staring into the direction from which the helicopter would come. As he sat there, he saw a small light on the horizon. It looked like a boat. It could not be a fisherman on Christmas Eve. Stornoway police would not send a boat to the island. What could it be Ian wondered? Officer McDuff had said Laura had been found after Mark had left her. Could he be coming back to the island to pick up whatever was unloaded a few hours ago? Why would he do that? They could have unloaded the shipment in Stornoway. It did not make any sense. Realizing that the boat might see the helicopter he radioed Stornoway and asked them to get the helicopter to change course so they would not pass close to the on coming boat. Stornoway assured him the helicopter had not seen the boat but to be sure they would land on the north end of the island opposite from where Ian had seen the boat.

Ian agreed to meet them on the north end and took off. When Ian arrived at the north end of the island the helicopter had landed and three people were climbing out of the aircraft.

Three figures walked toward him as Ian got out of

the car. The smallest of the three, a beautiful but rather small woman, said, "PC Mitchell, I am Sergeant Dill." I have two men with me. What are your plans?"

Ian was a little taken back by the appearance of a beautiful young woman on such a dangerous mission. Times had changed since the era when women were not allowed on police actions like this one. Over the past two years he had found the woman officers often much more responsible than the men. Maybe they still had to prove to the other policemen that they could do the job. Ian had nothing but good luck working with them. "I think the lorry with whatever was brought onto the island is hidden in a steading on a croft near the lighthouse. Our first step should be to reconnoiter the steading and see what they have brought onto Gealach. Without that evidence we have no proof of any wrongdoing. You did not think to get a warrant so we could search the McGiver premises? I hate for all of this to fall through because we missed a step somewhere." Ian stated.

"Way ahead of you PC Mitchell. I have the warrant in my pocket." Sergeant Dill replied.

"Then lets go and see if we can find out what is in those boxes I saw them load on the lorry." Ian said as he jumped in the car. The three officers joined him and they sped off leaving the helicopter and pilot sitting alone on the beach.

When they reached the McGiver house, the lights were all off. "Good." Ian said. "They have gone to bed. It will make it easier for us to search the steading. I think two of us should go to the steading and the others watch the house for any sign of activity." The other people shook their head in agreement.

"I will go with you while Mark and Hamish stay here and watch the house." Sergeant Dill replied.

The name Mark reminded Ian of the boat he had seen speeding toward the island. "Maybe we should put one of the men on the hill toward the sea just in case the boat I saw was heading for this house." Ian added. Sergeant Dill agreed as she ordered one of the men to head for the hill.

Ian and Sergeant Dill crawled to a door in the steading on the side away from the house. After looking in the window and not seeing any sign of life, Ian opened the door. Parked just inside the main door was the lorry he had seen down at the beach. "Sergeant Dill, you stay here and watch for any movement from the house while I check to see what I can find in the lorry?" Sergeant Dill nodded as Ian carefully turned on a torch and approached the lorry.

Reaching the vehicle he circled it three times checking to make sure there was no one around, or it was wired in some way to notify the house. Seeing nothing to be concerned about Ian opened the back door and saw the metal boxes he had seen on the beach. Laying his torch on the floor beside the boxes he raised the lid of one of them. "Shite!" He said.

"What's wrong?" Office Dill asked.

"It is not drugs. It is worse. Its guns." Ian answered.

"Why would they be smuggling guns to Gealach?" Sergeant Dill asked.

"I have no idea?" Ian responded. "My first guess would be to supply the IRA but that makes no sense. There are easier ways to get guns to Ireland than through the Outer Isles. Let me see what the other boxes have in them." Ian said as he lifted their lids. The other two boxes contained more guns and ammunition. "More weapons." He called to the Sergeant.

After placing the boxes back exactly as he had found them Ian went back to join Sergeant Dill at the door. "Smuggling weapons is illegal so they have broken the law but I honestly do not know what they are going to do with those guns. What ever is important enough to already kill one person and to kidnap a friend of mine? What do you think we should do?" Ian asked Sergeant Dill.

"I think we should arrest them and find out what is going on. I have no bloody idea why they would be smuggling guns. What concerns me now is whether they will use some of those weapons against us." She replied.

"I agree and I think the element of surprise is on our side if we do it while they are asleep, so lets get moving." Ian said as he walked toward where the man watching the beach was standing.

"Any sign of a boat?" He asked the officer.

"Yes, the light has been evident for the last couple of minutes but it is a long way out. What do you think we should do?" The officer asked the Sergeant.

Sergeant Dill turned to Ian for an opinion since he knew the situation better. "If that is Mark FitzSimmons then we would be able to get all of the smugglers at once by waiting for his arrival. On the other hand the boat might not be coming here and we would loose the element of surprise if we waited too long. What do you think?"

"I think we should wait about twenty minutes to see if the boat lands and who ever is on it heads this way. If not, then we can arrest the people in the house. It is five o'clock in the morning so I would guess they are going to sleep awhile longer."

"Okay, that is what we will do." The Sergeant replied. "Let's head back over the hill where we can see both the house and the boat. It does look like the boat is getting closer. What bothers me if the people in the house were expecting it you would think someone would be up." She said as she walked back toward their original hiding place.

The boat landed thirty feet off the shore. One person jumped into a dinghy and came ashore. The four policemen on the hill could see the man was carrying a rifle as he climbed the hill toward the McGiver house. As he got closer Ian recognized Mark FitzSimmons. He whispered to Sergeant Dill that this was Laura File's kidnapper and all of the activities must some how be connected.

There were still no lights on in the house but this did not seem to bother Mark as he walked boldly to the main door of the steading.

"He must be going in to check to make sure the weapons are there." Ian whispered to the others.

Only a minute later Mark reappeared and walked over to the house. Without stopping to knock he entered the small croft house. The policemen on the hill could hear a dog barking and people shouting as the lights in the house came on. Ian decided he wanted to hear what was being so he told the three Stornoway police to wait on the hill. He was going to sneak up close enough to listen. "I will give you a signal with my torch if I want you to join me." He said as he slowly and silently moved down the hill to the house.

Ian was able to get a few feet away from what looked like the kitchen window. He could see Mark; Steve McGiver; Jill McGiver with Moss; and Moira McNeill, Mark's secretary. Ian moved up until he was right under the window so he could hear what was being said.

"The job is done." Mark said. "I am taking the guns with me on the boat."

"What about us?" Moira asked.

"Well, I have thought about that and we have no other recourse but for the three of you to disappear. The movement cannot afford for anyone to suspect what we are planning until we are ready to move. You all know too much. I will take you to Stornoway where you can catch a ferry to someplace far away without raising too much suspicion. Go get dressed and pack a few clothes. We will leave as soon as you are ready and we can get the guns loaded." Mark answered.

As the three people inside went to get dressed Mark picked up the telephone. Ian could hear him tell someone the guns were here and he was taking the three problems with him on the boat and would shoot them when he was far out to sea and drop them over board. That would definitely keep them quiet.

Ian immediately crawled back to where the Stornoway officers waited. "We have a big problem I just heard Mark FitzSimmons tell someone he was going to take the other three smugglers including a blind lady and her guide dog on his boat and shoot them. And of course he is taking the guns. I think we should go down to the beach and jump Mark and the others as they make for the water. The others do not know they are going to be killed so we will have to handle it as if they were on Mark's side. What do you think?" Ian asked.

"I agree with but did you hear anything about why they were smuggling guns." Sergeant Dill answered.

"Yes, something about a movement." Ian answered. "I have no idea what that means."

CHAPTER TWENTY-NINE

Ian and the officers hurried to the shore so they find good cover before the smugglers made their way to the boat. The smugglers would be burdened with boxes of guns so they would move slowly. Each policeman was able to find a rock or hillock, which hid him. Their hiding places were spread far enough apart they should be able to surround the smugglers before they got into the dingy. They agreed as soon as the smugglers began loading the guns into the boat, Sergeant Dill should step out from her rock and tell them they were surrounded by armed police officers. If they did not show their numbers maybe there would be less of a chance of Mark FitzSimmons trying to use his rifle.

A few minutes later the smugglers came struggling down the hill in single file to the shoreline with Jill McGiver and Moss in the lead. They moved slowly because everyone but Jill had a box in their arms. It was obvious Jill's dog was leading the parade. Mark was the last in the row. His rifle was laid on top of the box he was carrying but was turned so he could easily grab it and shoot the people in front of him if they made a wrong move. When the four smugglers reached the shore, Mark instructed them to put the guns in the dinghy. Jill McGiver's nephew was helping her into the small boat when Sergeant Dill appeared from behind a hill.

"Put your hands in the air. You are surrounded by the police." She ordered them.

Mark FitzSimmons immediately raised his gun and pointed it toward the Sergeant. "If your fellow officers want you to live, they will lay down their weapons. Even if you shoot me, I can get a shot off that will kill or at the least wound you."

Ian knew what Mark was saying was true but he thought he would try to bluff him. "Don't try it, Mark. You might get her but do you want to go to jail for murder as well as smuggling and kidnapping. Think man of all the witnesses that are here."

"What kidnapping? I have kidnapped no one. Laura File is going to Paris with me. This beautiful police lady may be the first dirty copper I have eliminated though.

We will not stop until we have reached our goal." Mark explained with great emotion.

"What goal?" Ian asked trying to keep Mark talking.

Jill McGiver not being able to see what was going on answered with pride. "Why, the freeing of the Scotland from England of course. We are only a couple years away from the reestablishment of a free and independent Scotland. Now that the new parliament is in session, we have our own elected officials. We are bringing arms and ammunition into Gealach to be passed on to members of our group who are spread out over Scotland. If an armed resistance is needed we will be ready. It is our plan to free the islands first. From there we can supply arms and men for our patriots on the mainland. We are the William Wallaces or Robert the Bruces of modern day Scotland. Mark FitzSimmons is one of the organizers of movement. My nephew is a sergeant."

Ian couldn't believe what he was hearing. "You are smuggling arms into the Western Isles to start a revolution to free Scotland. You must be insane. Britain will be all over you with planes, missiles, and ships. There is not a chance in a million that you could succeed. It is too late for that we must rely on the parliament to make the moves which would bring us our independence,"

"This movement is not new. We have been in existence for over ten years and we have people in high places within the British Army. Places where they can slow the British response to any action we take. We have also been stockpiling weapons. It is easy to buy the weapons from the old USSR. They need money. For a few pounds they were glad to let us hide jets, battleships, and missiles in the Soviet Union. It is not very far by ship and air from the Russia to the Shetlands and we have a loyal group up there. We know we will succeed within the next two years. We have lots of patience since we have been waiting since Culloden to do our thing. First we had to get elected leaders and a system of rule and then we can run the English out for once and for all!"

Ian suddenly realized they had not stumbled onto a smuggling ring but people who believed in a major revolution. Ian was not sure about Mark. If he was going to kill some of the patriots what kind of leader was he. Ian wanted a free Scotland like most Scots and felt that the new parliament was a step in the right direction. An armed resistance might just destroy all the progress they had made. Mark and his kind must be stopped. Sergeant Dill was now only a few feet in front of Mark. Ian could tell she was shocked and angry by what Mark had just said. Without making a sound she rushed at Mark. Surprised Mark turned to fire and hit the Sergeant in the leg. She fell to the ground.

"Okay, does anyone else want to volunteer to get shot?" Mark asked. "I am not sure what to do since so many of you know about our little toy war."

"Toy war? Jill shouted. "This is not a toy war. We are going to get our independence and no one is going to stop us."

"Sorry, Jill. My job is to move guns I really don't have anything to do with freeing Scotland as such. My friends and I just pretended to be a part of the movement to get your cooperation."

"You mean the guns are not going to support an independent Scotland?" Jill asked with tears in her eyes.

"I have no idea where the guns will end up. All I know is we have buyers on the mainland for the guns. What they are going to do with them I do not know."

Jill became hysterical and began screaming "Traitor" at Mark. Mark paid no attention to her and instructed the rest of the "movement" to get in the dinghy. As Mark turned his back to Jill the ever obedient Moss feeling his mistress was in danger jumped Mark from behind sinking his teeth deep into the back of his neck. Mark went down when the weight of the dog hit him and his rifle went flying.

Ian grabbed the gun while Mark was still struggling trying to get the huge dog off.

"Good job, Moss. You saved the day." Ian said as he pulled Moss back.

The other smugglers saw a chance and started to run but the Stornoway officers grabbed them. That left Jill McGiver struggling to get Moss to come back to her. As soon as Ian had Mark handcuffed the dog went back and stood beside his mistress. Ian did not want to handcuff the old women. In many ways he felt sorry for her. "Jill, if you promise you will not run away I will not put handcuffs on you." Ian told her.

"What? What happened to everyone? Are we under arrest?" The old lady asked in terror.

"No one has been hurt except for one police officer and Mark who has a nasty bit on his neck where Moss grabbed him. But, yes you are under arrest." Ian responded.

"What about New Scotland? What about our independence?" She screamed.

"There will be a new Scotland but it will happen without blood shed and hopefully without any armed resistance. We have a parliament and they will lead the country toward being the best Scotland possible. No one knows whether this will mean complete independence from England. There is more than one way to independence and Scotland's will hopefully be accomplished by peaceful methods." Ian answered as he helped put handcuffs on the other smugglers. "Just be aware that people like Mark FitzSimmons do not care about Scotland they are only in it for the money."

"Moss did good work on overcoming this man without anyone else getting hurt. He would make a mighty fine police dog." Ian jokingly told Jill.

"No, I need Moss he is my whole world." Jill begged.

"I am only kidding. Moss is yours. He only attacked Mark because you were danger. He is a loyal and faithful friend."

"Sergeant, will you radio the helicopter and ask it to come over here and pick up these smugglers. Can you imagine if we had not busted up this little smuggling ring on Gealach what might have happened? I hope they can find who the guns were being delivered to before they can cause any real trouble."

"I have already radioed for the helicopter. It should be here any minute. I agree with you about finding the buyers of these guns as well as the rest of the people who work with Mark distributing them. We have one lead in the phone call Mark made from the McGiver house. I guess we will just have to follow every lead until we get them all."

"We have another big lead. Mark FitzSimmons kidnapped Laura File who lives at Gealach Point lighthouse tonight. He took her to a house northwest of Stornoway. She got away but we can stake out the house and see who turns up. I think the days of gun running in this part of the Western Isles are over. There comes the helicopter. You take the prisoners back to Stornoway and I will take the dingy out to Mark's boat and bring it back."

One of the officers had put temporary bandages on Mark FitzSimmons' neck and Sergeant Dill's leg so the Stornoway officers were able to load all of the smugglers on the helicopter without much difficulty.

As Ian took Mark's boat back to Stornoway he thought about the smugglers. He agreed with Jill about wanting an independent Scotland but certainly not in the method they had chosen. Mark FitzSimmons was the truly malicious one in all this. He had lied to Jill McGiver and had befriended Laura for the sole purpose of finding out what if anything she knew about the activities around the lighthouse. As Ian thought about Laura, he knew he wanted to become more than just friends with her. He was sure that this episode with Mark would make her even more reluctant to trust people particularly men. "In time she will come to trust me and that is all I can ask for right now." Ian told the stars.

Docking in Stornoway Ian went directly to the police station hoping Laura would still be there. He desperately wanted to ride back to Gealach with her and hopefully she would join his family for Christmas dinner. She had not had much of a Christmas and maybe he could make it up to her.

Laura was standing in the lobby drinking a cup of coffee talking to Sergeant Dill when he arrived. "Ian, I am so glad to see you." She said as she rushed over to give him a big hug. "Are you angry with me for lying to you? I was so wrong. I let a little flattery and a jeweled pin get in the way of my common sense. I will understand if you never forgive me."

"Everyone was fooled by Mark FitzSimmons. There is nothing to forgive. But, if you want to make me happy you have to promise to join my family and I for dinner later today. I do not want you to spend Christmas alone."

"Oh, Ian, thank you. I would love to have Christmas with your family but I will have to get some sleep or I will fall over in the pudding. How are we getting home?"

Sergeant Dill interrupted. "The helicopter is waiting on the helipad to take you back to the island. Ian, I will write up the incident at the McGivers and you can review the report and add anything I forgot. Are you ready to go?"

"Thank you Sergeant for everything and I do mean everything." Ian replied. "Laura lets go home to Gealach."

As they flew over the black sea with its canopy of stars, Laura seemed to want to talk.

"Ian, in some ways I have handled my move to Scotland poorly mostly in relationship to my son. I had sometime to think while I was waiting at the police station. Gary did not have to arrange for Jim to look after me but he did. Yes, he probably should have been more open and honest about it. I finally understand he did it because he cared. After the way I have treated him it is a wonder he cared at all. I turned my back on him after his father's death because I found him using drugs. Until tonight I never realized that the only way he could deal with his father's death was with the help of drugs. Then I ran off and left him. I know he is grown and not alone but it was like he had lost both his Mother and Father. He must feel exactly like I did when I thought I had lost both a husband and son. We need each other. The first thing I am going to do when I reach the lighthouse is contact him at the airport in London and see if can't at least begin trying to overcome our problems."

"Laura, does that mean that you are thinking of going back to the US? I don't want the events of the last few hours to scare you away from Gealach and the lighthouse. Remember King is half way through quarantine? Do you want that to be for nothing?" Ian asked.

"No, I love my lighthouse home. The smuggling has made it more difficult but it still is what I want to do. Gary has his own life and he can come visit. I can go visit him. My life is here now. Oh, dear I will have to find a new job as Mark FitzSimmons will not be around to give me work." Laura realized.

"I have a friend who runs a graphic design firm in Glasgow. Could you work with someone that far away? I know computers are making it easier to work separated by long distances. If it is possible I will contact him after the holidays and see what he says." Ian added.

"Oh, Ian that would be great. I could probably still work in the US and just may until I can get more business over here." Laura stated. "Oh, look, Ian! My lighthouse."

Off in the distance they could see the revolving light of Gealach Head guiding them safely home. Laura watched her beautiful home come closer and closer. The light was a beacon of safety for everyone who passed. It was so serene with the little house nestled at the foot of the tower. So sturdy from the ground but from the air it looked miniature, like the one on her Christmas tree.

"How could I ever leave my beautiful home, Ian?" She said as tears of joy stream down her face.

EPITAPH

Spring had finally arrived at Gealach Head. Gary had come over for his Spring break to begin the long process of building a relationship with his mother again. He and Jim Green were both going to come in the summer. Laura and Gary were planting Peter's roses around the sundial when they heard a car approaching. They looked up as the police car came down the crooked road to Gealach Head. Ian was not supposed to be back from Glasgow until day after tomorrow. He had gone to attend a training seminar that was a required part of his job. She had missed him while he was gone. Since that awful incident at Christmas she had seen a lot of Ian. He had helped her make friends on the island and had taken her into Stornoway a couple of times. Ian's friend in Glasgow had given her some work so she was gainfully employed. Laura was surprised at how glad she was to see the car coming down the hill. She had missed their local Police Constable.

Ian stopped way out by the garage instead of pulling right up by the gate. "Laura, can you help me unload the present I brought you from Glasgow?" Ian asked.

"What present? You did not have to bring me a present. But, sure I will help unload it." Laura said.

"At second thought, it might not take any help. You just stand there and I will get it." He said as he moved around to the back of the car and opened the back door.

As soon as he opened the door a big black streak of fur jumped out and made a dash straight toward Laura.

"Oh, my God, its King." Laura screamed as she ran for the dog. "King, King, oh, I am so glad to see you. But, how did you get out three weeks early? Ian, how did King get out three weeks early?"

"Sometimes the police can pull strings and I thought it was appropriate for the entire File family to be together here at Gealach Head." Ian replied with a shy smile.

www.ingramcontent.com/pod-product-compliance
Lightning Source LLC
Chambersburg PA
CBHW022059170626
46808CB00002B/500